MUMBO

GUMBO

MUMBO

A Madeline Bean Novel

GUMBO

JERRILYN FARMER

wm

WILLIAM MORROW

An Imprint of HarperCollins*Publishers*

Far

This novel is a work of fiction. Any references to real people, events, establishments, organizations, or locales are intended only to give the fiction a sense of reality and authenticity, and are used fictitiously. All other names, characters, and places, and all dialogue and incidents portrayed in this book, are the product of the author's imagination.

HarperCollins books may be purchased for educational, business, or sales promotional use. For information please write: Special Markets Department, HarperCollins Publishers Inc., 10 East 53rd Street, New York, NY 10022.

FIRST EDITION

Designed by JoAnne Metsch

Printed on acid-free paper

Library of Congress Cataloging-in-Publication Data
Farmer, Jerrilyn.
Mumbo gumbo/Jerrilyn Farmer. — 1st ed.
p.   cm.
ISBN 0-380-97889-X
1. Bean, Madeline (Fictitious character) — Fiction.   2. Caterers and catering — Fiction.
3. Los Angeles (Calif.) — Fiction.   I. Title.
PS3556.A719 M8   2003
813'.6 — dc21   2002027612

03 04 05 06 07 JTC/BVG 10 9 8 7 6 5 4 3 2 1

For Sam and Nick

Acknowledgments

Special thanks to Chris Farmer, first and always. I could thank you every day and it would still never be enough. Thanks to Elissa Lenard, who graciously lent her lovely flock to me for this story. Thanks also to Douglas P. Lyle, M.D., for help with the medical bits; Bruce Kelton, former federal prosecutor; and to Evan Marshall, my agent, and Lyssa Keusch, my editor, for their wisdom and help.

I am indebted also to Barbara Voron, Linda Urban, James Lamb, Barrie Trinkle, Jill Hinkley and Carolyn Lane, Michael Morrison, Libby Jordan, Lisa Gallagher, Debbie Stier, Erin Richnow, Jessica Miller, Richard Aquan, Victoria Mathews, Bernadette Murphy, Cindy Lieberman, Linda Venis, Barbara Jaye Wilson, Geraldine Galentree, Cubbie, along with Margery Flax, Doris Ann Norris, and each and every teabud, for their incredible support and inspiration.

And to all my friends in the world of game shows, I promise all the cool characters are inspired by you and all the rotten ones . . . I made up. We had a lot of fun, didn't we? On second thought, don't answer that.

MUMBO

GUMBO

JUDGMENT was bearing down on the beautiful Baker sisters like a freight train. The jury looked on. Beneath deadly hot lights, the young women awaited the verdict. They were doomed. Everyone knew it. But we still loved to watch them squirm. Sydney and Marley, the two elder sisters, wore the lowest-cut designer gowns. They clung to each other for support. Emily, the youngest of the three beauties, admitted she might faint from fear.

"Can you turn the sound up a little?" asked Drew.

I shot him a look. All the chefs were staring at the screen of our kitchen Toshiba, drawn into the drama that marked the final round of *Food Freak*, America's hot-hot-hot new cooking quiz show. I reached for the remote control and adjusted the volume.

"The guys from Jersey killed 'em," said Philip Voron, wiping his apron. "Is it too late to raise my bet?"

"Yes," came the answer from five other kitchen assistants and chefs.

On-screen, the celebrity judges tasted the food that had been prepared over the previous half hour. Tony and Frank from Jersey vs. the Fabulous Baker Girls.

"I'll take your money," I said, giving Philip a level gaze.

"All right," he said slowly. "Another twenty."

No one knows quite how these pop culture phenoms begin, but at the moment, America's TV viewers were just crazy about *Food Freak*, the show that pitted amateur chefs against one another in a hilarious send-up of feuding gourmands. Thousands of hot little office betting pools were springing up everywhere. Internet betting was also huge. For some reason, the idea of caring so much about who was crowned the best amateur chef in the U.S. had tickled us. The show was a riot for those of us who cook for a living, television of the absurd. Sort of like the Pillsbury Bake-Off on steroids.

Judgment was at hand. We all turned to the screen. And despite the knife-wielding prowess displayed earlier by the dance instructors from Trenton, it was not to be Tony and Frank's night. I two-finger-whistled when the guest judges, pop divas Destiny's Child, admired the sisters' shimmering chiffon gowns in sherbet colors as well as their mouth-watering take on fat-free tiramisù. I cheered on Emily, Marley, and Sydney Baker and whooped as they pulled out from behind and won the show by only a scant point.

There was some teasing and settling of bets, and then we all got back to work. This is what it is like to be an event planner in the midst of orchestrating a major Hollywood party. I was working in my own professional kitchen, one I'd had added to my home in the Hollywood Hills, preparing a spectacular Mumbo Gumbo and several other exotic dishes for a party of eighty to celebrate the close of production on one of TV's most memorable new shows of the season, the one whose final episode we had just screened early since we'd be working when it aired later tonight.

We would produce this evening's wrap party for *Food Freak*, but after this one last party, our schedule was alarmingly unbooked. The great blank calendar that was March loomed ahead. The country was not in a lavish, celebrating, party mood.

"We're definitely going to pull through this little slump," Wes said, looking up as he chopped a mound of okra. Throughout the past

month he'd said much the same thing, each time with the same upbeat tone. It never failed to make my stomach queasy at how hard he
was trying to cheer me the heck up. Wesley Westcott is my best friend
in the world and my business partner in our event-planning company,
Mad Bean Events.

I gave him a great cheery smile back. Wes is a tall, perfectly
groomed guy and you would hardly guess he was thirty-eight by the
boyishness of his good looks, the great hairline, or the energy of his
movements. He took note of my best smile and looked queasy.

I'm Mad Bean. Madeline Olivia Bean, actually. Twenty-nine. Single. Raised in a suburb of Chicago, trained at the Culinary Institute in
San Francisco, and finally transplanted to L.A. Wes and I began our
company a few years back, catering high-profile dinner parties in Hollywood, a town that rates a good party slightly higher than your average
fish rates water. The top-end party crowd has come to discover that we
are more than willing to be arty, outrageous, and temperament-free, a
perfect combination, it turns out, to prosper here amid hothouse egos
and insane party budgets.

But this town, like every town, has been changing. People are more
worried than ever about the state of the world and what the future
might bring. With fears about the economy, our best clients—the
movie studios and television productions—seem less inclined to want
to spend wildly. For the first time in, I think, ever, the Emmy Awards
decided to tone themselves down, banning the jewels and ball gowns.
And as for our business? No bookings. Our lack of income was something I was planning to be desperate about just as soon as this last party
was taken care of.

But not right now. Now, we had to cook and put on a terrific event.

I looked around. My kitchen is quite cozy in a brushed-stainless-
steel, white-tile, warm-wood-counters sort of way, but it is not pretty on
the day of a party. It's a battle zone. It is rather like the beaches during
the Normandy invasion, I imagine, only exchange the sand for
linoleum, the sweaty soldiers for sweaty cooks. A dozen prep chefs
were busy here and there, lifting great pots onto the fire, or shelling
fresh Santa Barbara prawns.

And yet, to me, the scene of culinary battle is also one of grace. The

energy in a working kitchen is thick with steamy rustic smells, with the
rhythm of aluminum whisks stirring against metal bowls, knives
pounding chopping blocks. Alicia Keys's soulful voice wailed out from
the CD player and kept the crew lively. With swift, graceful movements, a corps de ballet of white-clad cooks holding steaming colan-
ders zigzagged between fellow cooks rinsing greens, improvising their
efficient *pas de twelve* among the counters and sinks and gas flames.

I looked up to see a visitor to our frenzied workroom. There was
something odd about the way Greta Greene, *Food Freak*'s producer,
stood at the doorway. Anxious. Almost sad.

"Greta?" I said, walking swiftly toward her.

"Hi, Madeline. What a whirlwind in here. I'm afraid I need to talk
with you right away."

As I smiled at her, doing the party-planner-calm thing, I began reor-
ganizing the day's timetable in my head, just in case. Wes and I had
but ten hours to finish preparations and the clock was ticking. We had
staff to brief, sauces to stir, shrimp to butterfly.

Greta settled on an empty bar stool amid the clutter and announced, "I probably shouldn't put this extra burden on you, Madeline, but . . ."

Several of the nearby assistants looked up, Wes threw out a significant glance, and I joined Greta, giving her my full attention. A professional event planner hears this sort of thing all the time. Pre-party
problems and how to deal with them are exactly the reasons our clients
turn to us to plan their affairs. We take it all in stride.

Greta Greene looked tiny sitting at the vast butcher-block kitchen island, the one we'd rescued from the salvage yard and refinished, good as
new. She was small boned and attractive—the short-blond-hair-and-
small-upturned-nose kind of cute. She would have looked ten years
younger if her delicate skin hadn't begun to betray her with dozens of fine
lines—sort of the good news/bad news bargain of being a natural blonde.

Greta had risen steadily through the ranks of game-show jobs to become the television producer of *Food Freak*. When I first met her several years back, she had still been a PA, one of the many production
assistants who get the work done behind the scenes. Even in her PA
days, Greta Greene had always been the type to wear pressed linen

while the world around her wore faded denim. That morning she was wearing her size-two khaki pants with a neat dark blue blazer, a red silk scarf at her throat.

"This is awkward, really, Madeline," she said. "I've got news."

I gave her another reassuring smile. I had a closetful.

"The network called me three hours ago—you know, East Coast time. You won't believe our ratings last week. *Freak* is now officially bigger than *Who Wants to Be a Millionaire.*"

"You deserve all your success, Greta." Greta and I were business friends and, as we both had a tendency to work long hours, our casual relationship mostly consisted of two-hour lunches every few months to kind of keep tabs on each other and catch up. She'd fill me in on all the Hollywood gossip and I'd tell her what hot new restaurants and chefs were about to hit town.

Greta grinned, a little giddy with being on top, while her fine skin betrayed why they call them "smile lines."

"*Food Freak* is a great show," I said. I must admit, here, that we always say this. Even if our client produces *When Good Pets Go Bad.* But like most of the country, I got a kick out of *Food Freak.* I especially love it when a celebrity "chef" judge like Britney Spears tells a team that they maybe need to cut down on the butter.

"And, that's not all the news we got," Greta said. "The network wants us to do one more episode. A one-hour special. *Food Freak* just got an extension."

"Wonderful," I said, but then I stopped.

Greta waited until I fully understood.

"So then," I continued, "your shooting schedule hasn't ended."

She shook her head and hardly a blond hair moved. "I know. The network was actually begging us for more. Isn't that wild?"

"Congratulations, Greta," Wes called from nearby, following our conversation.

"Yes, congratulations," I said as sincerely as I could, considering that I had of course by then figured out the bad patch up ahead. If Greta's hot new television series was not, in fact, "wrapping," we could no longer throw a wrap party. I looked up at my work crew, chopping a hundred scallions, steaming a thousand fresh scallops, and gulped.

"Now the hard part . . . ," she said.

I waited for it.

". . . we've lost our head writer."

"Your head writer?" I took half a second to follow this new thread. "He quit?"

"No, no. We kind of can't find him at the moment, that's all." Greta smoothed her khaki pants, creasing the pleats between her slender fingers.

I waited for more.

"Tim Stock. Did you ever meet him?" she asked.

"Don't think so."

"Oh, he's a great guy. Very funny. He's young, thirty-six or -seven, and single, and, well, always doing some damn crazy thing." Greta seemed to shift gears and looked at me before continuing. "The problem is, Tim took off. He's probably in Vegas. He loves Vegas."

"Wasn't he going to be at the wrap party tonight?" It only made sense. I would have expected the head writer of the show to be there for the close of production.

Greta went back to work on her pleated slacks, smoothing, smoothing. She began speaking a little more quickly. "He wanted to get away early, he said. Tim had asked if he could skip the wrap party and I didn't see why not. I think he has some new girlfriend or other. Anyway, I have been calling him ever since six this morning, since I heard we have one more huge show to do. He's not at home. He's not answering his cell phone or responding to his pager. I wouldn't be surprised if he just left all his gadgets at home and took off with some new woman." She frowned.

All around us I could tell that my prep chefs were eavesdropping. The noise of chopping knives against boards had softened and cross conversations had ceased. We were all waiting to hear if our party was off.

"Madeline, I'm really in a bind."

I turned and gave the dozen chefs in my kitchen a bosslike glance and two dozen hands returned to work at a renewed frantic pitch. And why not? The party is not over until the client calls it off. And so far, what with her television series's runaway ratings and her runaway head writer, I had yet to hear Greta suggest our evening's party was to be canceled.

"Come on back to my office," I suggested, turning to Greta. "More private."

Greta seemed happy to follow me back through the house. It is a sweet old Spanish-style bungalow, all white stucco and arched door-ways, which was built in the Whitley Heights section of the Hollywood Hills back in the twenties. It has been reconfigured in a way that I can use the downstairs as my business space and the upstairs for living quarters. The original old kitchen was small, so I had it remodeled and enlarged to accommodate party-size cooking. In fact, most of the rooms downstairs are now used for a new purpose. The old butler's pantry is now a short corridor lined with glass-front cupboards. Here I display our growing collection of vintage serving platters and beautiful bowls in bright thirties colors like turquoise and cobalt blue and sun-shine yellow, all of which are used for the dinners we cater. As Greta and I passed through, she stopped to comment on one of the rare rose-pink-glazed cake stands.

Beyond the pantry, the former dining room is now transformed into the office I share with Wesley. I closed the door behind us as Greta and I sat down in this quieter part of the house. I took my usual seat while Greta sat opposite, across the antique partners' desk, in Wesley's chair. I offered Greta her choice of bottled water, and without further delay asked the big question. "Tonight's party. Is it off?"

"We need to cancel," Greta said, with a sigh.

A sigh, I daresay, certainly no bigger than my own.

Greta folded her beautifully manicured hands in her lap, stopping for once the constant creasing and recreasing of fabric. "Things at the office are going to be wild," she said, "just wild."

"Don't worry," I said. "It will all work out. I imagine it must be very hard to restart a show that is closing down."

"Exactly! We need to get our entire crew back—our camera opera-tors, our graphics guys, our ADs, our contestant department . . . And I've got to somehow book studio time immediately, which is impossi-ble. And not only that, everyone on the staff has already found new jobs. I have to lure them back and that means money. I need to set up a new tape schedule and figure out the budget and, and everything. We still haven't worked out a deal with our director. My God, Madeline, we were ready to strike our set tomorrow—which reminds me, I need to cancel our storage contract at NBC. And then our head writer is gone and I'm not sure, to be honest, if he's really all right, but . . . It's just a mess."

"I see," I said. I was sort of listening, but her point was clear from the moment she began. It was off, of course. I would have to stop the crew before they chopped their hearts out for a party that wasn't going to happen.

"But really, Madeline, I feel horrible about how this affects your group here. Please don't worry about the expenses. We'll pay for the entire party, anyway. We can afford it—I'll just bill it to the network and send them a copy of the contract. I know you've hired waiters and chefs, bought food, everything." She waved her delicate hand in the air in the direction of the kitchen. "But you will be paid, at least."

"That," I said, "will help. Thanks."

"And since *Food Freak* will still need to throw a wrap party when we come to the *real* end of the season, we'll reschedule the party. I'll let you and Wes know once we get our dates figured out, if that's okay. We'll do it right next time, too. Let's come up with a bigger budget. Hell, we were just given a new order for a one-hour special episode."

This had gone from one party to no party to *two paid-for parties.* "Wonderful," I said, without betraying a bit of whiplash. "And I'll get my guys to finish the dinner here and deliver it to your set. You can all take the food home. Maybe that little reward will help bribe your crew to stay with you."

"You are such a dear."

We looked at each other. It was so easy to deal with the little slings and blows when one's client was a good and generous soul like Greta Greene.

"There is one other thing, though," she said, pushing her short blond hair behind her ears. "One thing I was hoping you might think about."

"What's that?"

"This could be a neat opportunity for you, Madeline. You did tell me before that your bookings are down."

I didn't need reminding. It had gotten so bad that Wes and I and our full-time assistant, Holly, had speed-dialed through our entire contact list and called every client we've had over the six years of Mad Bean Catering, hunting for work. I even called the Vatican on a whim, since we'd once done a very nice reception for the pontiff's last visit to L.A. The pope was fine, I was told by Monsignor Reggia. He just wasn't in the mood to party. Money was so tight it was getting scary.

In fact, Wes and Holly and I had come to some difficult decisions. Wes revised his timetable on the house he had been restoring on the side. He hoped now to get it finished by next week in order to put it on the market as soon as possible. Holly was putting out feelers to her buddies, looking for something temporary. And that left me.

I have a lot of friends who own restaurants. But the food business was suffering all over and the same serious mood that kept the town's foodie clientele from throwing elaborate parties was keeping them home at night, eating take-out Chinese, instead of going out to expensive restaurants. Some restaurateurs I know had actually called *me*, looking for work. I had come to the worrisome conclusion that without being able to cook for a living, I had virtually no marketable skills.

"Here's the thing," Greta said, using her most winning manner, "would you come to work for me? Hear me out. I will pay you a fortune and I would never be able to thank you enough."

"Work for you how?"

"At *Food Freak*. With Tim away, we are down to just two writers. We absolutely need another one. We are dying for new material. It's only two weeks and then we're through. You could do it, Maddie. It's easy."

"What sort of material do you need?"

She smiled.

Wait. Did I just ask that? I realized how desperate to find a job I was when I discovered I was taking her suggestion totally seriously.

"Just recipes. And background on exotic foods and dishes. The history of pasta. Who invented popcorn. That sort of thing."

"Really?"

"It would be so easy for you, Madeline. I'll go over all the material;

Tim usually did that. And I'll assign the material into the show script. Tim did that as well. He'd pick from all the recipes and other information that we'd approved and he'd decide what went into each individual show."

"Is that difficult?" I asked.

"Well, time-consuming and picky. We have to be very careful or we might OD on lemon dishes in one show, or do too much Italian in another. That sort of thing. Tim is so good at it, he just keeps all the future shows in his head. He'd balance it all and none of us had to worry. I will just pick up the slack until we find him and bring him back. But I've been thinking, even if he's back by Monday, we're under the gun for new recipes and history-of-food material. And if Tim doesn't turn up, well . . ." Greta's eyes seemed to lose their focus for a second, but then she looked up and met mine. "We'll just have to be positive. So about this writing job . . . What do you think?"

Show biz. They always say if you sit by your phone long enough . . .

"I hate to admit it, Greta, but I'm kind of interested." Ha! Just when I was beginning to accept the lousy fact that I was probably good for nothing, along comes Hollywood announcing that that is precisely the skill set necessary in the game-show biz.

"Oh, good! You'll love it," Greta said. She took a dainty sip of water, smirking, I suspected, at how well it was all working out for her and the show.

I was smirking, too. This was a job, after all. Bills would get paid. And I'd get to find out what goes on backstage at one of the hottest shows on television.

"Of course," I added, "to be truthful here, I've never actually *written* anything before. I have absolutely no experience."

"Never mind," she said happily. "Not really necessary."

Hot diggety dog.

"Don't worry," Greta said. "We'll show you everything you'll need to do."

No wonder I love this town.

2

LAMOUR may still exist in the studios of Holly-wood, but if it does, it is not wasted on the pro-duction staff of game shows. Even if a show has taken but one short season to become the top-rated series, as *Food Freak* currently is. Even if the show has made a household name of its odd little star, Chef Howie Finkelberg. Even if the show has got all of America singing its theme song, "Who Let the Chefs Out?" Let it be known that even if the show is grossing hundreds of millions of dollars for its gimlet-eyed owners, the production assistants and contestant co-ordinators and question writers on that show work in run-of-the-mill squalor. These workers tread upon cheap carpet and work on ancient desks that have been recycled, production after production, from a time in the distant past before *To Tell the Truth* was even a glint in the eye of legendary game creator Mark Goodson.

I now sat at just such an old dark wooden desk, checking over the questions and answers I would soon be turning in as they came spitting out of the computer's printer.

"Hey!"

I looked up and saw Quentin Shore, one of the two regular staff writers on *Food Freak*, his face a fetching grimace.

"I'm going to kill you," he said, calmly. Only a madman would make the statement so coolly. Well, a madman or a frustrated game-show hack; take your pick. I had only known the guy for a week. It usually takes me longer to get someone this riled.

Quentin Shore had been passing by on the way to his office down the hall. Had been. Now, he stopped stock-still and stared at me. His perfectly oval head contained an overabundance of shiny forehead; his spiky brown hair was clearly running for its life. He was wearing his trademark, just-pressed Polo jeans with an oxford-cloth shirt tucked in. He always looked like this. Even after a workday that stretched past dinnertime, one had to give Quentin a nod for the high degree of just-pressed-ness he managed to maintain. I suspected starch.

Quentin sipped from a super-size cup of Starbucks and simmered with irritation. He was all the f-words: forty, fussy, forgettable looking, and at this particular moment, furious.

"Why?" I asked.

Quentin Shore seemed in no rush to tell me why he wanted me dead, but I could guess. In the world of television production, the stakes were high. Everyone felt vulnerable. Ratings. Each network passed along that particular sour stomach down the line to the folks who created the programming. Eventually this mass of passed-along pressure settled over entire studios. You could see it in the stress lines around every PA's tightly clenched jaw, hear it in the insistent buzzing of every runner's pager, and taste it in the dozens of half-empty coffee cups littering the consoles in every overtime edit bay.

My newness to the world of TV production provided temporary immunity, but eventually everyone in this world felt threatened. It doesn't take a Dr. Joyce Brothers to figure out why Quentin Shore was sputtering in my doorway. When a coworker moves ahead too quickly, someone may become threatened. Every extra square inch of office space—tacky carpeting be damned—mattered when gauging one's worth to the show.

I gestured to my temporary new quarters. "This office?"

"You're dead." He said it like the kid who catches his little sister eating cookies on Mom's good couch.

I tried reason. "This is only temporary. Until . . ."

He straightened up to his full five-foot-five height. "Don't give me that—"

We were joined at that moment by Greta Greene, who peeked into my doorway. "Morning, Madeline," she said to me. And then to the man standing beside her, angrily sipping his coffee, she said, "Calm down, Quentin."

Quentin forced his gaze from my newly assigned workspace to turn hurt eyes on Greta. "This is an outrage," he said softly. "I'm serious. How can you do this to Tim? You gave away his office! What's going on? Have you found him yet?"

Greta didn't answer right away. She looked uneasy, clearly not happy to be drawn into such a discussion in the middle of the hall.

"What?" Quentin insisted, trying to read Greta's silence. "Have you fired him?" Quentin lost a little of his peeved expression and was moving into the area of shocked. "Greta, that man was the best head writer in the business. He deserves more. He was my friend. He—"

"We're all worried about Tim," Greta said, cutting off any more of Quentin's tirade. "But those of us who are still here are also worried about getting the show together. We start taping this evening and, Tim or no Tim, the show must go on. You know that. You're a pro. Please try to stay calm." Greta was, as always, the definition of ladylike petite blonditude. She patted his hand. "Let's all stay focused, okay? It's Monday. You're a writer. Your deadline is"—she looked down at the Tiffany watchband on her small wrist, and back up—"in ten minutes." She gently shooed Quentin out of my office doorway, but he was loath to budge. "Let's meet in my office at ten o'clock. We need good stuff."

Quentin gave a lovely groan and muttered, "Great," his braces gleaming.

From her spot at the doorway, Greta sent me an inquiring look.

"Fine," I said, a neat stack of pages lying on the desk in front of me. The good girl. Competitive? Me?

I received a look from Quentin Shore as dirty and large as a landfill.

Then he hurried off down the hallway, careful not to spill his Starbucks.

I sighed. Me in TV Land.

I looked around my newly assigned office, tidy if threadbare, the prize that had sent a grown man into a tizzy of resentment and envy. It really wasn't all that much. But as carefully as I tried to resist the lure of Hollywood's seduction, I could not totally ignore the room's quirky coolness. It was like some large eccentric library you might find in a charming old hotel. But since it really belonged to *Food Freak's* head writer, Tim Stock, I felt a little awkward sitting among another person's possessions. I noticed a deep-blue glass vase, ready to accept a single flower stem. I instantly liked a guy who was ready to bring a flower into work. And it made me think again about the circumstances that might cause a man to remain missing for over a week. Something was nagging at me. Some old nightmare. "Missing" was a dangerous word. Was it really normal that an eccentric young writer should disappear on vacation for this many days? Probably. After all, none of his girl-friends or relations were calling here, looking for him. I was just scaring up some ghosts. I looked around the room again and tried to imagine what Tim must be like.

This office was actually two stories high, which gave it an open and majestic feeling. Floor-to-ceiling bookcases, old and dark, hugged three of the walls on the first floor, and rose up again from the second-story balcony. A spiral staircase was off to one side. I love libraries, and this one, devoted to the culinary arts, was exceptional. From its shelves, hundreds of books spotlighted every imaginable cuisine, diet, lifestyle, food group, or exotic ingredient on the planet. I leaned over to the nearest shelf and pulled down a few books. One could choose from the naughty (*Make Love to Couscous!*) to the cosmic (*The Scott Baio Diet for Inner Peace*) to the lethal (*Death by Frosting*) and beyond. This impressive cook's library stretched high, the top shelves almost scraping the large room's discolored acoustic tiles twenty feet above. It was that odd mix of great books and hand-me-down furnishings that made the whole thing offbeat. Take the sofa. Does anyone remember the horror called Herculon? That sad excuse for uphol-stery fabric rendered the brown sofa in the corner its seventies retro style and posed a skin-burn threat, all in one neat package. I sighed. I was there one short week and was already daydreaming about a little redecorating.

I came out of my meditation on Tim Stock's office with a start. It was just about ten o'clock—writers' meeting time. I grabbed my red canvas bag and quickly filled it with a file I'd kept of clippings from food magazines and newspaper food sections. I added a new yellow legal pad, and a folder in which I placed my game-show material—several pages of culinary facts and recipe histories that make up the questions and infotainment bites on America's hottest new game show. I was only now missing my lucky pen—a Sensa in black and blue—a real beauty, a gift from Wes. He'd told me it would help launch my temp career as a game-show writer if I carried a serious pen.

It still felt awkward opening another person's desk, but I didn't want to be late to our meeting. I pulled the drawer open and surveyed the jumble of Tim Stock's belongings. It was of *legendary* junk-drawer proportions. Pads of Post-it notes were crammed on top of a spaghetti tangle of multicolored rubber bands. Several spiral-bound notebooks squeezed against a sprawl of pink and blue index cards, all the worse for wear. A half-eaten Hershey bar seemed stuck to a knock-off brand clear-tape dispenser. Needless to say, dozens of cheap plastic stick-style pens shared the squalor with numerous capless felt tips. But my sweet little Sensa was not there.

Time was passing here, and I would simply have to make do with a ballpoint from Tim's cesspool of office supplies. I grabbed one, not terribly surprised that it was sticky, and wiped it thoroughly with a tissue from a small pack of Puffs protruding from the desk drawer. Handy. I dropped the cleaned pen into my canvas bag, ready to go.

"You planning on being late?" a voice drawled.

I looked up. At my doorway was that charmer Quentin.

"I'm on my way," I said, as I shut the desk drawer and grabbed my bag.

"Oh, joy," he said over his shoulder, moving up the hall in the direction of Greta's office.

Joy, indeed. I had fun at these gatherings.

Just last week, I'd attended my first writers' meeting, barely able to speak up and introduce my recipes. Greta sat behind her desk and smiled at me, encouraging her new little pupil.

"Go on, Maddie, what recipes did you bring in for us today?"

My first time up to bat, and I'll admit I had been a little tentative. "I studied the file that lists all the recipes you have used this first season of *Food Freak*, and I didn't see a show that featured *pasta al pesto*." Pesto is a favorite Italian pasta topping, but not terribly exotic. The sauce, which is made from fresh basil and olive oil and grated Parmesan cheese, appeals to many taste buds.

"Pesto?" Quentin smiled kindly. "Honey, we don't do anything as terribly *obvious* and *pedestrian* and—well, I have to say it because it's true—*clichéd* on *Freak*. Our standards, which I'm sure you can't possibly know about since you have absolutely no experience in television, are much more sophisticated. Nice try, though."

Jennifer Klein added quickly, "But personally, I love pesto." She smiled at me, a signal that she was not part of Quentin's vendetta.

"I love pesto, too," Greta said. "Why haven't we thought of using it in the past?"

"Well," Quentin said, muttering under his breath, "some of us *did* make a tiny suggestion of pesto at the beginning of the season, but then some of us were shot down by a certain head writer who found the entire idea of pesto, and I quote, '*nauseatingly* plebeian.' "

"Go on, Maddie, " Greta said, "what sort of background information have you put together for *pasta al pesto*?"

I took a deep breath. Whatever office politics ruled this kingdom didn't apply to a foreigner like me. I had diplomatic immunity. After all, the best part of a temporary job is that one never has to worry about "the long run." I opened my folder and began to read aloud.

" 'If you've ever driven or ridden the train from the French Riviera into Italy, you've been to Liguria, one of Italy's smallest and most charming regions. The sparkling Riviera di Levante, the coast from Genoa to La Spezia, is one of Italy's most famous. It features a collection of picturesque fishing villages, the most famous of which is Portofino. The Riviera di Ponente that stretches from France to Genoa is a flowering paradise studded with such turn-of-the-century belle époque resort towns as San Remo.' "

"It's a travelogue," Quentin commented. "Too many foreign words."

"I love it," Jennifer said. "I was in Liguria last year."

"Please continue, Maddie," Greta said. She was pleased.

" 'Traditional Ligurian food is some of the most refined cuisine in Italy. For centuries, sailors plied the seas as part of the spice trade, bringing to Europe the exotic products of the Far East and Africa. When they returned from their long voyages, the sailors had had their fill of fish and spicy food. What they wanted instead was fare that spoke of their homeland, made from vegetables fresh from the gardens and farms that cling to the Ligurian hillsides. As a result, the dish that is now most closely identified with this region is *pasta al pesto*, noodles bathed in an intensely green and fragrant sauce.

" 'Ligurians almost make a religion of their devotion to pesto sauce and its main ingredient, fresh basil. There is, however, no uniformity of opinion as to the best recipe for pesto or its best uses. Every village, and for that matter probably every family, has its own recipe for pesto sauce and its favorite shape of pasta to use with the sauce. For example, the Genoese prefer a sharp, pungent pesto sauce, which they serve with ravioli filled with veal and cheese. Many people opt for a mild pesto sauce, sometimes with cream or butter added. In many areas, the preferred pasta is *trenette*, a sort of plump local version of linguine. In still other areas, they dispense with the pasta altogether and add the pesto to their local version of minestrone or to fish soup.' "

"Okay," Quentin said. "That's our forty-six minutes, folks. Good night and sorry we don't have time for the game."

"But, Quentin, be fair. That's exactly what we are looking for," Greta said. "Madeline has given us some charming history of the dish, and at the same time she's opened up the possibility that our contestants might have their own versions of the sauce and their own ways of serving it. Of course we can cut that copy down to proper time. We always do." And she turned to me once more and said, "Excellent work."

"But," Quentin rebutted, "Tim said that—"

"Tim," she countered sweetly, "is not here. So let's move on." Greta wrote the words *"Pasta al Pesto"* on the large white board in her office, and next to those words she wrote "Madeline Bean."

That was one week ago and I am embarrassed to admit I still think of it. No wonder I have come to enjoy the daily writers' meetings.

I was like a tourist, just passing through, looking for a few thrills before I checked out. Normally, I might take a moment to reflect on how odious Quentin Shore could be. But in my tourist mode, Quentin was just one of the picturesque natives, irritating but quaint. I love to travel. There is the voyeur's delight in living briefly a foreigner's lifestyle. Knowing you are not stuck here, like the inhabitants are, it's fun to go native. There is also joy, when working in stress-pitted Hollywood, for those who charge in to the rescue. I had agreed to come "help out" an old friend in a deadline jam. My old friend was the boss. Under these artificial circumstances, what fun working in television was!

Still, no matter how many little triumphs I had had over the past week, I was still the new girl. I was not going to be late to this morning's meeting. I looked at my watch and vowed to speed up, but then had a little trouble shutting the darn drawer. After rearranging its contents in such a hasty manner, it just wouldn't close. I reopened the drawer and ran my hand over the supplies, settling them flatter. When I withdrew my hand, the drawer was able to close, but an errant Post-it note had stuck itself to the cuff of my black T-shirt. Clearly, the entire desk was booby trapped.

As I stood up and slung the strap of my red canvas bag over my shoulder, I pulled the little yellow note from my sleeve, rolled it in a tiny ball, tossed it into the trash basket, and walked out of Tim Stock's office. In the hallway, the show's other writer, Jennifer Klein, and the first PA, Susan Anderson, were up ahead. As they turned into the door to Greta's office, Jennifer saw me and smiled.

She gave me the sign to hurry up or I'd be late.

I knew. I was just shutting the door to my temporary office when I stopped myself. What business did I have tossing away that Post-it note? It wasn't, after all, really my office. It wasn't my desk drawer. And I hadn't so much as looked at the tiny yellow slip of paper.

Back into the office. Really, it would take no time at all. I quickly bent down to the black plastic trash can and stuck my hand into its fresh liner. Out I pulled the crumpled note. On my knees, red bag still hanging from my shoulder, I impatiently uncrumpled it. Was it trash or was it, perhaps, something I should replace in Tim's desk drawer?

The sticky note was not entirely blank, I saw, as there were several faint words printed in purple ink on the front. Thank goodness I'd scooped it out.

As I stood, I read the note. I steadied myself on the desk and read it again.

"Heidi and Monica might have to die."

F RANKLY," Greta Greene said to the team gathered in her office, "I had expected Tim would be back with us by now. It's been eight days. How long can anyone stand Vegas? Have any of you heard from him?" Greta's bright-green eyes settled on us.

The staff of *Food Freak* looked at one another. Several of us sat on chairs, which we'd drawn up to Greta's glass-topped coffee table. Others lounged on her black leather sofa. No Herculon, I took note, to scratch the executive staff's posteriors.

Murmurs of "Tim was born to be bad" and "That lucky dog" circulated. It suggested that Tim Stock, the show's apparently hard-partying head writer, had still not surfaced from what was probably stretching into a week-long bender. I looked over the small group and noticed that Susan Anderson, the chief PA, remained silent amid the rowdy suggestions of the others. Susan was a tall, curly-haired woman in her mid-thirties, with a great figure and wire-rimmed spectacles. Her yellow T-shirt had a saying on it: "Pull the Wool Over Someone's Eyes." Interesting philosophy.

About Tim Stock's current location, *Food Freak*'s full-time question writers, Quentin Shore and Jennifer Klein, seemed fairly clueless—a lovely irony since the two of them were, after all, in charge of clues. Quentin, in his spray-starched jeans, sat beside Jennifer, a sweet-faced woman, cute and plump, with dark hair and large gray eyes.

Greta answered her intercom's buzz and excused herself for a moment. As we waited for her to return, I took another look at Susan. The first PA was making furious notes on her legal pad. On a weekly prime-time game show such as *Food Freak*, the head production assistant has a massive job and she supervises the junior staff to help get it all done. During the tapings, she works in the control booth, taking editing notes from the director, timing the show in progress, and keeping track of the game-score readouts on camera to make sure the guy working the scoreboards is accurate. During the preproduction period, before the actual taping takes place, the first PA organizes all the approved game material, putting together the scripts for upcoming shows. Seemingly unaffected by the stress and the incredible amount of work, Susan looked pretty happy. She was a veteran of many prior game series and her curly-headed halo seemed to bestow on her a serene calmness despite the workload.

On folding chairs pulled close to Susan were her two assistants, the youngest members of the ensemble. Jackson Rush was the researcher, the guy who had to look up all the facts. Writers often wrote from their own memories, and that wasn't really reliable, I'd been told. No matter what you know, it's probably wrong half the time, Greta warned. That's why Jackson worked so hard leading up to every tape day. He verified every item to be used on the air with a second independent source. His heavy-framed glasses sat at a constant tilt to the level of his thick dark brows and he gave me a shy smile. Far slicker was Kenny Abernathy, Susan's second PA. He was a tall, wiry, good-looking kid just out of Stanford. Kenny's fine university education had earned him a job inputting game material into the show's computer database. A warning, if ever there was one, as to the job market for philosophy majors.

Greta Greene returned to her office. She took a chair between Jennifer and me and began the meeting.

"We'll be in the studio all this week, taping our final episode. I know you'll all help Madeline in every way you can, since she's playing catch-up while working so hard to feed us extra material." Greta looked up at her writers and PA staff, her gaze making contact ever so quickly with Quentin. "And by the way, Madeline, I went over this week's script with Artie and he absolutely loved the segment on *pasta al pesto*. I gave you credit for it, of course."

Arthur Herman was the show's executive producer and creator. A busy man in his early seventies, he rarely stopped into the production meetings, but I'd seen him around the offices and had been introduced to him on one occasion.

The group looked content. All but Quentin. He looked rabid. Or was that just a trace of foam from his latte?

"Now, let me just briefly go over our preproduction checklist with Susan's group before we look at new material," Greta said, and then went into a series of consultations about contestant biography data that needed to be added to the upcoming show. As they talked, Jennifer excused herself and left the office. There were innumerable delays and lots of waiting around in these meetings, so we often took our own rest room or phone call breaks when the getting was good.

As we waited for Greta to get to our new material, I wondered how each one on the staff had ended up in this offbeat branch of entertainment. Whether one was on a brief holiday, playing behind the scenes on a real television stage, like me, or sweating out the pressures of keeping a hit show on the air, like Greta, I doubt anyone who works on game shows is doing what they had originally intended to do in life. Whose college counselor suggests a future in games? I looked around the room.

A young guy like Kenny could probably go this way or that. Into feature films. Into prime-time dramas or sitcoms. He still had a few more years to find his place in Hollywood. But the others, those who were in their thirties and forties—my friend Greta, the two staff writers, Quentin and Jennifer, PA Susan, and researcher Jackson—they had all become game-show pros. They'd succumbed, this group, to the temptation of making good money on the outskirts of show business. In fact, there are hundreds of odd little jobs in the entertainment field that can

save one from the humiliation of going back home to Toledo and ad-
mitting to Aunt Ruth that one had not made it in Hollywood after all.
And so, one by one, I imagined, each had stumbled into working on
game shows and discovered they had a knack for doing the work.

As Greta was taking rather a long time to finish up her conversation
with Susan's group, Jennifer Klein returned to the black leather sofa
and smiled at me as Quentin slipped out of the meeting.

Frankly, putting aside any suggestions of redeeming social value,
the work of putting on game shows is fun. There is a wicked pleasure
in performing a task for which no sane grown-up could expect to get
paid, and in fact getting paid well for it. Like circus clowns or nuns in
a convent, this unique, offbeat employment lifestyle encouraged a
bond among the longtime staffers. Jennifer noticed me looking at her
and whispered, "Are you feeling a little more comfortable here this
week?"

I nodded and whispered, "Maybe."

She laughed. To these folks, I must seem like the next new shiny-
faced gal to pull a chair up to their lavish table.

Finished with the production notes, Greta looked up and suggested,
"Someone go find Quentin." As she collected our writers' pages,
Kenny ran out the door to track him down. Greta then began to read
through the material that Jenny and I had submitted. Susan and
Kenny chatted to themselves, going over some revised plans. A few
minutes later, Quentin Shore reentered the office.

"You're late," Greta said, keeping her eyes on the papers she was
reading.

Quentin walked over to her desk, handing over his material for the
day. As he returned to his seat, his beady eyes read the room, looking
for enemies, no doubt. He whispered to Jennifer, "Sure, when I take a
tiny break that's when she decides to go over my work."

"Relax," Jennifer said, under her breath. "The torture is only beginning." Jennifer had a quick laugh and a talent for the subtlest of sarcasm. She seemed fairly unruffled by the process at hand. I was frankly
just happy to be there, enjoying the show.

After only one week on the job, I had become accustomed to the
schedule for the writers of *Food Freak*. In the mornings, we met to go

over new material. After lunch, we were left alone to write up new recipes or rewrite something that needed work from the morning meeting. On this particular Wednesday, it took about ninety minutes once we got serious, all of us sitting in Greta Greene's office gossiping over each other's recipes, tossing out suggestions, offering corrections, for Greta to make her way through the material we had handed in. Once, when Greta was involved in a longish phone conversation with Artie, I stepped out to make a call of my own.

As I walked out into the hallway, I almost bumped into Kenny, who looked startled to see me popping out of the door. I smiled and pulled the door shut, and walked down the stairs to go outside for a moment and get some air.

My cell phone reception was slightly better outside, and I connected with Holly, our young and invaluable assistant at Mad Bean Events, after a few rings.

"What's shaking?" Holly answered, not bothering to ask who it was on the other end.

"Not much," I said.

"Ah, Madeline! You must be clever and sneak me onto your studio lot. I heard that U2 is shooting a music video there this week and I simply have to, have to, have to see them."

Holly is the sort of adoring fan whose enthusiasm could power a small city. Her devotion has prompted me, at times, to keep an extra-careful eye out, when one of her favorites shows up on the guest list of one of the parties we are catering. She's a mass of fan nerves when she actually meets them, saying "stupid fan things" and kicking herself for days after. She's hopelessly devoted to just about every celebrity she has ever met, and indiscriminately adores the guy who's on *Angel*, the guy who wrote the song "Short People," and the gorgeous guy who played the Royal Canadian Mountie on some long-canceled series.

"I'll see what I can do," I said warily.

"Please, Mad," she whispered, moaning. "I am going crazy. I can't find a single job. Can you believe it? I've spent the entire weekend helping Wesley move furniture around his spec house. If he tells me to hold the mirror an inch lower one more time . . ."

"Maybe I can get you a temporary gig here," I suggested. I could imagine that Wes and Holly needed a little breather from each other. He was probably overwhelmed with details before the real estate brokers held their open house tomorrow.

"Could you?" she asked. "That would get me onto the lot. I could scout around and see what other interesting productions might be going on over there."

"I'm sure. Look, I've got to go. I'll call you soon. Don't drive Wes nuts."

I trotted back up the stairs and reentered the writers' meeting. Greta was still on the phone with Artie and I noticed that Susan Anderson, the able first PA, had also taken advantage of their long conversation to take a quick break.

Quentin refused to look at me, but Jennifer brought me up to date. Artie was worried about Chef Howie's performance or some such thing. The star was unhappy.

Greta hung up her receiver and smiled at us. "Sorry. So many decisions and nothing, apparently, can wait. Let's get back to the fun stuff—the material."

Together, we discussed what recipes would work well, which ones had been done before, what recipes couldn't be repeated, and so on. The show was based on a simple concept: the celebrated star of the show, Chef Howie Finkelberg, challenged two small teams of contestants, talented home chefs, to cook extreme meals from Chef Howie's own stunningly fabulous recipes. Of course, it was our job to concoct those recipes, a job that I considered incredibly easy. But then, I was the new guy. Jennifer and Quentin had already worked for an entire season, coming up with hundreds of recipes. They were professional, pragmatic, experienced, expedient. By this time in the long season of shows, they were partially burned out. When my offering at this meeting, an off-the-wall recipe for Chef Howie's Confetti French Toast was praised and scheduled into the show's script, I felt terrific. I was having a ball.

Greta turned and said, "I am so glad you are here, Maddie," as she closed the meeting. The truth was, so was I.

As we all got up, and chatted, and stretched, and began filing out of her office, Greta held me back a moment.

"Do you have plans for lunch today?" she asked me quietly.

Quentin, who was hanging back, heard Greta's invitation and his shoulders seemed to sag beneath his heavily starched shirt.

"No plans," I said. "Would you like to discuss the new wrap party?"

"Fine. Let me take you out to lunch. I have something else I'd like to ask you about, too," Greta said.

She grabbed her purse and we walked together down the hall. My office—Tim's office, really—was three doors down, about thirty feet away. As we approached it, we both noticed something odd.

"Your door . . . ," Greta said, her voice perplexed.

I reached it first. The door to Tim's office was not completely shut. Greta looked up at me sharply. "Didn't I tell you that we always keep our office doors locked? It's a security issue. A precautionary measure when the game material is around."

"I usually pull the door shut and it automatically locks." I tried to remember if I'd done that this time.

Greta didn't look particularly disturbed but I made a mental note to double-check the door each time I left the office. Because the door was ajar, I simply pushed it in. "I'll just put down my files. It'll only take—"

I never finished the sentence. We both saw it at the same time.

"Oh, no!" Greta said, an intense whisper escaping like steam.

I could say absolutely nothing. A thousand tiny hairs on the back of my neck stood up and I began to feel sick.

4

TIM Stock's two-story office/library, neat when I had left it two hours earlier, was now a complete disaster. The row of tan-colored filing cabinets that lined one wall had been vandalized. Drawers were overturned and hundreds of manila file folders were strewn about the room, their contents scattered wildly.

We both just stared.

"What . . . ," I stammered, "happened?" I am sure there were any number of brilliant questions that might have been posed at this point. That, however, was the best I could do. It felt like someone had struck me. It was odd because it wasn't even really my office, or my possessions, or my papers that had been messed with, but still I felt sick. The office had been trashed. Pages in every color of the Kinko's rainbow were simply everywhere—piled on the floor, littering the old beat-up desk, a few awkwardly straddling the computer keyboard.

"Dear God," Greta said, stepping into the room.

"This is not good, Greta." I walked around the desk, trying not to step directly on a large pile of brad-bound documents, each one with a different pastel-colored cover, each about thirty pages thick. "Are these *Freak's* old scripts?"

Greta quickly shut the door behind her and reached for the script I held out. "Oh God, Madeline. This script." She flipped through it quickly and then rechecked the type on its pink cover. "This is *today's*. All the game material we're supposed to use in this afternoon's taping." She looked up at me. "It's today's script."

From her tone of voice, I got that this was a bad thing. I stood there, not knowing what to say.

"Sorry, Madeline. You probably don't know how serious this all is," Greta said. "The scripts for any upcoming shows have to be kept under lock and key. We must assure the network's Standards and Practices people that the outcome of each of our games will be strictly fair and aboveboard. It's not just that we are Goody Two-shoes about it. It's a federal law."

"A law for game shows?"

She sighed. "Yes. Naturally, they don't trust producers. Do you know anything about the old quiz-show scandals?"

Of course I did. Not from the actual fifties, of course, but I did rent the movie *Quiz Show* to prepare myself for my new temporary career. The quiz-show scandals occurred in the early days of television. Back then, certain "creative" quiz-show producers were caught tampering with their contestants. They fed the correct answers to individual contestants in order to heighten the show's tension and drama. Millions of viewers came back week after week to see if the same star contestants could keep up their winning streaks. When the cheating was uncovered and the shows were busted, these producers insisted that the shows were meant to be pure entertainment. That argument was frowned upon. Americans had been duped. They had been led to believe they were watching a legitimate competition. Some have suggested our innocence as TV watchers was then and forever lost.

"But, Greta, those old-time producers didn't go to jail."

"Because they hadn't actually broken any laws," she said, smoothing her navy blue pants. "But afterward, the government fixed that. Now, the entire staff of every game show must comply with federal regulations and sign form 509. That form, Madeline," she said, her voice as calm as ever, "promises that we'll keep the secrets secret or they can throw us in . . . well . . . in prison."

Man. Jeez.

I followed Greta's eyes back to the door. I was sure I had pulled the self-locking door closed when I'd left the office earlier, wasn't I? I know I was rushing, but . . .

Greta looked at me with a wan smile. "It's all my fault. I should have had you sign that form, too—the 509. My fault. An oversight. So now it all lands back in my lap, and I'll be lucky if all they do is fire me."

I blinked. How could this be? I had been having such fun playing in the world of game shows. I had found the greatest temp job on the planet. I was making a delicious amount of money and doing hardly any work. I simply looked up and fiddled with a few recipes a day. I sat in meetings and talked about food, for crying out loud. And it was good karma, too, since I was helping out a friend in need. How could it be that I was now suddenly on the verge of sending my generous buddy Greta to *prison*? How had I managed to do so much damage by simply forgetting to slam shut my freaking door?

"This is bad," I said, looking around at the disaster area that had once been a tidy office. And another, even grimmer thought struck me. What if this vandalism turned out to have a cause that was even worse than Greta imagined? Why had someone trashed *this* particular office? Was it just a potential game-show cheat, catching an unauthorized early peek at an upcoming script, bad as that would be? Or was the targeting of Tim Stock's office perhaps connected in some way to the disappearance of *Food Freak*'s head writer? There were too many possibilities for me to keep everything straight.

Greta, even under stress, never showed a feather ruffled. "There's a show-business term you may not be familiar with," she said, still her calm, soft-spoken self.

I may not have had any previous show-biz experience, but just living in this town, you learn to pick up a lot of these quaint show-biz terms. "We are screwed."

Greta nodded.

"Do we have to sneak out of the country?" I asked. Well, I can't stay serious for too long or it hurts.

Greta almost smiled and then got down to business. "Okay. We can fix this."

"Great." I stared at the pile of tumbled scripts.

"Okay," she repeated, firmer. "Let's not touch anything. For as long as we can keep this quiet, I'd like everyone on the staff here to stay out of it. I need to talk with Artie and he'll tell us what we can do. You okay with that?"

"Well, sure," I said. I imagined myself under bright lights, a federal prosecutor peppering me with questions. I saw myself looking rather strained, but never cracking.

"I have to make a phone call." Greta pulled her cell phone out of her purse and began dialing. She looked up at me and stopped. "You don't look so good, Madeline. You should go sit down."

"I'm fine. And I can't sit anywhere." The pile of papers and the green Pendaflex files with their nasty metal edges were strewn in such a way that they covered my desk chair. I was not terribly keen to try the Herculon sofa in the corner.

"You should leave, honey. Go sit down in my office. Wait there. Let's try to keep this contained until we know more about what really happened." We were both staring at the enormous mess, some pages ripped while other papers were crumpled and folded. "Damn, it looks like someone didn't care what he destroyed," she said, her voice tight. "Damn."

"I'll stay with you," I offered, one last time.

"No. I'm fine. I have to call Artie."

I opened the door and swiftly shut it behind me, glad to be away from the claustrophobic office with its worn-out furniture and its walls of bookshelves, with its yanked-open file drawers and an entire year's worth of paperwork barfed all over the tatty carpeting.

I walked quickly down the hall to Greta's office and pulled open the door. Susan Anderson was standing there with the two contestant coordinators for the show. They looked up as I came barging in.

"Oh. Hi," I said.

"Hi," Susan said. Her own office connected to Greta's and as long as the PAs were working, these offices could remain unlocked.

"Hi," said Nellie Lauren and Stella Tibbs—Nell and Stell, as they were called. They were almost always together and, frankly, I wasn't sure which one was which. I'd been introduced to them only once and only briefly, because the writing department seldom hangs out with the contestant department as a matter of security. I couldn't remember if Nellie was the tall attractive black woman in her sixties or perhaps the bouncy fifty-year-old with the bright-red pixie-style hairdo.

"Sorry to barge in," I said. "Greta asked me to wait for her here."

I imagined what Greta was going through, back in Tim Stock's office, her position on *Food Freak* suddenly threatened by a nasty act of vandalism. My head was pounding, but at a distance, I could almost feel it. I should have stayed there. I should have insisted on helping. I shouldn't have left her alone with that mess. I should have—

"   . . .she is, Madeline?" Susan was saying.

I looked up to see all three women staring at me. "Excuse me?" I had definitely missed something.

"Greta," Stell—or perhaps it was Nell—asked, perplexed by my confusion.

"Know where she is?" Nell or Stell repeated.

"Um . . ." Well, that was a bright response. If this was my clever answer to a simple staff inquiry, how the hell was I going to hold my own against the feds?

"Maybe she's gone to lunch," the tall, African-American Stell or Nell replied. She sounded agitated. As a matter of fact, so had the red-haired Nell or Stell.

"Stell and Nell need to talk to her immediately," Susan told me. "We've called her cell phone, but it just goes through to her voice mail. Either she's left the phone off or she's on another call."

"Right," I said, still trailing the conversation by at least three seconds.

"Hey," one of the contestant coordinators said, looking at me closely. "You look white as a ghost. Doesn't she, Stell?"

Aha! It was the red-haired woman who was talking. Red hair was Nellie. I felt enormous relief. I think I began to chuckle.

Stella said, "You do look pale. You having trouble, too?"

". . . trouble, too?" I echoed.

Susan filled me in. "Stell and Nell have to be onstage in ten minutes. Their contestants are giving them trouble. It's always something."

"It is," Stell confirmed. "I've seen it all and I still see something new every day."

"What kind of trouble?" I asked.

"What kind don't we have?" Nellie asked, running her hand through her short red hair. "Do you have any idea how hard it is doing this last-minute extra show? It's one hour and we need to find the best contestants, and we don't have the best. They've been used up! It's killing the contestant department."

"I hadn't thought about that before," I said truthfully.

"It's impossible," Stella said, raising one pencil-thin ebony eyebrow. "We simply don't have time to find the quality people we need. We use up to six contestants on every show. Now you go and multiply that times ten shows. Go on."

"Sixty!" Nellie picked up the complaint. "Sixty good-looking, outgoing, happy, talented, engaging, sparkling, smart, competitive people. That's who we have used up all season, Madeline. And now they say they need six more? Just where are we supposed to get six fresh A-plus contestants on such short notice?"

"And they have to cook," Stella added, her eyebrow still arched. "Don't forget they've got to cook, darlin'. They've got to cook good!"

"And answer culinary questions. It's impossible," Nell said, shaking her head. "We need plenty of lead time to place our ads in the Sunday newspaper. We usually do a cattle call and round up some possibles. We have to screen 'em all, of course, and hold callbacks. But all that takes time. We can't pull them out of our—"

"We've used up all our good ones," Stell continued. "This here season was supposed to be finished."

"So," I said, realizing they were waiting for my reaction, "you are having trouble finding good contestants." I hoped that was right. My mind had been racing around and around Greta's current problem. Thank goodness Nell and Stell weren't discussing something really complicated, like the weather.

"Girl, we gave up on 'good' last week. We're settling for live ones just about now."

"That's rough," I said, beginning to warm to this new problem. I had no idea it was a chore to find game-show contestants. It seemed like everyone I knew wanted to be on *Freak*. Of course, most of my friends loved to cook, but still. Who wouldn't want a chance to win half a million dollars just by cooking a nice meal? "Say, I could call some of my friends," I offered. "I know lots of excellent cooks."

"Aw, that's sweet," Stell said, twinkling her brown eyes at me. "But you work here now, pumpkin. Your friends are not eligible to be on this show anymore, now that you work here as a writer."

"It's in the rules," Nell said. "Those rules we all sign."

"The 509," I said, nodding in agreement, hoping no one suddenly wondered if I'd ever been obliged to sign them.

"Right," Nell said.

I realized, just then, the price my friends were now forced to pay so that I could work on a game show. I should have thought this through earlier. Heck, Wesley and Holly, my two closest friends, were excellent cooks. They could have come on this game show and won half a million. It seemed, suddenly, like such a better deal than having me work here for a tiny fraction of that jackpot. D'oh!

The door to Greta's office swung open and we all turned to look. I expected it to be Greta, ready to call a staff meeting, ready to announce what had happened in there, in that office down the hall.

Instead, in popped the star of *Food Freak* himself—Chef Howie Finkelberg. He and I had met only once before, but since the special episode was being taped this week, he would be in the studio a lot more.

"Hi, girls," he said. "Anyone know where Greta is?"

"No. We're all looking for her," Susan said and then, the gracious hostess, she said, "Chef Howie, have you met Madeline Bean yet? She's been writing for the show this past week."

"Hello, Madeline." The star of *Food Freak* turned to me and gave me his full attention. He was the sort for whom tight Levi's had been invented. He was dressed for the taping, wearing a custom-made chef's coat, cut to show off his muscles, over the aforementioned jeans. It was his trademark to leave the collar unbuttoned. Preteen girls pinned up "Chef Howie" posters on their bedroom walls and dreamed of crème brûlée and Chef Howie. "So good to meet you," he said, his contact-lens-enhanced green eyes meeting mine. Clearly he did not remember that we had been introduced the previous Monday. I chose not to re-mind him.

"My God," he said, never breaking our intimate eye contact, "you are gorgeous. That hair! You should be on camera! Do you act?"

"No," I stuttered, shocked. "Never." Can you believe this guy? How corny was that? What sort of green, new-in-town, stars-in-her-eyes, aspiring-actress type did he take me for?

"You're laughing," he said, amused. "I mean it, Madeline. You're a highly regarded chef in your own right, yes? You are a hot young Hol-lywood caterer. You are simply perfect." Howie spoke in a low growl. He did not stop looking at me.

"He's right," Susan said, a hint of excitement in her voice.

Nell and Stell kind of gasped, taken in by the power of Chef Howie's voice.

Here I was, my native skepticism on hyperalert, but how flattering, really, that Howie knew about my culinary business. Of course I was an event planner, not merely a caterer, but he still seemed to know me by my reputation.

I realized they were all staring at me, smiling at me, seeing me in perhaps a whole new light. I felt myself begin to flush and I brushed my long curly hair off of my hot neck.

Just my luck, I would get discovered and be on the brink of my big break just as I was on the verge of being thrown in prison for breaking federal game-show statute 509 or some such number. And, of course, much as I resisted everyone else's infernal dream about a career in front of the camera, I suppose it would be preferable to fifty years in the slammer.

Howie was waiting for my answer.

"What sort of thing did you have in mind?" I asked, annoyed to re-alize my voice did not sound anywhere near as skeptical as I had surely intended it to.

"Listen to Chef Howie," he said, referring to himself in the third person. If that wasn't a clear signal to *stop* listening, I'd never heard one. And yet, I continued to listen. I have no excuse. I just wanted to hear what he thought I might be able to do. Just in case this game-show writing gig was about to be flushed down the tubes due to my exceeding stupidity regarding closing doors.

"I think you should sing, Madeline," he said, with a completely straight face. "You could become the singing chef. It would be a sensation."

Yes. Right. I'm afraid with ideas like that one, I had better see what I could do to salvage the writing gig after all.

5

STELLA, Nellie, Susan, and Chef Howie waited for my response.

"That's not why I'm here working on *Food Freak*," I said modestly. "I may be the one person in Hollywood who has no Hollywood dream."

"Really?" Chef Howie asked, teasing.

"Really. I have no desire to be discovered," I said, smiling. "And, truth be known, I don't sing. At all. But that's awfully nice. Thanks anyway, Howie."

"No, no!" Stell and Nell insisted in unison.

I was startled at their insistence. Me? A singing chef? It was really . . .

Stell said, "It's *Chef* Howie."

"What?"

Nell continued in a lowered voice, "We all say *Chef* Howie."

"All his fans call him Chef Howie," Stella explained. "It's simpler."

"Oh," I said. "You're not joking."

Howie, with a dashing smile, winked at me. Yes indeedy. *Chef* Howie. Right.

The door banged open and we all looked up, expecting Greta. But this time, a tall, snaky-thin woman entered. She wore black leather jeans and a zebra print halter top, not actually appropriate for office attire, but then again, not actually appropriate for *any* kind of attire after, say, 1983. She had the sort of skin that had no doubt spent many a summer slathered in cocoa butter. It had the leathery look for which one pays extra when buying expensive luggage.

"Chef Howie," she said, her voice like a cheese grater. "What the hell are you doing here? I've been looking everywhere for you."

"Hey," Howie said, "chill. I'm waiting for Greta."

Susan did her introduction thing. Susan was indispensable. "Fate Finkelberg, meet Madeline Bean, our newest writer."

"Fay, nice to meet you," I said.

"I'm *Fate*," she corrected. "F-A-T-E."

I avoided a spontaneous smirk and congratulated my self-control.

"A new writer?" Fate turned to Susan and her lips curled downward. "You mean Greta replaced Timmy Stock already? Shame on her!" Fate exuded disapproval and dissatisfaction, elevating the concept of negative energy to an art form.

"Madeline is just helping us out. It's temporary," Susan explained.

I checked out Fate Finkelberg, who was frankly wearing too much jewelry and exposing too much old skin to be taken very seriously. She might have been something twenty-five years back, but by now it was difficult to tell what. She was trying to pull off that disco look and I shuddered to imagine that she had been stuck in those platform shoes for the better part of three decades. I took in her streaked blond hair, cut in the same shaggy style that Rod Stewart used to wear long ago. I turned to study Howie again. He looked to be young thirties and I did the mental math. Fate must be Chef Howie's mother.

As for Howie, with his thick brown hair and his devilish grin, there was nothing I could find wrong with his looks. In *People* magazine's "Sexiest People" issue, they said Chef Howie was bringing back Elvis sideburns single-handedly. His hands were rough and scarred, the way tough-guy chef's hands always are, very sexy. He could have been a rock musician with that lean build and those clear green eyes. Very bad-boy chic. Some insisted it was Howie's hip, casual machismo in the kitchen that had ratcheted *Freak*'s ratings higher and higher. Staring at him now, up close and personal, I couldn't say I'd argue.

"Come on," Fate said, turning back to Howie. "Let's go to the trailer. We need to talk. One of these girls can tell Greta you want her."

Howie seemed very used to following her orders, because without a murmur of dissent or skipping a beat, he told us, "Ladies, I'm outta here. Tell Greta I need her right away. Good to meet you, Maddie." He gave me a slow TV star smile, and winked. Twice.

"See you later . . . Howie." I know. I am bad.

Fate Finkelberg turned slowly; her light eyes traveled over my white jeans and blue tank top, stopping for a moment as she checked out my unruly red/blond hair, which, for once, I was wearing down. It's curly and heavy, and when I'm cooking, I almost always pull it back in a braid or clip it off my neck. As a newly minted game-show writer, however, I was experimenting with the whole long pre-Raphaelite hair look. It was a pain to fuss with, but I'm trying to get into the pain. Fate Finkelberg, queen of the spiky shag cut, was not impressed. At all.

"You call him *Chef* Howie, sweetie pie, or you're out of a job." Ms. Finkelberg didn't raise her voice and didn't blink. She was taking me on, perhaps hoping I'd snap at her bait and get myself fired.

What to do . . . I was being ordered around by *Chef* Howie's psycho mother. Something inside of me just wanted to resist. But I shouldn't. I knew that. I did. I knew it.

Old bat Finkelberg held my gaze, a slight smile playing at her lips. Stella felt the need to fill the silence, explaining, "Madeline is just getting the hang of things around here, Fate. We're trying to fill her in."

She looked nervously at Nellie, who chimed in with, "That's true!"

What terrifically weird dynamic ruled this world? I hated this sort of power play. I tilt at windmills. I tilt at Chef Howie and his mom! This desire I have to oppose idiocy is one of my weaker people skills. It's a very good thing that I am my own boss in my own event-planning company, I realized. But I was not my own boss now. And the truth was, I needed this particular job. With that in mind, I used what little maturity I could scrape together and struck a nonresistant pose. Alas, my act of restraint was not a complete success. I couldn't keep my honest eyebrow from arching a fraction of an inch higher than its more mature mate. Ms. Finkelberg, taking note of my absent apology and my uneven brows, smiled to herself and turned quickly, following Howie out of the room.

"Chef Howie's mom does not love me," I said as soon as the door closed.

Susan Anderson broke into a delighted smile. "Madeline!"

"You are perfect!" Stella said.

"Perfect," Nellie said.

Susan's eyes twinkled. "Fate Finkelberg is not Chef Howie's mom."

"She's his wife," said Nellie.

Oh, man. The handsome young chef and the dried-out old showgirl with the fist of iron—there had to be some terrific story behind this bizarre Hollywood marriage.

The door to Greta's office opened and in walked Greta Greene herself.

"Greta!" Stell said. "Oh good!"

"Thank God you're back," Nell said. "We have got to talk."

"Look at the time," Stell said, seamlessly taking over. "We've got a major contestant problem. We are terribly late getting today's contestants to the set, but—"

Greta interrupted her. "I know. I know. Everything's running late today. I need to talk with Madeline first. Then I'll come find you two and we'll straighten out your contestants."

Nell still looked worried. "We're running so far behind, I'm—"

Greta gave them both a sunny smile. "It's just that kind of day. I'll be by later, okay?"

What could the two contestant coordinators say? Even Susan, who was standing by, waiting her turn to ask Greta a question, seemed surprised. It was rare for Greta to seem so little concerned at being behind schedule. Nell and Stell, no less baffled, left the office.

"Susan," Greta said, looking down at her notepad. "How many scripts are out now?"

"How many have I handed out to our crew today?" Susan asked, "Nineteen, why?"

Greta pantomimed, spreading her arms out and then scooping them up again.

Susan tensed, like she had just been pinched by a sudden, but very familiar, pain. "Changes?"

"We'll talk later, okay?"

Scripts were distributed to the show's director and all the behind-the-scenes technical people in the morning on tape days. Any changes made after that distribution were issued as separate pages, each subsequent version a new color so everyone could keep track of the fact that the green copy of page eleven was fresher than the pink one, and so on. The only reason scripts were collected outright, like Greta was now requesting, was when major revisions were in the works. And on the day of a taping, such an ominous move signaled a fight-against-the-clock workload for the head PA.

"Let's gather them all quickly, please," Greta said, and added, "I've got Advil or Tylenol, take your pick."

"I've got my own," Susan said, across the office and reaching for the door. She was a veteran of these wars and had already donned her professional face. Before she left the office she turned and added, "Chef Howie and Fate were looking for you. So you may want to save those painkillers for yourself." Then she quietly left the room.

Greta sat down behind her desk. "Maddie, is it hot in here or has the stress just pushed me into menopause?"

"What happened to Tim's office? Have you figured it out?"

"Not yet," she said. "I've been too busy working out what to do with our schedule." She tapped a gold pen on her notepad. "I have an idea, but I'm going to need help."

I nodded.

"We have to be very careful how we handle this. It will only bring the dogs of hell down upon us if the staff hears about what happened in Tim's office."

Did no one in this line of work consider understatement?

"I mean," Greta said, rubbing her hands together as if to get warm, "we don't actually know what did happen, do we? In all that mess, we can't even be sure it was the show material they were after."

Maybe she was right. Maybe someone was angry with Tim. I thought it over.

"You see, Maddie, we are living in a fishbowl. The tabloids are looking for dirt. We're vulnerable here."

It was a particularly fetching picture, us the fish, our brewing scandal the crud at the bottom of the bowl, and what, I wondered, was the little statue of Neptune with his tiny trident? No matter. Greta, a great one to offer up metaphors, was on to another one.

"It's like we're Mr. Clean but sometimes there is just too much dirt for even Mr. Clean to, um, clean. We work so damn hard to keep our show beyond reproach, to earn our good name."

While the jaded among us might question whether a game show might indeed have a "good name" in need of protection, I admired Greta and her desire to salvage the good name of hers.

"You're afraid of what *Entertainment Tonight* will do with this story?"

"Of course I am. I'm embarrassed. I'm worried. We're the *Titanic*, Maddie. And out there are icebergs."

"Like this office break-in," I suggested.

"Right. News of our office break-in would be disastrous. *Food Freak* is big, but we could sink. It happened on my watch, after all. And Artie would just about die if this show went down." Greta's voice got softer as she toted up the potential damage. "And the network would take a lot of flack. And the whole genre of game shows would appear to be untrustworthy, again, like ocean liners were back in the old days. Can you imagine?"

Almost seasick with symbolism, I shook my head in sympathy.

"And I'm afraid," she continued, even more kindly, "it wouldn't be at all comfortable for you, Madeline. It was the office you were assigned to that was vandalized."

Of course, she was right. I couldn't even remember if I'd heard the damn door click shut. "I'm so sorry, Greta."

"Don't blame yourself," she said, but her tone of voice reminded me of what one might say to the poor underpaid fool up on deck whose job it was to watch out for ice.

I did blame myself. In only my first week of working on the country's most popular TV show, ladies and gentlemen, I had made quite a contribution. I might have destroyed the network's biggest asset by failing to pull a lousy door a quarter of an inch tighter. "Well," I said, hoping for some hope, "where do we actually stand? What is missing from Tim's office?"

Greta sighed. "It will take hours to go through that mess. I don't know what exactly Tim kept in the office to begin with, so I can't know what might be gone now. I've tried to call Tim, again and again, but there is still no answer on any of his phones."

"It might not be so bad," I suggested.

Greta looked resigned. "As long as the script for today's show was there, we're in deep trouble. We'll never know if they looked at it or not. We have to scrap that show."

"The script," I said, thinking of all that work now gone completely to waste.

"The script," she echoed. "Anyone could have seen the questions and the menus and the secret recipes we had planned to spring on the players in today's taping."

I nodded. In *Food Freak*, the teams could earn bonus advantages by correctly answering questions about gourmet cooking. In the second half of the game, they had to cook special surprise recipes. If one team had the questions in advance, they could easily win all the extra bonus ingredients. And if they knew in advance what recipes they'd have to prepare, they could plot out their strategies ahead of time.

Greta looked miserable. "I'm really royally screwed here," she said, shaking her delicate head. "Think Queen Victoria. Wasn't she the one who had eleven children?"

"I believe she had nine," I said.

"Still, I made my point," Greta said. Then she checked her notes and went on. "But I think we may just have a chance to get through this without it all hitting the fan. Will you help?"

"Of course."

"First, you'll sign the 509 form immediately, which will take care of the show's obligations to adhere to all the federal regulations, okay?"

"Of course."

"And, clearly, we can't tell anyone we had a break-in."

I looked around Greta's corner office. It was decorated in beautiful, classic furniture. The art on the walls looked expensive. She had earned the right to call the shots on a big television series, I knew, and she also had a lot to protect.

"What will you do about today's taping?" I asked.

"We have to cancel it," she said, shaking her head. "I can't really believe I'm saying this. It's unheard of. We never cancel."

"The show must go on."

"Do you know why?" she asked, instructing me kindly.

"Tradition?" I guessed. "There's no business like show business?" I was pretty sure there was a classic show tune that had this sort of thing explained.

She smiled. "No, it's the budget. To cancel a taping at this point will add about seventy thousand dollars to the cost of this season, damnit."

Poor Greta.

"There's studio time. Then there are salaries. Our production crew gets paid union wages and this will add another day. Same goes for talent, warm-up, craft services, meals . . ."

I watched as she ticked off the items on her notepad.

"Well, we have no choice," Greta said, more to herself than to me. Deep creases etched her pretty forehead. "We have to write another show's worth of new material and reschedule the taping. Damn."

Greta seemed extremely disturbed, but then, so was I. There went my pesto recipe. Poof. There went my Confetti French Toast, too. Damn.

"We will not break any laws," she assured me. "We won't take any risks. But we need to give everyone a good, convincing reason for why we are canceling today's taping, a story that won't invite suspicion. Can you think of anything?"

"I'm good at cover stories. There are always last-minute disasters in the party business and always a great need for discretion."

Greta smiled back in a distant sort of way.

I continued, "Like the time we threw a launch party for a new CD. One of my waitresses found the drummer of this terrifically famous British band stoned out of his mind, dancing naked in the ladies' lounge."

"Really?"

"To hear her tell it, old tattoos on old drummers do not make for the most pleasant viewing. Anyway, we needed a polite way of getting the guy out of there."

"You didn't tell his record company?"

"No, no. The problem was, the drummer wasn't inclined to put on his jeans and go home. But my friend Holly had a great idea. She told him reporters from *Us* magazine wanted to do a feature on the sexiest men of rock and roll . . . and they were waiting to interview him—with his clothes on—back at his house in Holmby Hills."

Greta said, thinking of her own problems, "We need a clever story like that."

I do love to solve problems. It's just that in my normal line of work, I usually know something about all the variables before I try shuffling them. Here, I was lost.

"I'm particularly worried that Fate Finkelberg will get wind of the truth and get herself in a ferocious snit. That woman. If she suspects we've got a real problem with the production, she could hold up our negotiations with Chef Howie for his next contract. Damnit."

I had seen Greta deal with difficult problems all week, managing the large operation. The problems weren't growing any smaller.

"Are you okay, Greta?"

Her hand found the box of tissues on her desk, and whether she had a speck of dust in her eye or a tear, I couldn't say for sure. "I can handle it," she said, her voice still strong.

"I know you can."

Greta Greene looked up and asked aloud, "Where is Tim? Why can't I find him? He should have been in contact with someone on the staff by now, even if it was just . . . ."

"When someone is missing . . . ," I started, but I couldn't finish it. The not knowing is the worst feeling in the world. Any kind of final answer would be better than wondering and worrying and tearing yourself apart inside. I knew that. I had felt that when I was a child. Someone missing was a terrible thing.

Greta said, "I don't want to give in to panic. I don't. But why was

Tim's office searched? Is there something worse than stealing scripts going on?"

We were finally talking about the real issue that was causing Greta so much grief. "You're worried about Tim Stock."

"I don't know. He's just disappeared. What if he—"

She was interrupted by the ringing of her phone. As she answered it, I thought about the problem of the missing head writer. What if all the troubles had not started with today's office break-in? What if the troubles stemmed from the man who had occupied that office for the past six months?

Greta hung up her phone with a tight frown. "Fate and Howie. He's waiting for me and I just can't get to him right now. If Tim were here, I'd send him. But he's gone. He's gone. So now you are officially our 'acting' head writer."

"You're kidding, right?" You have to love this television business, really. A man is missing, a production is in crisis, seventy grand has just flown out of the window because a door is left ajar. If you screwed up badly enough here, you could very quickly wind up running this town.

"Greta, I don't think this is such a good idea," I said. "Fate and Howie were here a few minutes ago. I am not Fate's favorite staffer. Not at all her cup of tea, to tell you the truth. Really. She'd rather stomp on me with her silver platform boots than listen to me."

"This show is my life," Greta said, finding perhaps one more speck of dust in her eye. She dabbed. "I know how pathetic that must sound, but this show is all I have. I have worked so hard, so hard to get a hit series. And here it is, Maddie. I just need a little time. I need your help."

I'd gotten us into this mess and now Greta was counting on me, however misguidedly, to get us out. But what was really going on here in Game Show Land? The head writer of the show was seriously missing, his office was turned into a rubbish heap, and what about that Post-it note that read: "Heidi and Monica might have to die." Were these events connected?

"Greta, about Tim Stock—"

"Oh, don't worry about Tim," she said, her face pale. "Forget what I said. He'll turn up. I know it. But I honestly don't think I can handle one more thing going wrong right now. Once the *Hindenburg* has crashed, it's down, you know? Will you go see Howie for me? I need a miracle, here. Maybe some little white lie to stall him while I think of a way to cancel today's taping that won't arouse suspicion."

"I'll try my best."

With all the backstage drama swirling around *Food Freak*, I had a lot of questions. Another visit with the show's charismatic star might lead to some answers. And that sent me searching for Chef Howie. And Fate.

6

A FAVORITE TV show is like a pal. It is an intimate relationship. You invite it into your living room or den in the evening and it tries hard to entertain you.

To the people who package those half hours and send them to your house, however, time stretches out. It takes a week of days and nights to produce each twenty-two minute package of fun, minus the commercials. And while it may seem like we're in your bedroom or your family room, we're not. We're on some hot soundstage in some dusty studio in an industrial-looking neighborhood of Los Angeles.

Arthur Herman Productions leases office space in the old part of Hollywood, east of Highland. *Food Freak* is made on what is now the KTLA lot, located at the corner of Sunset Boulevard and Bronson. Here, a scattering of eighty-year-old buildings covers twelve acres of studio space, all enclosed like a medieval fortress by high, barbed-wire-topped walls that go on for blocks. The guards on duty are not so much occupied with fighting off medieval dark knights as they are mostly busy painting over the rude spray-canned markings of those knights'

present-day equivalents. Sentries posted at the entrance gates keep out
the passersby, mostly neighbors, recent arrivals from El Salvador or
Guatemala or Mexico who live in the surrounding dusty apartment
buildings. Only those who are employed on one of the productions
that are shot at this studio are admitted into this small kingdom, or
those lucky ones who have business here and have had their names left
at the gate, a pass waiting.

When I worked as a caterer, arriving with dinner for casts and crews
at studios like this one, I'd often have a pass waiting. But now, for my
tiny stint as a writer on *Freak*, I actually belonged here. I ran down the
dozen stairs from our second-floor offices, and opened the exterior
door, exiting our building onto a private alleyway. It might not look
like much, but I loved being on this lot. Like many transplants to Los
Angeles, I have a crush on Hollywood. I enjoy its strange history.

And this particular studio on the low-rent side of Hollywood, ragtag
as it appears today and obscure to tourists, has more history than most.
Not many folks know that this very lot was the original Warner Bros.
movie lot, built in 1919. Although the nine old soundstages have gone
through half a dozen owners since that time, it remains one of the old-
est production studios in continuous use in this town.

I looked back at our office building, one of several three-story, tan
stucco units, and then headed off on my errand, crossing a small parking lot on my way to soundstage 9, which contains the sets for *Food
Freak*, awaiting the next taping. I should have been concentrating on
my task, figuring out some way to correct the trouble I'd started, thinking about what I might say to Chef Howie that could possibly fix
things. But instead, I was daydreaming. I always am while walking
along these small, private streets, bewitched by the romantic history of
early Hollywood.

In 1914, two brothers in the Warner family started a film distribution company in New York. Their two other brothers, Sam and
Jack, came west. It was here, on this very lot, that they produced
their first silent serials. Here, I thought, looking at the buildings
around me, they had once hired Charlie Chaplin's brother, Sydney,
to star in one of their first features. By 1923, the films that were produced by the brothers became highly respected. Here they shot

Babbitt by Sinclair Lewis. All the early stars worked here. Barrymore. Swanson. Rin-Tin-Tin.

I walked down one of the trafficless streets on the lot, shielded from greater and lesser Hollywood, and from reality, and from the twenty-first century by the tall walls. Alone on the lot, I forgot for a moment the glorious southern California spring weather, lost in the studio's no-less-glorious past. The movies found their voice in 1927, a most important year in film history, I thought, as I passed by the very soundstage where *The Jazz Singer*, starring Al Jolson, was shot. That first film to have dialogue and music was a stunning hit, and an entire era of talkies followed. This little studio on Sunset produced many of those early musicals, like the hugely popular *Gold Diggers of Broadway*, in 1929.

On this bright afternoon, I could imagine what it might have been like once upon a time, when dozens of chorus girls in marcel waves and glittery tap shoes hung around these quiet studio streets. Back in '29, here, at this very corner I was now passing, a young woman might have caught a smoke, hoping to flirt with someone who could boost her to stardom. I stopped, wondering if it was possible to conjure up such ghosts in the strong sunshine.

But Hollywood's history is a saga of boom and bust and this particular piece of real estate's heyday was soon past. By 1933, the Warners moved to large new quarters in Burbank. By World War II, these production facilities in Hollywood were leased to independent producers, just like they are now. Back then, they were home to war-training films and Warner cartoons; the big feature films had moved on.

When I reached soundstage 9, I took a look around. Each immense, dome-roofed soundstage squatted on an entire block and I couldn't immediately see what I was looking for. I checked down the side street. No Chef Howie mobile home. So I continued walking up the block, recalling the stories of this lot's past.

As television took over this town, a local station moved in and today KTLA continues broadcasting their morning show and newscasts from here. The station accounts for the two huge white satellite uplink dishes now settled like giant upturned mushroom caps next to one of the newest of the buildings. There's an eclectic mishmash of entertainment facilities here. It's the home of L.A.'s number one news radio station. KFWB began life right here, and—no one knows this!—its call letters stand for Keep Filming Warner Brothers! My friend Wesley and I love to stump each other with such trivia about the old days.

Since the sixties and seventies, these soundstages have been used to film television series, as well. In early 1961, an immense set was built on three of these stages to accommodate *Gunsmoke*, while the production's horses were stabled on yet another soundstage. It must have been terrific to spend those years filming here, driving your car through the studio gates and then changing into costume to live in the Old West.

I turned the corner, expecting to see Miss Kitty hanging around. Instead, down the block, I saw Kenny, one of the assistant PAs, exiting the door on this side of soundstage 9, balancing a stack of scripts. He waved.

"Hi, Madeline."

"Hi, Kenny," I said. "Say, did you know that *Donny and Marie* was taped here?"

"Excuse me?"

"And *Jeopardy!*" I continued. I was on a jag now. "And *The Dating Game.* And *Supermarket Sweep.*"

"No kidding."

"Bet you thought they shot that in a real market, but no, they built a perfect replica of a supermarket in soundstage two, the better for its contestants to go racing down the aisles, looking for expensive groceries."

Kenny looked at me for a beat before he offered, "Cool."

Alas, not everyone is a history buff.

"I'm on my way back to the office," he said. "Susan told me to collect all the scripts."

"Right."

"Um," Kenny said, checking me out a little more closely. "You lost?"

"No," I said, quickly. "Not really. Well, I'm looking for Chef Howie. Can you point me in the right direction?"

"He's still in his trailer," Kenny said. "He wouldn't give me back his copy of the script."

"Oh?"

"It's just around the next corner," Kenny said, pointing back the way he'd come.

"Thanks."

Kenny continued toward his office and I turned back to my quest, following his directions, eventually rounding the corner and discovering the white, twenty-five-by-eight-foot motor home that doubled as Chef Howie's dressing room.

I stepped up to the door and heard an argument coming from inside the trailer. A male voice was saying, "I disagree totally. This is perfect for Chef Howie." I tapped lightly on the white door, but got no response. I knocked harder and waited.

I could make out the sound of Fate Finkelberg's cigarette-hoarse voice inside as she yelled, "Who the hell is that, now?"

The door opened a crack and I was surprised to see Quentin Shore's squinting brown eye. An awkward moment passed as he neither opened the door any wider nor shut it in my face. I suspected he wished to do the latter.

"Open the door, for God's sake," Fate's voice ordered from inside.

"Hi," I said, walking into the overly air-conditioned main cabin. On the far side, a makeup station and professional clothes racks filled the corner. In the larger area, four white leather captain's chairs surrounded a white marble table. Fate was sitting at the table while Howie and his makeup artist occupied the dressing-room corner.

"What do you want?" Fate asked.

"Greta asked me to go over the material for today's taping with Chef Howie," I improvised, ever the ingratiating one when I wanted to be.

"Waste of time!" Fate said.

"There is really no need," Quentin whispered, still standing close to me by the entrance. "I'm on the job here. Chef Howie wants me."

"Yes, but I don't think you know—"

Okay. Just a quick word of advice. If you should ever be in the presence of a game-show question writer, never, ever begin a sentence implying that there might be something they do not know. Quentin looked like he had swallowed a lemon, whole.

"Look," I said, acutely aware of how "not well" this was going.

"Greta wants me to take over for Tim. I'm the acting head writer and—"

Quentin Shore's shiny face turned red. "That's . . . that's not fair." He turned to Chef Howie, but at that moment the star was checking his mirror to see if his legendary sideburns were even. Quentin turned again to me. "I've been kind to you. I've been helpful. But you have just gone too d—, well, too far."

Quentin Shore couldn't seem to bring himself to curse.

"For your information," he said, his voice tense, "I've been working on *Freak* since the pilot. Did you know that? Furthermore, Tim Stock is my good, good friend. He dropped me a note and asked me personally to look after the show while he was away. So it's my duty and my responsibility and my job to brief—"

"Tim Stock?" I asked quickly. "Where is he?"

I noticed that Fate was watching us closely as we bickered back and forth, her hand dipping into a can of Planters cashews.

How had I gotten in the middle of a catfight? As an event planner and caterer, I had taken pride in my tactfulness, in my good relations with both clients and staff. Heck, I like to make people happy. But the emotions in this line of work clearly ran hotter. People here liked to brawl. My friendly little "get-along" personality wasn't serving me at all well, I was discovering, in this extreme sport of Hollywood ego wrestling. This temp recipe-writing job, which should have been a breeze, had already pitted me against a good number of combatants, each with an agenda the size of Mount Wilson. And why? Because in this arena, I was an unknown, a rank amateur. Everyone wanted to take me on. Here, on this turf, I had zero credibility.

But every problem must have a solution. If my rational approach wasn't working, I'd have to adapt to the culture, and, lucky for me, this was a world where outsiders could move up fast. Acting was called for, and I'd have to change my vocabulary, too. I looked at Quentin coolly and tried the New Hollywood–version Madeline out on him. My voice lost every ounce of its calm and friendly tone. "Cut the bullshit, Quentin."

"What?"

"Stop fucking around. Stick with the topic, okay? Tim Stock. Just where the fuck is he?"

At the table, Fate Finkelberg stopped chewing her cashew, and in the makeup corner, Chef Howie's hairdresser stopped spraying Freeze and Shine on Chef Howie's perfect hair.

"I don't know where he is right this very minute," Quentin pleaded, a tinge of hurt now creeping into his belligerent tone. "I don't. I got a card," he explained, "from Vegas. Tim asked me to look after Chef Howie, and that's all. I'm not trying to give you a hard time, Madeline. Honestly," he lied.

I blinked. Quentin had responded perfectly to the New Madeline. So this is what it took—being willing to be more obnoxious than the other guy. I realized why people hated what Hollywood did to them. But now, even the New Madeline's silence threatened Quentin.

"It's the truth. I swear," he said. Quentin's eyes darted over to Fate. She sat there ignoring Quentin. She was, instead, checking me out. Recalculating, I hoped.

"Go," I ordered him. The dominatrix approach seemed to be working, so why change it? "Talk to Greta. Talk to Artie. Just get going."

Quentin, head bowed, turned to Howie and said brightly, "Well, I'll leave you now and get back to my meetings at the office." And with that, he left.

Two f-words. That seemed to be all it took for anyone to be taken seriously in Hollywood. You simply need a competitive nature, which I clearly proved I had, and a willingness to sink to that level. I swallowed.

"So," Fate said slowly. "What do you want?"

That was a good question. My original plan had been to get Chef Howie alone. He had seemed like a nice guy. I had hoped I could convince him to be a pal and call off the taping. Perhaps it could have been implied that he wasn't feeling well. Getting Howie alone, however, would be a challenge. In the meantime, I had to stall. "Let's go over today's script," I suggested.

"That's a laugh." Fate popped another cashew. "This script is total garbage, which we just told Quentin. The script is unacceptable. We hate it."

"Oh?"

"Chef Howie," she called out. "This new girl was sent here to go over the script. Tell her what a complete and utter piece of crap it is."

"I'm not sure it's total crap, Fate," Howie called cheerfully, turning back to check out his reflection in the mirror. His makeup man had finished with Howie's hair and now picked up a large brush and dipped it into a jar of powder.

"Well," she said, speaking loudly across the room to him, "that's because you haven't read the thing yet, darling." She turned back to me as I took a seat at the table. "It's crap."

"Okay," I said, taking out my pen, looking earnest. I had suddenly hit upon a whole new plan.

"Why is it crap?" she bellowed. "Because the show is based on a man, my husband, who is famous for just one thing: New American cuisine. That's the gold mine, doll. New American. This script you want to shoot today is full of recipes that are supposed to be from Chef Howie, but they are dishes that Chef Howie would never in a million years cook."

"That sounds particularly stupid," I said.

Fate eyed me, surprised. "Yes, it is. As you know, Madeline, Chef Howie's name is revered on seven continents. He is the leading star of New American cuisine."

I wondered, briefly, how many gourmets in—say—Antarctica were praising Chef Howie's expertise with grilled pork chops, but held back from actually asking.

"So which of the writing geniuses on *Food Freak* decided," Fate continued, fuming, "to have today's cook-off recipes feature a 'little Italian café lunch'?"

"Good question," I agreed, matching her irritated tone and volume. Then I gave what I hoped was a properly smug smile. "I'd like to know what Quentin had to say when you asked him that!"

A cashew was held arrested in the air as she got my point. "Quentin wrote that Italian dreck? Those nasty *bruschetta aglio e olio, al pomodoro*? That sad, sad *cozze all'aglio e prezzemolo*? No wonder that damned little toad defended this script and sang the praises of today's pathetic menu. No wonder!"

Despite her rant, her Italian pronunciation was perfect. Fate Finkelberg obviously knew from her Italian dishes. But "nasty" and "sad"? Who could despise a simple and satisfying *bruschetta*, crusty toasted Italian garlic bread with a topping of fresh tomato and basil salad in olive oil? And why hate the *cozze*, a perfectly marvelous dish of fresh mussels sautéed with garlic, lemon, parsley, and wine? Since she had chosen to get riled about them, and since she didn't actually know I had written those very recipes, I kept it to myself and let Quentin take the rap.

"I'm new here," I said with a sigh, "but honestly, how do you both put up with this?"

Howie was actively listening to our conversation now. He waved at his makeup man to stop powdering and I suspected he didn't want to miss a word.

"Exactly," Fate said. "My God, Howie, she understands us!"

I smiled at her sympathetically and became Fate Finkelberg's new ally.

"Madeline, you know food. You know how hard my Howie has worked to make this show the top show on the network. You go and tell Greta we will not ruin Chef Howie's credibility. He owes it to his fans to stay true to his damn muse."

"Chef Howie stands for something important," I said. "And no network or producer is going to make him break his word to the American public."

"That is goddamn right," Fate said.

"But they'll never postpone a taping to make corrections to the script at this late hour," I said, my voice thick with disgust at the horrid network. "They would rather ruin an artist than pay a crew overtime. Damn them," I said, in deep frustration.

Fate smiled at me in friendship. "Let me tell you something, sweet pea. There is nobody and nothing on the face of this earth that can force Chef Howie to do something that's just plain wrong. Chef Howie has principles, damn it to hell."

"You are just amazing," I said.

"The truth is," Fate said, pushing the half-empty tin of nuts across the marble tabletop, "Chef Howie is a sweetheart. He loves everyone and everyone loves him. He's buddies with the head writer, Tim Stock, so my Howie just lets a lot of this crappy writing go. I always tell Chef Howie he's gotta put his foot down or they'll figure they can roll right over him, like damn battle tanks. That's the way it works if you show any kindness, am I right?"

I nodded, watching Fate warm up to the problem. Her mounting frustration reminded me of the mercury in one of those bulging old Warner Bros. cartoon thermometers, which had been inked right here on this very lot, over half a century ago.

"Believe me when I tell you, Madeline, I know what is happening here," she continued, the mercury edging higher. "Sure, the network loves *Freak*. They love the ratings. But they think they can push us around. If I don't watch out, they'll destroy Chef Howie. It's maddening, honey. It kills me."

In my several years as a professional caterer and party planner, I'd run into plenty of clients like Fate Finkelberg who had some huge gripe that they couldn't let go of. However, in my former role, my task was to settle the client down at all costs. This new job was actually a hell of a lot easier.

"It is simply sickening," I said, disturbed to my core. "But they have the power. In the end, just what can you do?"

Fire burned behind her leather lids. "What can I do?" she said, raising her voice even louder and looking to the back of the trailer.

Chef Howie met her eyes. "It's okay, Fate. Come on, honey. It's okay."

"Tell me something, sweetie," she said, her voice edging higher. "I forget. Who calls the shots around here?"

Howie waved away his makeup guy. He walked over to the table and crouched down right beside her. "Fate," he said, soft and low. Chef Howie flashed her the kind of smile that would have stopped a female elephant on the veldt in midcharge.

"No, Howie," she said, but her voice had softened. "No. I mean it this time. How much longer, darling, are we gonna let these game-show jerks screw with you? Italian food? *Bru*-fucking-*schetta*? We're walking, baby. So they lose a day of production. What the hell do we care? It's not coming out of our pocket. Madeline knows how these things work. This is the only language they understand, believe me."

And so it escalates up the chain of command, I realized. A little drama just to get some attention and respect. First a little swearing, and next, the stakes had been raised so high that a star walks off the set.

"Fate . . . ," Howie started again, but she simply wasn't going to be Fate'd.

"It's just dandy," she said, hot and determined, "that the network is begging us for one more show. Wonderful. But we are walking until they give us a script worth doing, Howie. I know you hate this, but trust me. Your buddy Tim Stock isn't here today. There is not one person here that you have to please," she said, staring him down, "except *me*."

Fate Finkelberg's thin, tanned body, encased in its zebra-striped halter top, quivered with anger. Chef Howie knew when to stay quiet. Like me, he must have caught a glimpse of the cartoon thermometer, its bright red mercury now past the point of stopping. We watched it throb almost to the top and then, under the pressure and heat of Fate's enormous ambitions and bitter disappointments, explode.

E'VE got some serious news," Artie Herman said. "Very serious, so please settle down, people."

The entire staff of *Food Freak* was assembled in the executive producer's office. They were gathering there, on the third floor, by the time I got back to our building. I never made it back to my office, in fact, but instead joined the throng as we marched up the flight of stairs and found spots to perch, some leaning, others standing or sitting around his large quarters. I had never been in Artie Herman's office before and he and I had met only briefly. I was impressed by the art on his walls, mostly enlarged stills taken from famous old-time commercials. A large portrait of that cartoon imp, Speedy Alka-Seltzer, took the spot of honor behind Artie's desk, while a colorful frame featuring a blow-up of Lassie eating Pro-Patties hung over the credenza.

"First, a little background," Artie said, as the group settled down. "You all know how proud I am of this show. We've done what no one else has done. We've made a game show number one."

No one rushed to correct Artie Herman. No one bothered to remind

him of all the quiz shows that had been at the top of the ratings heap
fifty years ago. No one mentioned the new monster reality games like
Survivor, or dared to whisper the names of such recent game champs
as *Who Wants to Be a Millionaire?* or *Weakest Link*. The little man
with the white curls who had created *Food Freak* could be forgiven for
a little *Freak* chauvinism.

"We have done a wonderful job this season. Wonderful," he said,
beaming at us. "We deserve a lot of credit. We worked damned hard.
Now you all know, we were set to wrap the show last week. You all
know that. But when the network asked me, 'Artie, will you save us one
more time? We need one more episode of *Freak*.' What was I going to
tell them? Should I have told them no? Of course we could do another
show. It's our pleasure and our responsibility to do another show. Sure
it is. We want to help."

Artie Herman was in his seventies, a man who had made a fortune,
so I had heard, in the advertising game back when television was just
starting out and when Madison Avenue doted on its creative kooks.
With his soft jowls and his frizz of tight white curls, Artie Herman
struck me as a jolly elf, the type who hosted kids' cartoon shows. He
spoke with a charming accent, part Brooklyn, part lisp—like a fey
Henny Youngman. The rumors had it that despite his office artwork,
he had not actually created those famous campaigns. But then, lots of
gossip was mean.

Artie stood in front of his desk and slipped his manicured hands into
the pockets of his khakis. "Here's the thing, my dears. Here's the thing.
We've been hit with some pretty rough news today. That's why I called
you all in here."

The staff was alert. According to our production schedule, we were
all due on the soundstage in about ten minutes, to start taping today's
show.

"I'm sorry to tell you two sad things. Well, the first isn't really so sad,"
he amended. "First, we must cancel the taping today."

Everyone from the most senior lighting director to the youngest runner looked shocked. Murmurs of surprise circulated among the forty or
so staffers present.

"It's a shame, sure," Artie said, responding to the reaction. "A shame.

But you must understand, it is no one's fault. Chef Howie called me from his trailer. He was not feeling well. He really was a sick man. This happens, sometimes. Not, God willing, too often, you understand, but it happens."

Sick? I looked at Greta, who gave me a slight nod.

So that's how it was to be explained. Perhaps I actually had a talent for this business. I felt a mixture of thrill and queasy.

"Sick?" The question came from *Food Freak*'s director, Pete Steele, who was leaning against the door frame, cool and aloof.

"All of a sudden, Pete, yeah," Artie said, his voice sounding very sincere. "What are you gonna do? So we'll see how he is, and we'll reschedule. Nothing to it. Don't worry."

"When?" Pete sounded just a little peeved. "I'm not available for the next two days. I'm already committed to *Bloopers*."

"Don't worry, Pete. I understand that. Greta will figure out the schedule, won't you, Greta?"

We all watched Greta nod.

"Good, okay then," Artie said. "And of course you all get paid for a full day." There were some sighs in the crowd. "Sure. Of course. We have insurance that covers all of these costs in the case of a talent getting sick, so we won't be losing any money. Good. Then the next order of business, before I let the crew go home, is to tell you more disturbing news. This really hurts me and I know you will all be concerned, too, but I found out this morning very disturbing news about our good friend and writer, Tim Stock. For the past week, he could not be reached. And, well, we are getting worried."

Not the first on the staff to be told, now was he? I looked back at Greta, sitting next to Artie's desk. Greta liked to hold her cards tight to her petite chest, but at some point she had had to break the bad news to Artie. Of course, our office staff knew that Tim was out of contact, but everyone else in the room, from the cue-card woman to the props guy, was startled.

"What happened?" Pete Steele asked.

"We, uh, don't know all the details, of course," Artie said, in his phumfering way. "Sure, it's a shock to us all. Tim is like my own son. He's never missed a day of work on this show since the first day we went into development, over a year ago, and it was just Greta and Tim and me. He's a champ. He needed a vacation after all the work we loaded on him. He deserved a break, so maybe he went away on vacation. Sure. But that doesn't explain why no one can find him at all. So I had to tell you. It's a shock."

Greta spoke up for the first time that meeting. "Let's not get worried yet. Tim left before we heard from the network last week. He didn't know we had been asked to do one more show. He's probably . . . I'm sure he's just fine. But we'd like to hear from him. If anyone has any information, Artie and I would be extremely grateful."

I looked around to catch Quentin Shore's reaction. After all, he'd just received a postcard from Tim Stock. As I scanned the group, all murmuring now, I realized with a start that Quentin was not present.

"Okay, so that's it," Artie said, looking old and tired. "You can all go home. Greta will reschedule our taping. And our darling Susan . . . ," he said, looking over the crowd and finding the first PA, Susan Anderson, sitting on the floor by his coffee table, "ah, there you are, my dear. Susan will phone each of you with your new call times for the taping."

Susan gave a little wave.

"What about the contestants?" Nell asked.

"They've been sitting in makeup for over two hours," Stell added.

"Tell them to clear their schedule this week. We'll let them know when we need them back," Greta said. "And of course, we'll prepare an entirely new script for the next taping, just to be careful."

How smoothly she played the game. I suddenly had that whooshy feeling that a bishop must get when he finds himself scuttling diagonally all the way across the chessboard. There he is, startled to find himself landed on such a dangerous square.

In this game, moves upon moves were in play. First, Greta moved me into range of the Finkelbergs. There, I tempted Fate to make a move. Soon, Fate was agitated enough to capture her favorite chess piece, Howie, and take him right out of the game. Artie Herman knew how to respond to losing his star piece. He sidestepped the facts and called it a sick day. Greta was quite a player. Using this gambit, she protected our secret about the office break-in, canceled taping without losing the show a cent, and made it possible to discard our possibly tainted script, without ever appearing to have made a move at all.

And before anyone else could raise a loud gripe, Artie announced, "That's all. Let's go home."

Conversations picked up as the three stage managers and sound engineer, the art director and set decorator, and the others cleared out of Artie's office. As I had been the only one there who hadn't known Tim Stock, I was not included in the wash of gossip and concern as it spread over those who had obviously been close to Tim. Jennifer Klein, the other staff writer, looked paler than usual, and Jackson and Kenny, the two assistant PAs, were huddled together, talking.

Greta Greene caught up with me in the hallway. We were surrounded by those who were leaving, shuffling down the stairs, and she pulled me gently into the small supply room off to the right. We huddled next to the large copy machine and found a tiny bit of privacy.

"Madeline," she said, "great work. I mean it. You saved my life."

"I hope it all turns out well," I said. "Chef Howie is sick?"

"Insurance claim. They always say the star is sick. Who can argue? Fate made her protest gesture and now she can cool off. It was just perfect."

"Are you sure?"

"Of course. There was nothing wrong with those recipes. She'll calm down."

"But what's really going on with Tim Stock?" I asked, finding myself uneasier about the fact that he still hadn't been found. "Is he in Las Vegas? Have you heard anything new?"

She pulled a distracted hand through her short-cropped blond hair. "Nothing. I'm really getting mad. Why hasn't he checked his messages? I've left so many, the tape is full."

"Talk to Quentin," I suggested. "He just heard from Tim."

"What?" Greta looked more startled than I would have expected. "Are you sure?"

"That's what he claimed, but then I didn't see him in Artie's office."

"Artie," Greta said, shaking her head. "Artie took the news hard. He got emotional. Artie's a sweet old guy in many ways. He's been very attached to Tim. He was close to tears when I told him that Tim wasn't answering any of our pages or messages and we just didn't know what was up."

Everyone suffers when someone goes missing. It's the terror of not knowing how to respond. Has something horrible happened? Is the missing person in need of our help? Or has it only been some mix-up? Some thoughtlessness. Some missed communication. Should we rush off in rescue mode, or simply accept the fact that we'd been stood up? The anxiety of waiting to find out which is the appropriate response, fear or anger, can be excruciating.

The hallway outside the supply room had cleared. The staff had disbursed.

"Look," Greta said as I was about to leave, "hold on for another second. We still have a problem. Tim's office."

I thought about the papers and files and books lying everywhere.

"I've been thinking," Greta said. "It seems more like a crime of opportunity, doesn't it? Someone, some contestant or someone else who shouldn't have been within fifteen yards of our writers' department, saw the door ajar . . ."

I winced in a ladylike fashion and Greta patted my hand and continued. "Anyway, they grabbed the chance to take a look around. I don't know if they were after the script or just looking to snatch a wallet. Whatever it was, they made that mess as a cover-up and got out of there fast."

I nodded, considering it.

"The thing is . . . I can't just call maintenance to clean it up. The office has obviously been trashed and the fewer people around here who know about it, the better. You're the only one I can turn to."

"To clean up the office?"

The chess master nodded. "Can you stay late and take care of it? Please?"

"Oh, man."

"I know. It's vile. But let me think . . . Why don't I throw in a bonus? How about a perk?"

Hollywood was famous for throwing around outrageous perquisites, extra little luxuries above and beyond one's salary, when they wanted to butter someone up. Stars often demanded them in their contracts: bowls of M&M's with the green ones removed, fresh tulips in the dressing room, or a stretch limo to take them to work. A limo. Being picked up for work each morning in a limo could be nice. That is, if I didn't live only five minutes away in the hills of Whitley Heights, and if my street wasn't so narrow and twisty no self-respecting stretch could climb up it.

"I need your help so badly, Maddie. I'm moving on to bribery." Greta grinned at me. "I have an idea. I've heard you complain about the filthy old furniture in Tim's office."

I had renewed respect for how Greta managed to work her way up the ladder of life. "You'd get rid of the sofa from hell?"

"It could be arranged. And I might be able to find something more suitable to replace it."

"It's tempting. And I'd like to help you. But that office is a nightmare."

"Look, you don't have to do this alone. Maybe you know someone who could help you. Just no one from here."

At last, Greta sparked my interest. "You'll pay them?" I asked.

"Sure."

"I mean in money, Greta, not by tempting them with Naugahyde love seats."

"On the payroll! As our fourth PA. Done. Who do you know?"

"I can call Holly Nichols. I think you know her. She works with me at the catering company. She's been looking for a temporary gig until our busy season." I used my most optimistic phrasing. "Maybe Holly is still available. What's the salary?" I was hoping Holly could pick up a few hundred dollars for one evening's tidying up. I felt so responsible for the business slowing down and all of us having to scramble.

Greta always clenched tightly on to the show budget's purse strings, but she was pretty much out of options here.

"How much?" I picked up my cell phone.

"I'll pay her one thousand dollars for one night's work."

Had she just said one *thousand* dollars? That couldn't be what I heard.

"Okay, okay. Twelve hundred. But that's it, Madeline."

"You're offering twelve hundred to face that mess?" I asked, quickly adjusting to the inflated numbers and protecting my protégée.

"All right. I'll give her fifteen hundred. Are you happy now?"

"I'll call her," I said.

"You are amazing." Greta gave me a little hug. "And while the two of you clean up in Tim's office, just be careful."

I stopped dialing and paid attention.

"We think we know what's going on, Maddie, but we don't all the time."

That was for sure. Since I'd been working on *Food Freak,* I felt I didn't really know what was going on most of the time.

Greta put her hand on my arm, kindly. "Sometimes it's just a string of bad things, random and annoying, you know?" she suggested hopefully.

"I really hope you're right," I said. But we both had our doubts.

The producer of *Food Freak* walked me out of the little supply room and down the stairs into the now empty hallway outside our offices. Everyone on the staff had been eager to take advantage of their surprise day off. "I won't let anything harm this show," Greta said. "I've still got a few moves left."

And so had I. I punched the last number into my cell phone and waited to hear Holly pick up the phone.

"Yo!" Holly's husky voice came over the phone, breathless from whatever she was doing, whether it was from step aerobics or chasing her kitten around her apartment, I couldn't be sure. Ever since she had broken up with her boyfriend several months back, Holly had become a homebody.

"Are you able to meet me here, at the studio? Right now?" I asked. "You've got a command performance on the lot, if you want it. Nothing improper involved, just schlepping."

"No way," she squealed.

"Way. And while we're cleaning up my new office, we're going to be doing a little snooping around. Are you up for that?"

"Sure."

"I have a feeling that just about nobody has been telling me the truth around here, Holly."

"Big surprise," she said. "Hey, Mad, this is, like, *it,* you know? The phone call. My big break. 'Come down to the lot, Miss Nichols.' And I'm all, like, 'I'm ready for my close-up.' "

"Right. Cool, isn't it? Oh, and don't forget to bring a mop."

HAT a dump," Holly said.

"Especially from that angle." I looked down at her. Holly was on her hands and knees making neat piles of manila envelopes on the floor.

"From any angle," she suggested. "But maybe it looks better when it's straightened up." Holly reacted to my doubtful expression. "Worse?"

"You wouldn't think it was possible. I know."

Holly Nichols sat and looked at me. As a creative soul, she often dressed as if to pay back her parents a hundredfold for sending her to a private girls' school that required uniforms. Tonight was no exception. I smiled at what Holly had considered the right thing to wear for this occasion, an evening of playing janitor in a frumpy office on a closed television studio lot. Her long, lean legs were covered in snug, white silk capris slashed with lime-green stripes. Not many women could handle the illusion of width such a horizontal pattern projected across the posterior, but Holly Nichols, thin as a wisp, managed to look stunning, if offbeat. Her white crop top exposed a lovely midriff. She had kicked off her lime-green sandals and I noticed she was wearing several toe rings and a fresh pedicure in matching lime. In this dazzling outfit, more suited, perhaps, for a disco party at some Palm Springs country club than housekeeping, Holly began straightening the books that were flopped all over the floor, their spines splayed, and placing them into neat piles. She sorted them quickly into stacks of cookbooks or trivia books or foreign phrase books. "It sounds like this missing Tim guy is the key to the whole thing."

"Maybe."

"Where did he go?"

I had asked myself the same question all week. "Maybe Las Vegas, but they've called all the hotels and he isn't checked in anywhere."

"Not under his own name," Holly guessed.

"No one seems to know where he is. And since I have never met the guy, I can't even guess."

Holly sat back on her heels and took a break. "The fact that a guy is missing and his office has been trashed . . ."

"I know. I know." There were just too many coincidences and secrets.

We looked at each other. Holly's white-blond hair fell over her forehead in long straight bangs, while the rest had been caught up in the back at a jaunty angle in a sloppy topknot. "So what do you think is really going on with this missing dude?"

"He's not technically missing. He's just . . . well . . . *not here*. He could be on a two-week cruise to Mexico or holed up drunk as a skunk in some cheap motel in the desert. That's what all his coworkers think. The one who is most upset is Artie Herman, who is just a sweet old guy."

"The executive producer?"

"Right. He seems very concerned, but in a fatherly-bossly kind of way."

"I didn't know you were going to be doing any undercover investigating here," Holly continued, now on her knees handing me books. "Your trouble is, you don't seem to be able to leave any puzzles alone. You are a problem solver, Maddie. It's your gift and your curse."

I bonked her on the topknot with the pamphlet on "Peas!" I was about to shelve. As we talked, I took each book she handed me and shelved it according to the simple organizational system Tim's office library employed. All the cookbooks for any particular single subject were filed alphabetically by subject. I stuck the "Peas!" pamphlet and a thin volume offering *101 Simple Carrot Recipes* onto the low "Vegetables" shelf, and the book espousing the *He-Man's All-Steak Diet* up on the "Meats" shelf.

"I'm not really getting too involved here," I said. Denial is my friend. "I'm out of here in a week. I just want to be helpful. You know me." After only a week in a foreign land, surrounded by aliens, I had already lost my bearings. How had I come to accept all the nonsense? Perhaps it was the pace at which everyone worked, and the intensity. It kept one dizzy enough to begin to doubt that up was up and down was down. "I'm so glad you are here," I said, taking another book from Holly, this one about Asian cuisine. The "Foreign Food" section was against the far wall, and as I walked across the room in my stocking feet, I continued explaining the bizarre set of circumstances. "The truth is, Holly, the mess here probably has nothing to do with Tim Stock. I think it might be my fault that this room was broken into."

"That's dog poop! None of this is your fault, Mad," Holly said, sorting through the books she had collected from the debris. She held up another cookbook featuring international cuisine—this time Greek—and flung it, Frisbee style, across the room at me.

"Holly!" I caught it, and imagined the simultaneous flinches of every blessed librarian across the country as I snatched the book out of the air as gracefully as I could.

"Good catch," my assistant commented, with a grin.

Despite her unorthodox library skills, Holly was making sense. I couldn't believe how much more grounded I felt talking with someone who came from my own world. "Anyway," I continued, "the big secret here is how paranoid game-show people behave when it comes to their clues and answers. They have this bunker mentality and seem to worry all the time that their game material might leak out."

I had come back to stand next to Holly and her stack of books, the better to reduce the likelihood of any of them going airborne.

"And that's why someone broke in here?" Holly asked. "To cheat on the game? Who would do such a thing?"

"The contestants on *Food Freak* can win half a mill," I said.

Holly countered slowly, "But aren't you even the teensiest bit suspicious that something else has gone wrong here, something bigger than a cheating contestant, and you and I might just be the dumb idiots brought in to cover up someone's dirty work?"

"It would make me feel a lot better if I could talk to this Tim Stock. I wonder if I put my mind to it, if I could track him down."

"Oh, dear . . ." Holly held up the little yellow sticky note she'd pulled off a mass of pens and notebooks in the corner behind the desk where someone had overturned all the desk drawers. The one that said "Heidi and Monica might have to die."

I gave my assistant a stern look, which, thanks to several long years of practice, she quite easily ignored. "Oh my God, Maddie. Oh my God. Who are Heidi and Monica? Do they kill the contestants around here?"

"I don't know who they are. That note could mean anything," I said. "Don't go overboard, okay? Tim Stock is a writer. This could be the premise of a new script idea. Everyone here is extremely dramatic."

"Really?"

"I think that's most likely a story idea, a little Post-it creativity."

"Right," Holly said, "I get it."

"Wait." I said. She was just about to discard the Post-it note. "Let's keep this . . . just in case."

"Just in case, huh?" Holly said, warming back up. "What do you really think? Is anyone around here acting weird?"

"Everyone acts weird here," I said, sighing.

"List all the suspects," Holly requested, getting comfortable.

"There's this writer—Quentin Shore—and he's the most aggravating, frustrated, silly person you've ever seen. But he's not evil. He's more like afraid of his own shadow. I used one classic four-letter word, and he just ran away."

"Mad," Holly said, looking up from straightening a loose-leaf folder of notes and clipped recipes labeled "How to Gumbo," "you have already cussed at your new job?"

"I'm ashamed. They made me do it."

"Man! I would have loved to hear that! You swore at some writer?"

I nodded sheepishly.

"Just once?"

"Okay. Twice."

Holly hooted.

"But, honestly, he had it coming, Hol."

"Don't tell me. I know it. They *all* have it coming."

"And Quentin is not the only Froot Loop out of the box. You would not believe Chef Howie."

Holly looked upset, "Aw, schnitzel. Don't tell me Howie Finkelberg's a jerk. He's so hot."

"He's okay, Holly. But he's got this very strange wife. She's completely nuts."

"Really?"

"Her name is Fate. Fate Finkelberg."

We just looked at each other. "Maybe," Holly suggested, "that name alone pushed her over the edge."

"And I have to admit . . ." I lowered my voice. "Even my old pal Greta has me worried at times." Although the office door was closed, we were both aware that Greta was working late in her own office down the hall.

"Take my advice," Holly said. "Trust no one."

"Amen."

Around us, patches of floor were now clear. We'd been at work for almost three hours, and the place was looking much better. Reams of disheveled papers had been picked up and placed in two industrial-size trash barrels. We had spent the first hour reading through most of the papers as we chucked stuff. The bulk of it was pages and pages of past scripts, which had come undone, the metal brads now scattered here and there. Many sheets were folded. Pages from different past shows were mismatched and mixed up together. Greta had told me earlier that these extra copies of old, used scripts were not important to the show anymore. One set of back-up copies was kept by Susan Anderson, another set by Greta. Holly and I had neatly stacked the hundreds of stray pages in the trash bin. Often, we'd find a page with handwritten notes scribbled on it. I became accustomed to deciphering Tim Stock's scrawl. On one page that featured a recipe, he'd written: "Tell H to make the garlic sexy." On another, he'd written: "H can flirt with the eggplant." Each show featured tidbits of information right before the first commercial. Often, Tim would write in corrections in his flowing peacock-blue fountain-pen ink, like, "Fix this! Should be 1, not 8 teaspoons!"

"Do you think anyone would mind if I took these?" Holly asked, her blue eyes lighting on the old mix-and-match script pages.

"Well . . ." I looked at the trash can, neatly stacked to the top with a season's worth of jumbled show scripts. "Why not?" Greta said they were all worthless. They were scripts for shows that had already aired.

"Bonus!" Holly whispered, cheering to herself.

"But what will you do with them?"

"Sell them on eBay." Holly had decided to support herself through our tough financial times by becoming an Internet entrepreneur, putting all sorts of odd items up for auction on-line. In this way, she offloaded a thirty-seven-inch mirrored disco ball, a vintage Bakelite mah-jongg-tile bracelet, and two acrylic paintings she had created back in art school during an experimental asparagus-stalks-as-paintbrushes period, and made over $300 in her first week as an eBay auctioneer.

"Be back in a jiffy," she said. Holly put the last of the hardcover books into a pile on her left and sprang up from the floor. I've never felt short at five foot five, but when Holly stood, I had to look upward about five inches to make eye contact. And that was when she was barefoot.

"Where are you off to?" I asked.

"I'll just take this junk out to my car." She backed up, pulling the gray plastic trash barrel on its heavy-duty wheels, and carefully maneuvered it to the door between the tall piles of cookbooks.

"Okay. Come back soon," I called. "Greta said she'd stop in and help us if she could."

"Gotcha." Holly pulled open the office door and was quickly through it and down the darkened hallway.

"You want me to go with you?" I called after her.

"Hell, no. I'm illegally parked in an executive's parking space right near the door downstairs," she called back. Her voice faded so that I almost didn't catch her last line. "Who's gonna bother me on a security-patrolled lot?"

Who indeed? Perhaps that was the most worrisome issue in today's office break-in. Who had been able to penetrate studio security to get into this office during the middle of a busy workday? Of course, anyone who was already authorized to be on the lot could have done it. Anyone on the *Food Freak* staff or crew. And anyone who had been given a day pass, like the contestants who had been waiting to be taped before they were sent home.

I turned to dust off the top of Tim's desk. There was one last paper, a Xerox copy, to be dealt with. I picked it up and wondered where it should go. The trash? A file drawer? Tim had made a copy of a small packet of one of those old-fashioned berry-flavored drink mixes that kids used to like. Perhaps an errant piece of *Food Freak* reference material? I pulled open the now organized center desk drawer and placed it there. I'd figure it out later.

It was nice to see the desk so spotless, all the debris and papers finally cleared off. I had a feather duster and gave the old oak surface a quick brushing. But why, I wondered, would any contestant risk being caught in the head writer's office? It would mean immediate disqualification from the game. And how would they know the office wasn't occupied? It made no—

And that was the very last thought I had before the shocking flash and the vivid pain and the room tumbled inward suddenly and melted into black velvet.

9

THE faint, high-pitched drone of a tiny siren seemed to move farther and farther away, becoming softer and more familiar, and exactly like the sound of Holly's breathy voice. A murmur. As the words came into focus I noticed that the voice held a terribly concerned tone. "Maddie? Maddie, are you all right?"

I wasn't sure I really felt like opening my eyes. Nicer to snooze awhile longer.

"I'm going to tell Artie." That voice seemed to come from a different direction. I realized it was a different voice. I was so pleased with that discovery, I smiled. "Something is wrong," said the voice. Why, it was Greta Greene's voice. What was she doing in my bedroom? I'd have to wake up to find out and I wasn't really in the mood.

"I'll stay with Maddie," Holly's voice whispered from somewhere.

"No, that's okay," I mumbled. "I'm waking up. I'm—"

I opened my eyes then, and instead of my small cheerful bedroom with its maize-colored walls and white lace curtains, I saw a two-story-high wall of bookcases, a big oak desk, and mottled gray industrial carpeting.

"Madeline?" Holly said softly. "Were you napping?"

"I'm . . ." I reached down to touch my soft, vintage quilt and was startled to feel my fingers brush against the stiff Herculon fibers of Tim Stock's office sofa. I looked down and saw tweed, mixed fibers of burnt orange and brown.

"What happened?" I asked.

"I got back and here you are," Holly said, talking low, "asleep. Then Greta came down the corridor and we couldn't seem to get you to wake up."

"Ow." I reached back and felt my head. A tender, egg-shaped lump was taking shape. "Did you happen to see anyone, Holly? Some guy, maybe, running down the hall or down the stairs or out in the parking lot?"

"No, nobody. What's going on, Mad? Was somebody here?" Holly asked, her voice unsure.

"See," Greta called from the open doorway. She had returned, accompanied by Artie Herman, who pushed her aside to see me for himself. He had apparently been working late, too, staying past nine P.M., up in his executive office on the third floor. Artie wore his gray hair longish, and his curls were slightly disheveled. For a seventy-year-old man working late, he seemed surprisingly youthful in his typical uniform of khaki pants and work shirt, the sleeves rolled up. The faded blue denim shirt was loose everywhere except where it stretched to cover his small paunch of a stomach. Artie put his hands in his pockets and sighed through his nose a few times, like he was thinking things over.

"Are you all right, Madeline?" Artie asked, pronouncing the end of my name "lyn" instead of "line," with a long *i*. "You look—you should excuse the expression—like crapola, darling. What the hell happened?"

"I'm just resting," I said, unable to actually get my mind around the answer to Artie's question. Had I fainted? Or had I been struck from behind? I looked around and noticed a large, glossy, coffee-table-size cookbook on top of the desk. That desk surface had been cleared off

the last I could remember. "I'm fine," I repeated. "Who else is working late here tonight?"

The production offices for *Food Freak* occupy three floors of the
west wing of building 12 on the KTLA studio lot. On the ground level
is the public area of *Food Freak*'s domain, including the main entrance
and a large reception area, along with the contestant department.
Stella and Nellie and their assistants have offices on the first floor, next
to two large contestant audition rooms and another game run-through
room. There are stairways on both sides of this wing that lead to the
floors above.

Freak's offices are mostly on the second floor, including the large
head writer's office and research library, normally occupied by Tim
Stock, where we were presently assembled. Also on this floor, Jennifer
Klein and Quentin Shore each had an office. Greta Greene's large
corner office was down the hall. Her outer office held the three desks
used by her production assistants, Susan, Kenny, and Jackson.

Upstairs, the top floor contains Artie's large office and the second
story of Tim's office/library rises to that third level, too. But in such an
old building, with all the remodeling and reconfigurations done over
eighty years to accommodate hundreds of productions and their vary-
ing space needs, there were more than a few oddly shaped rooms without windows that were used as supply rooms and storage space. Several
offices on each floor had been locked and were apparently not in use,
or were used only occasionally by the custodial staff.

"So you're fine?" Greta asked, not sure if she should press me
further.

"Fine," I said. More or less. Someone had hit me over the head, of
course. Some unknown someone had crept up behind me, and, as the
other great TV chef Emeril Lagasse might say: "BAM!"

"Anyone else working tonight?" I asked casually, feeling more like
myself every minute.

Artie looked at me as if I was nuts. "You mean anyone crazy like you
and your friend here, working way too late? I know you are new here,
young lady, but you don't have to work so hard."

"Okay," I agreed affably. Greta was trying to keep all the problems
associated with Tim Stock's office below Artie's radar so I didn't try to

deny that Holly and I were just a couple of crazy show-biz workaholics with ambition.

"There is no one else here," Greta answered, looking over at Artie and back to me. "Just Artie, who has been upstairs in his office, and me down the hall in mine. Why?" Greta sounded worried. Any moment Artie might discover things were starting to go very wrong. What if he suspected that his production offices were not as secure as they should be? That his shows' scripts had been messed with? That his head writer was gone and the writer's replacement was found out cold in her office? Would he blame his producer for all these random acts of strangeness? Of course he would. "Did you hear something, Maddie?" Greta asked.

I began to doubt myself. Had I heard anything? "No. I didn't." Had I really been attacked? It sounded far-fetched to me, sitting there, and I was the one with the sore noggin and about ten missing minutes. I wasn't so sure that telling my weird tale and showing them the lump on my skull was my best option.

"I've had my office door open all evening, Maddie. I haven't heard a thing on this floor for over an hour. Except for Holly. I heard Holly coming and going ten minutes ago and looked out to see who it was."

"What's happening?" Artie asked me. "Did you faint?"

I looked over at Greta and saw the tense little lines on her forehead and remembered my task. She had a mess on her hands and I'd agreed to help her clean it up. Until I figured out what was really going on, I was not going to make more waves for Greta by freaking out her boss. A woman working in a man's world has it rough enough. I could relate. But, clearly, something else was going way wrong here, at the offices of *Food Freak*, and it was bigger than Greta Greene had imagined. No mere unscrupulous contestant had broken into Tim's office this afternoon, of that I was now sure. The intruder had to be someone with more access to the locked-down KTLA lot, day or night, than a contestant would have.

I sat up on Tim's old sofa and found my head didn't really ache as badly as I'd feared. "I must have imagined it. Maybe I just drifted off for a moment. But I thought someone stepped into this office," I said slowly.

"What?" Greta looked frightened.

"While you were resting?" Holly asked.

"That's outrageous! No one is allowed on this floor," Artie said. He was a shortish man, but he could make his voice boom with authority. "I'm going to have a word with security. This just cannot go on. They know we work late on *Food Freak*. They have orders to patrol our hallways but never, ever to enter our offices. I'll see what they have to say."

Artie left to call security, muttering that he simply wouldn't have this, and Greta remembered a question she needed to get answered and followed him out, leaving Holly and me alone once more in Tim Stock's office.

I looked over at Holly. "Someone was here. I just wanted to keep it quiet for now. Somebody attacked me when you were gone."

"What?"

"From behind," I said. "Hit me hard on the head."

"Oh my God! Who was it?"

"I don't know. I didn't hear him enter the office and I didn't see him."

"Oh, man!"

"It was a few minutes after you left. Are you positive you didn't see anyone on the stairs or in the halls?"

"Not a soul. Oh, Maddie. I can't believe it. And you didn't yell? What happened? Where were you? What were you doing?"

"I was dusting," I said, trying to remember. "Over there. The desk."

We both looked over. It was covered with a clutter of papers and folders, and one large, heavy, oversize cookbook.

"Remember?" I said. "That desk was completely cleared off. Don't you remember?"

"I don't," Holly said unhappily. "It might have been. I was too preoccupied with clearing the floor of all the books and the script pages. Damn."

I stood up and walked over to the desk. How long had I been knocked out? What had the mystery man done in here while I was unconscious? Was he the same guy who had broken in to search the office earlier in the day? With the job somehow incomplete, had he come back tonight to finish it? Had he been startled to find me here, working so late, and then panicked and knocked me out before I could turn around and identify him? And what the hell was so important in here that he was looking for?

"Where were you standing?" Holly asked, bending down to pick up the feather duster from the floor in front of the desk.

"Here," I said, joining her. "I was standing like this, with my back to the bookcases, leaning over and dusting. Like this."

"Then?"

"Then, nothing."

"And you fell?"

"I must have," I said, not remembering a thing.

"Right down here?" Holly asked, pointing to the rug below our feet. "Or over there, ten feet away, onto that awful sofa?" Holly wrinkled her forehead.

I looked down. I looked at the ugly sofa. Now how the hell had I gotten all the way over there?

"He must have picked you up and carried you to the sofa," Holly said.

"This is really too weird. And then what?"

"I don't know," Holly said, worried. "You weren't . . ."

"Absolutely not. I'm telling you, except for the bump on the head, I'm fine."

"So what do you think happened?"

"I guess he carried me to the sofa. And then he made this little mess on the desk." I gestured to the stack of envelopes and memos and heap of paper clips. "And then the guy vanishes into thin air. You heard no one and Greta heard no one."

"Well, you know what I think?" Holly asked. "I think Greta is lying."

"I don't know."

"And we should get the hell out of here," Holly suggested.

That wasn't a bad suggestion. I was thinking we had done enough for one night. I was thinking I might call my friend Honnett. He was the guy you could most accurately say I've been dating. Except for the fact that we don't actually go out on dates. And the fact that he hadn't called me in over three weeks. The truth was, our relationship was sort of on uncharted seas, and if this had been any old regular night, I would have kept to my resolve to let him make the next move.

Chuck Honnett had long-standing reservations about starting up with me, had some weird notions of our age difference being an issue. He's over forty, had been married twice. There were maybe fifteen years between us, but I have never been a stickler for numbers. Still, the guy comes from a different sort of culture. He is a detective with the Los Angeles Police Department, and I descend from a long line of antiauthority types. On paper, we don't work at all. However, recently, we'd moved off paper and into bed. I know how complicated that move always made things between friends. I knew it a couple of months ago, too. And, yet, it's what I had wanted and so I did it anyway. I guess you could say "impulse control" is not my strong suit.

"I'm going to call Honnett," I said, looking up at Holly.

"I thought you were giving him time," she said, concerned once more. I hate it when my younger associate with the freaky hair and teenage fashion sense sounds like my mother.

"You're right. What was I thinking?"

"That you don't want to go home all alone tonight?"

"Ah, yes. Thanks. That." I gave Holly a cockeyed smile and then noticed something odd, right behind her left ear.

"What?" Holly saw me shift my gaze and turned around to look behind her.

"That bookcase, Holly." On the wall behind Holly, the floor-to-ceiling bookcase, its shelves crammed with old books, seemed wrong. Slightly off-kilter.

"Hey," she said, checking it out. "It's askew."

"It is." I walked over and tried to see what was up. It seemed like the wall was made up of a solid row of built-in bookcases, but this one case, four feet wide and ceiling tall, was now pulled out on one side about half an inch. "I didn't realize it wasn't attached to the wall. Maybe . . ." As I spoke, I pushed against the side of the bookcase and it easily clicked back in place, flush against the wall, fitting seamlessly into the long line of bookcases. Then I tried pulling the bookcase forward. The heavy case, its shelves full of cookbooks, swung on invisible hinges toward me.

"Oh my gosh." Holly stood transfixed. The bookcase opened out smoothly, like a gate. We stared at the section of wall that was now revealed. The mystery of my secret attacker was instantly solved.

A DOOR." Holly's shock had reduced her to just a smidge above speechless. I had pulled the swinging bookcase completely open and we found ourselves staring at what was simply, plainly, and unarguably a small white door set flush into the wall.

"A secret door," I elaborated. "Holly, have you noticed that this whole scene is getting very . . . very . . ."

"Scooby-Doo?"

"Exactly."

"I know." Holly scratched her head, which caused her blond top-knot to wiggle from side to side. "First some ghost hits you over the head in a creepy old office building and now this mysterious door. I mean, what next? What's on the other side of this wall?"

A good question. In my short tenure on *Food Freak*, I hadn't studied the office layout in great detail. I couldn't be sure if this hidden door would connect to the next office over, the one occupied by Jennifer Klein, down the corridor to the right. I had visited her several times over the past week, receiving game-show writing tips and sympathy. I couldn't recall seeing any interior office door on her side that would align with this one, but then again, such a door could have been covered up in some long-ago remodel. Perhaps, in some prior life, this section of the old studio had once been configured as a suite of offices and this blocked door was a vestige of that past arrangement.

"It's probably something completely mundane," I said. "Like from some long-forgotten production office. And the door probably just leads into Jennifer's room next door."

"Did that bump on the head knock the freakin' romance completely out of you?" Holly asked, still whispering. "Come on. Aren't you going to try the handle?"

"I'm sure it's locked . . ." I took a step closer to the door, reached for the small brass knob, and twisted. To my surprise, it turned easily. "Or not."

"Let's check it out." Holly was always eager to plunge ahead. "C'mon. I'll cover your back."

"Jinkies, Holly," I said calmly. "Hold your horses." And with that I pushed on the plain white door and watched it swing silently inward into pitch blackness. Holly and I stepped inside, and just as we moved forward, the plain white door shut tight behind us, pulled by a lever, locking us in and cutting off all light from Tim's office. There were shrieks in the darkness. Ours.

"We need a key from this side," Holly said, jiggling the doorknob.

"Great," I said helpfully.

But we shut right up as we soon bumped into an obstruction—just three feet in front of us we could feel a wall, and feeling around it, we realized it was only about four feet wide and so acted as a screen across the entrance to the new room. Feeling our way, we moved a few feet around it and into the room itself.

"Lights," Holly's voice called out testily. We both patted down the walls just inside the door and around the vestibule wall, searching for a switch. All I felt was the cool, rough-textured walls. Holly's escalating curses indicated that she hadn't found any light switch either. It was extremely dark in that room. Excessively dark. Oppressively dark.

"Cell phone?" Holly whispered, hoping I had mine with me.

"In my purse. Back in the other room."

"Permission to scream?" Holly asked, her voice edging up to the higher octaves.

"Soon," I said. "I think I can almost see something." After several seconds of feeling around blindly, our eyes were gradually becoming accustomed to the pitch dark. I was beginning to get a sense of what this room might be. Faint, faint light was seeping in from Tim's office next door, along the cracks between the bookcase, filtering into the gloom. Slowly, the space began to form itself into shapes. My eyes strained, searching for something familiar, as objects began to emerge in darkest relief, charcoal gray against the inky blackness.

"I am not scared," Holly's voice said from somewhere in the darkness.

"I'm proud of you," I whispered.

A large, low object took shape ahead of us, on the north side of the room. My brain loves a puzzle and this object struck me as being about the right height and size for a sofa. But, wait. That would be all wrong. The sofa in Jennifer Klein's office is set against her west wall. Unless I was somehow turned around.

"What's that odor?" Holly asked, her voice sounding like she had stopped breathing through her nose.

"I'm not sure. It's musty in here," I replied. "We have to find the light switch." I took another tentative step forward and confronted another familiarly shaped object. A small wooden table seemed to jump up and knock into my shin. "Heck!"

"What is it?" Holly asked. Her voice was nervous and jumped out at me from back near the wall that masked the door. "Mad, I can't find any light switches."

"Why don't you try the door again?" I suggested softly. "I can manage here. Feel your way around that little wall and then try feeling around the door for a dead bolt . . ."

"No," Holly called out stoically. "I'm having fun."

Holly always knew how to make me laugh. "I'll bet," I said, smiling in the dark.

"Do you think there's a lamp on a desk or something?"

I took another step forward and froze. Something cold and snaky brushed against my cheek. "Schnitzel!"

"What? What is it?" Holly's voice hissed at me with some urgency.

My hand, out of reflex, rose up to my face to slap away whatever it was that had touched me, that slither of something thin and cold and evil which had shocked me in the dark and caused the hair on my scalp to go tingly. Blindly, I slapped at the air. And there it was again, swinging away and whipping back to strike me. I had swatted something, something dangling from above, some unimaginable trap set to spring at me in the dark.

"Mad Bean, tell me what is going on with you or I'll go insane," Holly's voice rang out from somewhere close behind me.

"Wait. Stay where you are." As I thrashed in the air above my head, I found it swinging away from me again. What was it? The thin, metallic coldness reminded me of something. Like a chain, or a necklace, or . . . I realized with a certainty what was taunting me in the dark. I had been engaged in battle with an old-fashioned, hanging metalchain pull cord, the kind that looks like a long row of BBs, the kind that was often attached to ceiling fans. Or antique light fixtures.

"Maddie, I'm freaking out. What's going on?"

"Wait." I waved my hand above my head in the darkness and found the cord, dangling innocently. One sharp tug and the darkness was instantly replaced with a well-lit, windowless room.

Holly and I had to squint in the sudden brightness, but we could clearly see that we weren't in any writer's office. Come to think of it, the door to Jennifer Klein's office was at least twenty feet down the corridor from mine. Between them, I now realized, was some unaccounted-for space. This room.

The secret door behind Tim Stock's cookbook library shelves had led us to a small and neat little bedroom—a bedroom out of another era. The hulking low shape against the north wall was a twin-size bed, not some office sofa. And on the bed was a fawn-colored chenille bedspread with blue flowers.

"Wow," Holly muttered. "This looks just like a movie set. Like from the fifties."

"More like the thirties." The floor was carpeted wall-to-wall in an eggplant-purple rug that featured a swirly sculpted design. There was a roll-armed club chair in gold-colored velvet with a matching ottoman, and a small Chinese-style writing desk in black lacquer with gold trim.

"This place is cool," Holly said.

"In a *Twilight Zone* kind of way." The space was narrow, but ran the entire length of Tim's office next door. However, its size and its furnishings were not as remarkable as what the room *didn't* have. There was no door out to the main hallway. There were no windows.

"What should we do?" Holly asked, still standing back.

"Since we don't have the option of leaving right at this moment, anyway, let's give ourselves a minute or two to check this place out."

"What are we looking for?"

"Well, either Tim Stock's disappearance is suspicious or it isn't. Either somebody wants to sabotage *Food Freak* or they don't. But whatever is going on, I'm not about to stand around getting bonked on the head again. I need to know what is happening. Look underneath everything and in every drawer."

"You always know what to do, Maddie," my loyal assistant said, always eager to give me props for leadership.

"Now that we've got light, go back and check that door, will you? See if there's a way to unbolt it from this side. Report anything you find."

Holly disappeared behind the vestibule wall and then reappeared. "This little wall blocks all the light from that other room. Isn't that odd?"

"Or perhaps it was designed to keep all the light from this room from being observed from Tim's office?"

"That's true." Holly, like me, seemed to be lost in thought.

"Any way out?" I asked.

Holly shook her head.

Since we were sealed into our newfound room, I didn't plan to waste any more time. "You take the desk," I said. "I'll check the bed."

Holly nodded and went over to the Chinese lacquer desk, sitting down on the small gilt chair. She pulled out the center drawer and looked up at me. "Nothing."

I'm not sure what we were hoping to find, but this discovery was a letdown all the same.

Holly began opening up the side drawers of the desk as I turned to the twin bed. It was neatly made up, with its bedspread folded around one plump pillow. I pulled back the spread and saw nothing but a dark gray blanket tucked under crisp white sheets. I smoothed my hand underneath the blanket and pillow, but there was nothing out of the ordinary to be found there.

"These drawers are all completely empty," Holly said, disappointment in her voice. She closed them one by one.

"Nothing in the bed, either."

I surveyed the small space. There were few other objects to search in the sparsely furnished room. No closet. No other furniture with drawers. Just one framed picture on the wall over the bed, an old faded engraving of a girl sitting on a porch swing, circa 1932, the kind of cheap decoration that might have been found in a hotel of the period.

Holly stood up. "It's surreal. Like maybe this place was set up seventy years ago and no one has been in here since then. That's why it has that musty, dusty smell."

Perhaps. But I had another idea. I'd been hit over the head twenty minutes earlier by some intruder, and whoever did it was neither seen nor heard anywhere near the outer hallway. What were the chances my attacker might have been lying in wait in this room? I pulled the mattress back off the bed frame with a strong heave and there, lying between the old bed boards, was a copy of a magazine. *Gourmet*. Last month's issue.

"Let's keep looking," I said softly, replacing the mattress carefully on its frame.

"Looking where?"

"You take the carpet. I'll check the picture."

"You mean like I should pull up this monstrous purple plush?" Holly grinned at me. "All right!"

I kicked off my shoes and climbed up onto the bed. I tried to take the large picture down from the wall. It wouldn't budge. "This is strange. I can't figure out how this picture is attached."

"Yeah? Well, this is strange, too," Holly said. I looked down and saw her sitting back on her heels on the floor. At the corner of the room, she had managed to pull back a corner of the carpet. "It's tacked down all along that wall," she said, pointing, "but then I found it was loose over here. Look at this."

I climbed down from the bed, stepped back into my clogs, and went over to look.

There, beneath the carpet, were the unmistakable seams of a trap door. Holly pulled on a ten-inch length of rope and the trap opened up, revealing an old wooden ladder, which stretched down below into another darkened space.

"Madeline?" From not far away, a voice was calling, but the sound was muffled. Holly looked at me and I put my finger to my lips. It was Greta Greene. She was in the office next door, Tim Stock's office, and she was calling my name. There was no reason to keep our new discoveries a secret from Greta, and yet I felt the need to find out more before I decided whom I could trust. Besides, we had found our own way out.

I pointed down the ladder and Holly's eyes grew wide. Holly looked down at the old ladder and made an "after you" type of gesture as Greta's voice called my name once more. I couldn't resist giving Holly another "after you" sweep of the hands. Maybe it was the ghost of Charlie Chaplin who was goading me on. Greta's voice was closer, now, just on the other side of the wall, so I surrendered the pantomime wars by stepping into position at the top of the ladder. Taking one rung at a time, I descended quietly into the darkened room below. Holly, always the adventurer, began her descent just above me, her bright lime-green strappy sandals almost upon my fingers, permitting me no time to second-guess my course of action.

When I reached the floor below, I jumped off the ladder. Holly was soon beside me, and together we tried to get our bearings. It had occurred to me that we had taken one step beyond exploring. We had clearly escalated our adventure into prowling around the hidden regions of the old studio building. Holly, silent in the tradition of our new prowler status, gave me a look—a look that said, "I thought we were going to be spending the night cleaning up a few dumped files, so why am I following you down some freakin' ladder into the bowels of a darkened studio late at night like we're two fugitives from Alcatraz instead of lucky girls who are working on the greatest hit cooking show on television?" Or at least, that's what her look said to me. I've known Holly a long time so I was pretty sure I had it right.

I responded with a look that said, "Don't get all distressed. We're fine. We'll talk later. Until then, let's just look around and figure our way out of this mess."

Holly's return look, I'm afraid, can't really be interpreted in polite company.

Holly mouthed the words silently: "Where are we?"

Luckily, enough light escaped through the open hatch above so we could look around in the dimness and get our bearings. We seemed to be inside some old studio-props storage room, piled high with dusty furniture and worn-out file cabinets. Open shelving along the walls revealed manual typewriters and adding machines from the forties. There was other vintage office equipment, like water coolers and old wire wastebaskets and dozens of heavy black dial-front telephones. It was hard to say if these sorts of props were likely to be used by any of the studio's current productions, but if they were, I'd bet the call for them was minimal. Holly followed me through narrow aisles between the stacks of furniture, until we came to a door.

We were pretty far away from the ladder in the corner or its open trap, but still we kept to stealth mode. Holly gestured like I should try to open the door, while I paused to try to figure out where we were in the building. Were we near *Food Freak*'s front reception area? I knew the receptionist's desk was located on the first floor, beneath our offices somewhere, but I had the sense that it was off farther, in a leftward direction.

Holly gave me another of her twisting-a-phantom-doorknob gestures, and I looked back at the door. I wondered if it might lead to some interior hallway, or if we'd run into a studio guard and have to explain just what we were doing creeping around. But with Holly getting impatient and me unable to figure out in my head where we might be, I decided to just go ahead and open the door. It had an old-fashioned dead-bolt lock with a manual switch, and I slowly unbolted the lock.

Instead of landing us in someone's private office, or in some restricted corridor, the door opened into an alleyway. And only six feet away was Holly's Volkswagen Beetle, its backseat crammed with mismatched old *Food Freak* scripts, blatantly parked in some gone-for-the-day executive's prime parking spot.

"Well. Hunh!" Holly looked around, amazed.

"Nifty way to escape without anyone seeing you, eh?"

Holly nodded. "So, should we go back in and tell Greta about all of this?"

"Wait." I looked over at Holly's red Bug. "Do you have your car keys with you?"

Holly pulled her key chain from her pants pocket.

I looked down at the *Gourmet* magazine I was still holding, the one I had picked up from under the mattress in the secret bedroom. Its glossy cover featured a tantalizing, steamy copper pot filled with a bubbling Louisiana Cajun gumbo. Affixed to the lower right-hand corner was a small white subscription label: MR. TIM STOCK, 12226 LEMON GROVE DR., STUDIO CITY, CA 91604.

"Holly," I said, "I have an idea. Let's go for a drive."

S TUDIO City. Naming a community after a row of soundstages lacks poetry, sure, but it underscores how proud 1920s Los Angeles was that the movie trade was moving to town. Why dream up some sweet and evocative name like "Valley Blossom," or honor a town founder by naming it "Sennettville"? Studio City said it all. One must only be thankful that other neighboring suburbs didn't fall in line, or we'd be driving from Studio City into Bank City into Beer City and so on.

In those early days, the movie business was pushing out in all directions from Hollywood proper. Boomtowns sprang up overnight in many of the outlying areas where land was cheap. In 1927, Mack Sennett built a new movie studio on two hundred acres just north of the Cahuenga Pass. Soon his Keystone Kops were knocking into each other and falling down in front of silent film cameras on the lot. Success and employment came to town. Studio City was prepared to welcome all the stars in their shiny cars. The first traffic signal in the San Fernando Valley was placed at Ventura and Lankershim Boulevards.

Holly steered her VW onto the northbound Hollywood Freeway and headed for this nearby Valley town. As she drove us to Studio City, I considered what I really knew about Tim Stock. I had heard stories— that he had taken off on vacation, that he wasn't returning calls, that he'd sent Quentin a postcard from Las Vegas—but I could get better information on my own.

You can tell a lot about a person from just observing how they live. Neat or messy? Affluent or broke? One name on the mailbox or two? That sort of thing. And, then, what if Holly and I get to his house and his lights are on? What if his car is in the driveway? Checking his address on the magazine label, I guided Holly to transition to the Ventura Freeway and exit at Laurel Canyon Boulevard.

Holly is a careful driver, despite her freewheeling ways in most other pursuits, and she obeyed the speed limit as she steered us out of Hollywood and into the San Fernando Valley. In the glare from the halogen streetlamps overhead, we cruised along at sixty-five, enjoying the rare 10:00 P.M. treat of minimal freeway traffic.

This section of Los Angeles has changed a lot since it was cheap land for the studio's grabbing. For one thing, it was no longer cheap. In the intervening decades, Studio City had been joined by a string of neighborhoods that choked and crowded down Ventura Boulevard. Clearly, no sort of sane zoning had controlled these towns' hodge-podge development. But, despite its daytime congestion and its propensity to plop a Volvo dealership next to a shrimp restaurant, Studio City was filled with authentic old Hollywood character and charm. The Mack Sennett Studio soundstages were still there, but after several transformations, they now provided filming space for TV sitcoms. The studio had evolved, in seven short decades, from *The Keystone Kops* two-reelers to *Seinfeld* episodes. Studio City was also home to many small businesses. Yolanda Lee's Studio City Psychic Predictions is located just a few blocks down from the Euphoria Bridal Salon, which is close to The Hound's Lounge pet emporium, which is down the block from Art's Delicatessen, and not far from the address we had discovered for our missing head writer, Timothy Stock.

"I haven't been around here since Donald and I . . . ," Holly said.

"Ah, Donald."

"You're probably tired of hearing about him, right?"

"What are you talking about? Vent."

"You're the best, Mad. I loved that idiot. I don't now, of course. But I did."

I had had great hopes for Holly and Donald Lake. He was a likable guy from Indiana or some state like that, a good guy, Wes and I had thought, a young screenwriter with a lot of talent. But Donald had found himself on the Hollywood roller coaster for maybe one long ride too many, and after getting jerked around through all those extreme ups and downs, who wouldn't be ready to puke?

It's not that Donald suffered or struggled. The problem was that Donald had a lot of luck. His first script, an intimate betrayal story set against the backdrop of Nazi Germany, got a green light almost immediately. Only it was jiggled and rewritten into a spectacular sci-fi epic adventure. But again, Donald had been lucky. Even twisted inside out, his film became a huge success, which was shocking enough for a first script by a naive young screenwriter. His second script, about a free-spirited woman and the struggling writer she loved, hadn't fared as well. It had not yet—as it is euphemistically phrased around these parts—found a studio. Such is the sharp way of the world here, and the cotton-wool words we have learned to use to smother the pain.

"I heard Donald bought a house around here," Holly said, her eyes scanning the hills south of Ventura Boulevard as we turned west onto Studio City's main drag. "With the money he made from *Gasp!*"

In the best part of the Studio City hills, even tiny houses bring over half a million dollars. "He bought a house with what he made writing that one movie?"

"From just what he'll get off the video rentals." Life could be hell for a screenwriter, but the royalty payments weren't so bad.

"Have you called him?" I asked, looking at Holly's profile as she drove, the passing streetlamps flooding the car interior with pulses of light and dark.

"What's to say? He's a creep. End of story."

"Men," I said. It was an appropriate final comment for any number of our conversations. Lately, Holly's and my own male-female entanglements had taken on a puzzling, doomed quality. While we searched for our partners in romantic comedy, we kept accidentally wandering into melodrama. "It'll get better," I said, ever the optimist, "we've just hit a slump."

"What I need is to get my tarot cards read," Holly remarked.

"One-two-two-two-six Lemon Grove," I read off the label. Holly turned up a side street, which she declared would eventually intersect with Lemon Grove Drive. It appeared that Tim Stock's house was, in real estate terms, fashionably south of Ventura Boulevard.

"Are you sure you know where we are?" I asked.

"Let's check." Holly pulled over, steering her car up to the curb in front of a tidy California bungalow–style home, dark for the night. She reached under her seat and grabbed the Thomas Bros. guide, a thick book of street maps that require at least a bachelor's degree in map-reading skills to decipher. Most Angelenos keep this book handy, since it's virtual insanity to try to navigate in a city that doesn't get the concept of north-south and east-west streets. With all the hills jutting here and there across the county, there is no hope for a nice easy grid.

It was a quiet night, just a dog barking down the street. From a distance, we heard the faint wail of a siren. I looked over and saw a tear drop onto the page of the map book.

"Hol?"

"You have to admire the art of cartography," she said softly.

I was certain that the artful maps contained in the Thomas Bros. guide, accurate though they may be, had not moved my friend to tears. "Donald?"

Holly made a circle with her forefinger on the open map page. "Here's Donald's new address. One-one-nine-four-nine DeMille Drive. I never even got to see the house, Maddie. He moved in there a few months ago."

I found the tissue box wedged under the backseat and offered it to Holly. She took three, one-two-three, and wadded them into a pale pink ball and honked.

"I wish I could say I had always known that Donald would turn out to be a jerk," I said, "but I had liked him. Maybe it is impossible to have a good relationship with a writer."

Holly began giggling through her tears, sitting beside me in the dark. Parked on this quiet side street, with only the growing sound of more sirens in the background, we found it easy to talk about such a painful subject, so close to Holly's heart, and to mine. Holly's laughter was both at herself and at me. I had broken up with a guy not long ago, too, a sitcom writer I'd been with for four years. I ended it, finally, but I should have done it sooner. Despite the long time we had been seeing each other, neither Arlo nor I had wanted to make any kind of permanent commitment. When that's the case, you should know it has no future. And then I met Honnett. And then . . .

"Maddie? Um. Would you mind if we drove by Donald's house?" asked Holly. "Just to see what it looks like? If she's there, we'll just keep on driving. What do you think?"

This would really be the worst sort of self-destructive, emotional, soul-destroying journey for Holly. It would be taking a step backward instead of moving forward. Donald had been seeing someone else. He was the last guy in the world you would expect to be unfaithful. He came from a very together home and had gone to a great university. He was funny and modest and even had gee-whiz farm-boy good looks with dimples and everything. But things had begun to look iffy when Holly discovered Donald alone in a locked room with an actress. Still, Holly heard him out. Even though the actress had been stark naked, Holly had believed Donald's story. Anyone could believe that a forty-something woman might hit on a great young guy like Donald, even if you didn't add in her dwindling career options and the fact that he'd written a movie that grossed over $100 million in the first week. Holly chose to be understanding.

It had been much more devastating when Holly had walked in on Donald and a film student he was mentoring at UCLA Extension's Writers Program. After that discovery, easygoing, in-and-out-of-love Holly had accepted no explanations. She had simply left with her heart broken. In the past six months, she had seen guys on and off but no one had stuck. Lately, she had even given up going out to clubs. I had really not known what to think.

"C'mon," Holly said, her voice all innocence and persuasion. "We'll just cruise by. Nothing wrong with that. We're in the neighborhood, right?" Holly turned her red-rimmed eyes to me. "I looked on the map. It's only a few blocks from here. Can we go?"

"Oh, sure," I said. Well, what else could I say? Who hadn't done a million unhealthy things while pining for a lost love?

"Cool. Thanks. We'll just drive by. I promise." Holly looked carefully down the street and then pulled her Beetle out onto the road. I rolled down the passenger-side window and noticed that the air was cooler, the heat of the day having lifted, and that the breeze coming into the car had a slightly smoky flavor.

"Here it is," Holly said, pulling onto a winding uphill road. "De-Mille Drive. It should be up on the right somewhere." Holly drove very slowly as we both tried to catch the address numbers on one of the houses to get our bearings.

"Look," I said, "11945. It has to be that one, two houses ahead."

Holly pulled over to the curb and stopped the car. We could see 11949, Donald's house, clearly. Its front porch light was on. It was a small wood-shingled three-bedroom affair with a sweet little front garden and a white picket fence.

"He has hydrangeas," Holly said, in a strangled voice. She loved hy drangeas.

The night was still and quiet, except for the sound somewhere of sirens again.

"Do you smell smoke, or is that just me?" I asked.

"You mean coming from the ashes of my burnt dreams?" Holly asked.

I laughed. "Yeah."

She laughed, too, and then reached for the tissue box, pulling one-two-three more pink tissues and wadding them up. "I would have loved this house," she said into the ball of tissues. "I would have loved those hydrangeas."

"Hey, Holly. New car?"

We both looked out Holly's driver's-side window. Walking up to the car from behind was Donald Lake.

"What are you doing here?" Holly demanded.

"I'm walking my dog," Donald said, gesturing to the puppy at the end of the leash he was holding. "I do it several times a day, actually."

"Oh. You got a dog," Holly said, stunned. I was stunned, too. We were busted. Caught stalking an ex-boyfriend. It just doesn't get any lower than that.

"He's cute," I said, trying to act like it was a normal thing that Holly and I should just happen to be sitting parked at the curb on a practically deserted dark residential street deep in the hills of Studio City at ten-thirty at night.

"She," Donald corrected, cheerfully. "She's a beauty, isn't she? Six months old. Part poodle and part something else, we think."

We. He said "we." He was probably living with the film student, Danielle, and Holly was in for another colossal bruising. I wondered if the next step might be Donald inviting the two of us in to have coffee with the two of them. That I could not bear.

"What's your pup's name?" Holly asked, finding her voice and spirit. She must have missed that fatal "we."

"Well," Donald said, "I hope you don't mind. I named her Holly."

"You're kidding?" Holly squeaked, and then hopped out of the car to see her namesake and scratch her darling ear.

Well, say! It didn't seem all that likely Donald could be living with a new girlfriend if he was hauling off and naming his new puppy after his old one. Hot diggety dog.

"Holly, huh?" she asked, smiling at the puppy, who was quite naturally wagging her tail at the attention.

"I have missed you so much," Donald said, looking at the human Holly in her silk hip huggers and bare midriff. "I called you and left about a million messages. You never returned any of my calls. I didn't know what to do . . ."

"That's a whole 'nother conversation," Holly said, her voice low. "You were horrible to me, Donald. I trusted you and you were horrible."

I felt like an eavesdropper on a discussion that was getting too intimate, too fast. "Excuse me, Hol," I said, calling through the open car window. "But we really need to get going, remember? Got to get over to Tim's house."

"Oh." Holly spun around and bent down to look at me sitting in her car. "Oh, Mad."

"Can't you stay a while and talk to me?" Donald said. "Let me show you the house, at least. You, too, Madeline."

Holly wanted to stay. Of course she did. And as things had gone so far off course anyway, how could I question providence?

"I really need to get to this other guy's house, actually," I said. "Maybe another time, Donald. But I could go over there alone, Holly. If you want to stay here for a while . . ."

"Oh, could you?" Holly said quickly. "That would work. Take my car. I'll just go and look at Donald's house and you can come back and pick me up in a few minutes, okay?"

I slid over to the driver's seat and buckled the seat belt. With a quick wave, I pulled out into the narrow street and headed toward Lemon Grove Drive, aware that I had left Holly in a very tender trap.

The address on Lemon Grove I was looking for was only about nine blocks away, as determined by the Thomas Bros. map. I pulled around a corner and headed in the proper direction up Knotty Pine Street. With the passenger window still open, I got a large whiff of smoky air as I approached the corner to Lemon Grove. I remembered the sirens and slowed down. At the corner, I made a right turn but a policeman standing in the road stopped me almost immediately. He waved me to turn around. Instead, I rolled down the driver-side window. He reluctantly walked over.

"Sorry. Can't let you go any farther," said the officer. "We've got a fire down the road and we need to keep access clear for emergency equipment."

"That's terrible," I said, "but I live on this street. It's late and I'm just coming home from work at the studio." I gave a quick wave at all the old scripts Holly had piled up in her backseat.

He looked at me and the scripts and asked my name and address.

"Madeline," I said. "Madeline Stock. I live at 12226 Lemon Grove. Just down there." I waved in the general direction of "there" and looked serious.

"Stock?" he asked. Then he spoke into his Motorola radio.

I waited to be busted, wondering how long it would take and whether there was a law against fibbing about one's address to a traffic cop.

"Say, Mrs. Stock." The officer was standing in the street next to my open window. "You better get down there. Sorry to give you such bad news, but they say it's your house that's been burning. And I'm afraid, ma'am, your husband may not have made it."

"My husband?"

"Yes, ma'am. Sorry. They're pulling his body out of the house right now."

12

THE officer who approached the car was female and wore an LAPD uniform. "Are you Mrs. Stock?"

"What happened here?" The aftermath of chaos filled this block of large residential properties. The smell of smoke was everywhere. Lemon Grove Drive was slick with water and crisscrossed with fire hoses. Neighbors, roused from their evening television programs, stood around in twos and threes, subdued and watchful as the emergency workers went about their tasks. *Food Freak* had aired about two hours ago. It was an odd thought. Two fire trucks and a few other emergency vehicles were parked at odd angles, filling the street. Several firefighters were working cleanup, pulling equipment from one of the trucks. Others were still hosing down the smoldering shell that only an hour ago must have been the garage attached to Tim Stock's home. No other residence on this affluent block of houses appeared to have been affected, but I noticed that several roofs nearby dripped water. A precaution.

"I'm Officer Blackwell," the woman said.

A helicopter circled over our heads, rotors loudly chopping through the air, directing its searchlight on the burnt, smoldering structure. In the bright illumination a new burst of puffy white smoke billowed upward.

"I'm sorry to have to tell you this," the young officer said. "We don't know yet what caused the fire. Garage fires aren't that uncommon. As you can see yourself, there's been a lot of damage, but it's mostly contained in the garage, as far as we can tell. The car is a total loss. The BMW M3 coupe. Was that your husband's?"

It took a moment for me to realize she was talking to me.

"I'm sorry. There's plenty of time for these questions. I'm just wondering if you know what time your husband got home tonight?"

I took a deep breath. "I didn't know anyone would be here tonight, actually. But you are saying that Tim . . . he *was* here and now . . . now he's dead?"

"I'm sorry for your loss, Mrs. Stock," Officer Blackwell said kindly. "You're in shock. If you'd like to come sit in my squad car, you might be more comfortable. With a casualty, there will be detectives out here soon to take charge of things. They'll want to ask you some questions, but why don't you just rest until they get here."

"No, thank you. I'm fine."

Tim Stock. I tried to get my head around it. Tim Stock was no longer missing. Tim Stock was dead. The poor guy. It seemed impossible, and yet there had been something odd about the whole setup. I had felt all along that something might be terribly wrong.

An ambulance was pulling up to the front of the house now. This one was from the Los Angeles County Coroner's office. I watched as two large paramedics lifted a gurney from the back of the still smoldering property and wheeled it over to the vehicle. One of the neighborhood men pulled his young son around so he wouldn't see the shape of the body under the thin blanket. But I couldn't turn away. This was as close as I'd ever been to the man whose office I had been borrowing, the man who had spent the last year writing the country's favorite game show, the man who had disappeared without a word to anyone.

I'd heard a lot about Tim Stock over the past week. Jennifer Klein told me about him, what a good guy he'd been. How he read several books a week, everything from Shakespeare to Vonnegut to Dorothy Sayers with pleasure. How he'd often fly to New York for the latest musical, and he'd always take a less affluent buddy along as a treat. How she figured he'd never settle down, he was one of those guys who flitted from one beautiful young woman to the next, but how great a friend he'd been. A bike enthusiast. An animal lover. A talented amateur chef.

The gurney was raised, the stretcher was shifted into the back of the coroner's van, and the rear doors were slammed shut. What had Tim Stock been doing here in his garage when he was supposed to be drunk in Las Vegas? Was he hiding out? From whom? From Greta or someone else at work? I couldn't make any of it fit together. Why had he died tonight?

There was nothing left to see here. I turned away and began to leave.

"Madeline?"

I swung around. Lieutenant Chuck Honnett of the LAPD stood in the street, staring at me. His eyes were cautious.

I hadn't seen in him in a while, and I hated how my breath seemed to get instantly shallow and short. Absence and all that. I checked him out: the same tall and lean frame, the same wide mouth. Honnett was Honnett. His tanned face had seen too much sun, but he had this great jaw and these sexy hollows beneath his sharp cheekbones. His dark hair had begun to show some gray, but on him it looked good. Chuck Honnett, the guy who hadn't called me in over three weeks. Of all the cops in all the cities in all the world.

"Hi," I said.

Honnett seemed unable to hide the puzzled, assessing expression that had found its way into his laser-blue eyes. This—my being here—was not computing. He looked down and tried on a frown. I didn't often score one on the poker-faced cop. "What are you doing here?" he asked finally.

"That's your greeting?"

"Look, I can't really talk now. I just got here, Maddie, and I need to take over the scene." He looked uncomfortable, but perhaps that was because he had jumped to the conclusion that I was here tracking him down to demand things. Like some time alone to talk about why he had been avoiding me. Like why a little thing like our going to bed together and having incredibly good sex had to mean our relationship must go instantly to hell. He cleared his throat and spoke in a low, intimate voice. "This isn't a good time, you know?" And then, he finally found a smile for me.

"Okay," I said, extremely agreeable, backing up. "No problem." If Honnett was worried about some messy public scene, he was way, way off. I had other "issues" right now. I was pretty sure someone would be along any second and call me "Mrs. Stock," and I'd be exposed as a fake and a liar. I gave a little wave and turned to walk over to Holly's car. I was pretty sure Honnett would find my involvement, not to mention my deception, here at the location of Tim Stock's death peculiar and unseemly and just a big fat LAPD embarrassment. All would be best if I could just . . .

"Oh, Mrs. Stock? I see you have met the detective in charge."

At Officer Blackwell's introduction, Honnett adjusted his expression and turned to meet the victim's widow. Naturally, there was no one there but me. By the time he could react, I had made it all the way over to Holly's car, parked across the street.

Honnett kept his eyes on me as he stood, head bent down, questioning Officer Blackwell. He spoke to her again as I got into the Beetle and turned the key in the ignition. Unfortunately, at that same moment, the coroner's van began backing out of the driveway. Another uniformed cop at the site stepped out into the street, blocking my easy escape, while the van pulled out. So I sat there, watching, as Tim Stock left his house for the last time. The poor guy. It was unlikely this fire was going to turn out to be a simple accident, not with all the mysterious troubles over the past week. Things always connect. When a guy hides out and then winds up dead, it adds up to trouble. What sort of trouble had Stock been involved in? Was there something going on at *Food Freak* that could get a recipe writer killed? Or was it something else, some personal problem that had become fatal?

I was just shifting out of Park, when Honnett called out, "Wait."

He walked up to the car and checked it out for a minute before speaking. "Why don't you step out of the car, Madeline?"

There's something so impersonal when they use that officer-speak. "I thought you were in a hurry to get rid of me," I joked, staying put behind the wheel of Holly's red Beetle.

"Not anymore." His voice sounded gravelly and tired. "Please?"

I turned off the ignition and left the keys dangling as he opened the car door for me. I stepped out and then leaned back, resting my body against the cool lacquered sheet metal. Honnett took a step closer. I could smell the fresh scent of lemon soap on his skin.

"What is it?" I asked, meeting his eyes. The chopper above drowned out the words as it roared closer overhead and then moved off a little. Its search beam washed over us, lighting us up as if we were onstage for a few moments, and then leaving us in the dark as it moved off, hunting for the source of the white smoke billowing again from Tim Stock's garage across the street.

"Are you planning on getting me in trouble with the department?" he asked quietly.

"Why would I do that?"

"Look, you found me here, right? You seem to have done a pretty good number on Blackwell, pretending you are related to the victim, for Christ's sake. So if you went to the trouble to scam your way onto a crime scene to see me, I've got to figure you are plenty pissed off. And, hell, Maddie, you have every reason to be. But can we take this somewhere private?"

"I'm not mad at you." I looked at Honnett. He hadn't called me in almost a month. Why was that? "Well, I guess I am, but that's not why I'm here."

"Oh, yeah?"

"Yeah. I was in the neighborhood"—I almost laughed at how it came out, but what else could I say?—"and thought I'd visit a friend."

"In the neighborhood?" He smiled. "Right. Who were you visiting around here this time of night?"

"I dropped Holly off at her ex-boyfriend's house down on DeMille Drive. She needed a few minutes so I thought I'd just stop off and see this guy I work with. And now, I think I'm in shock." Nothing sounds as fake as the truth. Nothing. I'm not sure why I even tried.

"So your story is, you were stopping in to see some guy. What guy?"

"This guy, Tim Stock. When they told me his house was on fire, I just hurried over to see if I could help or something."

"Aw, Maddie. That's bullshit. Stock didn't work with caterers and party planners. He worked for some TV show."

"Right. *Food Freak.* I know. I work there, too, Honnett."

"What's that?"

"Yeah. And you would know where I was working these days if you ever called me. But I guess you've been busy."

He didn't actually blush, but he paused and took the hit before he went on. "So you really do work with Stock?" he asked. "Since when?" He had begun to relax. In fact, he was checking me out, his eyes wandering down the front of my black T-shirt, down my white jeans.

"Just about a week. I've been helping them out as a temporary thing. Writing recipes."

"So you weren't out looking for me?" he asked, beginning to buy into my story.

"Just a coincidence," I said. Which was a mistake. Detective Chuck Honnett believes in coincidences just about as much as I do.

"Uh-huh," he said slowly.

I reached out and put my hand on his arm. The strong, hard muscles beneath his black shirt were tense. If Officer Blackwell was checking us out from across the street, I wondered what she would make of the grieving widow now. "I had no idea you'd be here," I said honestly. "But naturally, if I didn't have so much work going on right now, I'd be missing you terribly. In fact, I'm definitely stalker material when my hormones are acting up."

"You're looking good, Maddie," he said, almost breaking a smile. "You always do."

Why, if I could still get to him like this, hadn't he called me?

"I gotta go back to work," he said.

"Right."

"Sorry about all this, Maddie. Sorry about your friend Stock. And, well, sorry about a lot of things."

I like it when men apologize. It may be one of my favorite things. I pushed my heavy hair off my shoulders and waited to get the whole enchilada. "You are?"

"Yes. Sorry about us, too."

"How about that," I whispered.

"I'll call you."

"You will?"

"Tonight. Later."

"Want to stop by?"

"Maybe." His smile was slow and friendly. "See how late this thing goes."

"So I can leave now, Lieutenant?" I asked, rubbing against him almost by accident as I stopped leaning against the car and slowly stood up straight. I reached for the car-door handle, but he beat me to it and opened it for me.

"I know where to find you," he said. The perfect cop exit line.

I slid back behind the wheel and again turned the ignition. Honnett put his hand on the open driver-side window. "So," he drawled, "how do you suppose Officer Blackwell there got the wild idea that you were the *wife* of the deceased?"

"Well . . ." Honnett had a better view of the low-cut V of my T-shirt from his present position, so I took a little extra time to answer. "I had to tell the officer down the street something. Tim was a friend. I was upset. I can't stand being kept away. You know me."

"I know you," he said, watching me pull out from the curb, "too well."

13

I T was close to midnight when I pulled up in front of my house on Whitley Avenue and parallel-parked Holly's little red punch buggie so it blocked the driveway. My garage is so crammed with odd pieces of furniture I pick up at swap meets, dozens of table rounds that we use for the parties we cater, and boxes of dishes from the thirties that I haven't been able to actually park a car in it for years. My old Jeep Grand Wagoneer had been left parked on the KTLA lot, but Wesley had come to my rescue. He got a ride over to the studio and picked it up for me. It was back home now, as usual, dealing with the night air out in the driveway.

I walked up the flight of stairs to my front door. Hillside homes require a little more exercise to access than others, but the view is usually worth it. In my case, I have a nifty view of the hills on one side. However, my property actually borders the Hollywood Freeway on the other side, so from *that* angle I have the view of a particularly prosaic sound wall. Such real estate challenges make for that ultra-rare affordable property. One man's disgusting anchovy becomes another's delicious Caesar dressing. I say it's all a matter of taste. The sound of eight lanes of rushing freeway traffic coming from just beyond the sound wall was something I'd learned to get used to, and now it blurs into a sort of ocean roar. Billionaires pay millions for that very sound, when it's coming from the Pacific.

After I'd left Tim Stock's house on Lemon Grove Drive, I got around to checking my cell phone and realized I'd missed a call. I retrieved my voice mail to discover that Holly had decided to stay on at Donald's for the night. No reason to stop by and pick her up, as Donald had offered to drop her off tomorrow. They had a lot of "talking" to do, she euphemistically chirped in her message. I shook my head, and yet, I could hardly fault Holly for doing what I was doing, allowing the men we cared about one more chance.

Before I could put the key in the door lock, my front door opened. Wesley was in the house, waiting for me.

"Hey, you," I said. "I didn't see your car."

"My contractor drove it over after he dropped me off at the studio to pick up your truck. I told him to park up on Iris Circle," Wes said. "I figured we might have too many cars down in the cul de sac tonight and I didn't want any of our friends getting tickets."

"Thanks, Wes." I gave him a hug. "I'm so glad you could come over. I'm just incredibly awake and there are too many thoughts." I had phoned Wes from Studio City and filled him in as best I could. He'd agreed to come over and talk. We had a lot to catch up on. As I followed him back through the dim hallways to the kitchen, I was glad once again he was so fabulous with food.

"A little midnight snack?" Wes asked, giving a Vanna White gesture in the direction of the center island.

"Oh, man. I don't think I've had anything to eat since breakfast."

Set out on the old worn butcher-block countertop was a beautiful antique linen napkin positioned like a place mat. Atop the crisp ivory napkin was a cobalt-blue plate heaped high with a seafood medley.

"Ceviche?" I asked.

"Maine lobster, sea scallops, and Pacific oysters marinated in lime juice and cilantro," Wes confirmed.

Beside the plate of the most lavish ceviche on the planet, was a

large, shallow bowl containing one of my favorite things, green as-
paragus risotto with wild mushrooms and aged Parmesan. Wesley knew
I loved it. Steam was still rising from the wide-rimmed white bowl.
"I'm embarrassed to tell you how starving I am."

"Start eating," Wes said, pleased. There are no words sweeter to a
chef than those of a hungry diner. "And I have a chocolate tart with
orange-caramel sauce for dessert. I brought you my leftovers. I ate
hours ago."

"You cooked all this tonight at your place?"

"Well, I was celebrating. Go ahead and eat. I'll have dessert with
you."

Setting down my red canvas bag on the end of the island, I pulled
out a chair and quickly picked up my fork. The sweet lobster in Wesley's fabulous ceviche was completely sinful. "Wes. So fresh. So light.
This is incredible. We should do this for a luncheon, don't you think?
Those ladies in Bel-Air would love this for their mah-jongg party."

He smiled. "I've really missed you like crazy, Mad. Tell me everything. What the hell is going on at *Food Freak?*"

"It's like a whirling, swirling feeling every minute I'm there, Wes.
And I can't always tell if it's a giddiness type of swirling, you know, from
mainlining Hollywood glamour, or if it's more like a disaster-upon-us,
toilet-flushing type of swirling . . ."

Wes began to laugh out loud.

"Don't laugh. It's like the water is rising and I'm in way over my
head."

"Elegantly put."

"I'm learning from Greta Greene. She has a way with a metaphor."
I finished the ceviche in record time and began on the risotto. "I'm
dying, this is so good."

"Ah," Wes said, giving me an affectionate smile. "So tell more.
Details."

"I'm eating here."

"I don't care. You tell me you're being flushed down the tubes, I
want to know everything." With that, he poured each of us a chilled
glass of Chalk Hill Sonoma Chardonnay, a '98, and I told him all the
odd things that had happened that day. As we sipped our wine and I

finished my meal, I told him about Tim Stock's office and the secret bedchamber we discovered behind the bookcases; about the office break-in and the necessity of canceling today's taping; about Chef Howie and his manager-wife Fate; about Greta's concern that everything be kept quiet, no matter what; about the office cleanup with Holly and getting knocked out; about Artie Herman and Susan Anderson and Jennifer Klein and Quentin Shore; about finding the recent issue of *Gourmet* magazine under the bed in the secret room and going out to see Tim Stock's house for myself; about the fire in Studio City and Tim's body, found at the scene. By the time Wes was serving each of us a generous slice of the chocolate tart, I had run out of story, but not out of questions.

"You know what bothers me the most?" I asked.

"Not knowing everything," Wes answered. "You like to know how everything works and who everyone is and what it all means."

"Yes," I said. Wes understood me better than anyone, but of course, we had been friends a long time. We met in northern California where I had become a sous chef at a legendary foodie restaurant that is now a gourmet mecca. I'd just finished at the Culinary Institute in San Francisco. Wes had been doing graduate work in chemistry at Berkeley, but he has many talents and interests and had always been an artist at heart. In those days, he wasn't very happy. He used to hang out at the bar of the restaurant where I worked, order the best wines on the menu, and then offer me a glass as we closed the place.

Timing is everything. Wesley Westcott and I became friends at a time when both of our lives needed major course corrections. I'd had a serious disappointment. I had just been let down by the one man I'd ever loved, the man I was planning to marry. Things were dark for me that year. And Wes had come to a crossroads of his own. After years of scholastic achievements and awards, Wes wanted to skip out on academia and start over. He had more of a taste for the world and a riskier nature than was satisfied teaching lecture halls full of college freshmen. He suggested we go down to Los Angeles, and I agreed to be his partner in a start-up catering company when we could afford to start a business.

With a few local references, I was able to land a job cooking for a little café in West Hollywood while Wesley began tutoring at UCLA. Before long, customers at the restaurant began asking me to cook for their private parties. One fan of my cooking was a producer who offered Wes and me the chance to cater the meals on the set of his soap opera, and soon we found ourselves too busy to keep up with our day jobs. We had a business. But through it all, Wesley and I had vowed to keep our friendship above our work relationship, and we had settled into a most compatible arrangement.

"It is so frustrating," I said. "If I knew more about things on *Food Freak*, then I'd know if I could do anything to help," I continued. "Frankly, the way I've been going at it, I can't tell if I'm helping or hurting." My teeth sank into the deep, dark, chocolate tart filling, and somehow, everything seemed a little better. Chocolate will do that.

"Well, I think you're learning plenty," Wes said. "Hey, you've only been there for a week."

I was ready for some tea and went to fill the kettle. I placed it on the gas burner, and began clearing the plates and tidying up. "Now you have to tell me about you," I insisted. "What did you say earlier? You cooked this amazing meal to celebrate? I need some good news."

"I don't even know where to start," Wes said. "It's about the house."

Wesley had begun buying wonderful old distressed houses and then renovating them with an architecture fan's sensibility back to their original grace and beauty. Then, Los Angeles real estate being what it is, he turned around and sold them for a very nice profit. There were many successful people with good taste and deep pockets but without the time or talent to fix up a house. In the present boom market, finding tarnished real estate gems and polishing them had become Wesley's hobby. With a good credit rating and the help of bank loans, it was also an excellent way for Wes to invest his down payment and fix-up money along with his design genius and hard work and make a good return. On the other hand, there was always a risk. Wes was in a perpetual state of concern about when the real estate bubble would burst, but so far he had not had to face that dilemma.

Each new project pushed his luck a bit further. If between the time he bought a wreck and the time it took to fix up and sell, home prices went steeply downward, he might not be able to pay back the mortgage. But Wes loved houses. He loved bringing an old neglected beauty back into her glory. Normally, he considered the risk one he could manage. But with our party bookings practically nonexistent, Wes now needed to make a profit on his hobby and quickly turn over his current fixer.

His latest project was a big old mansion in Los Feliz, but what he had originally estimated would take two months to refurbish had dragged on and on. He'd had a double crew working on it for about four months now, and it seemed it would never be completed. He had been discovering new problems that needed to be corrected every week, from the foundation to the attic. I would never have the patience.

"Don't tell me it's done?" I guessed. "Are you listing it?" That would be ample reason to celebrate. This had been the largest project Wesley had ever taken on, maybe too large. The house was 4,800 square feet of mess. Everything needed to be done to it, from refinishing the floors to reroofing. If it was ready to list with a broker, Wes might be able to sell it in a month or two and get his money out a few months after that. Which, let's face it, he dearly needed. Wesley's side job required that he sink every spare penny into a big old unlivable house, and until this house was sold, Wes had very little money to live on.

"It's better than that," Wes said, accepting the cup of tea I presented. "It's sold."

"What?"

"Sold." Wes stirred in two packets of Sweet 'n Low and smiled.

"How? When? What happened?"

"A guy has been cruising by the house. I've seen him go by. And last night he stopped and asked when we would have the house ready."

"Some guy who lives in the neighborhood?" I asked.

"He lives about two blocks up, on Chiselhurst. He actually thought about buying my house when it was listed for probate last year and I bought it, but he couldn't stand how filthy it was."

"The wimp," I said. "So now it's beautiful and clean and he wants to buy it from you?"

"No. Now he already bought it from me. We're in escrow."

"What!"

"I can't believe it, either. And it's an all-cash deal, Madeline."

All cash. The holy grail of real estate sales. It meant the buyer didn't need to qualify for a bank loan. It meant the house needed only to pass inspection.

"How did you do this?" I asked, amazed and so happy for him.

"I live a clean life," Wes said, virtuously.

"Who is he?"

"Erik Whalen. Know him?"

"Why is that name familiar?"

"He's got a band. The Golden Crows. He's going to move into my house, apparently, and then tear apart his house up the street and turn it into a recording studio or something."

"Oh, man. That's so hot. The Golden Crows are huge, aren't they?"

"I don't know, Madeline. All I know is the man has a British accent and over two million dollars in cash. He stops his car at the curb and buys a house out in the street. I love that guy. I love the Golden Crows, whatever music they play. I'll even go out and buy one of their CDs."

I raised my cup of tea to Wes. "Congratulations. This has got to be the start of good news from now on."

"Here, here." Wes raised his teacup and sipped.

"You tired?" I asked him after checking my watch. It was after one-thirty.

"Are you kidding?"

"I wanted you to look at something." I reached over and grabbed one of the handles on my canvas purse and dragged it closer. From inside I pulled out Tim Stock's copy of *Gourmet* magazine.

"So that's the magazine you found in that hidden room next to Stock's office?"

"Yep. I have flipped through it and there's something funny."

Wes moved his chair closer to mine and I paged through the glossy magazine, filled with exotic recipes and lush photos. "What are those?" Wes asked, stopping one of the pages I'd been fluttering and pointing to a headline. It read: "Culinary Quickies in Ten Minutes or Less." The word "Culinary" was marked with a yellow highlighter pen.

"I know. There are dozens and dozens of them. Just single words or even a few letters, but they aren't necessarily important words. What can it mean?"

Wes took the magazine and started again, from the beginning. "You have a pen?"

"Sure." I found one in my bag and then grabbed a blank pad of paper from the kitchen counter.

Wes began to read off words, finding all the highlighted ones. "Take these down: 'the . . . professional . . . seven . . . culinary . . . America . . .' " He stopped. "It doesn't mean anything."

"Wait a minute. No. That sounds like something. That book from the Culinary Institute. You know. Their bible, *The Professional Chef?* We've got that here." I jumped up and surveyed my little kitchen bookcase. It was one-one-hundredth as grand as the cookbook library at *Food Freak,* but extensive enough for us just the same. I hefted the thousand-page volume I had been searching for off the shelf and brought it back to Wesley. "Look at this. *The Professional Chef,* Seventh Edition, by The Culinary Institute of America.' "

Wes made a half-whistling sound and went back over the issue of *Gourmet* more carefully. "Well, I'll be damned. Look, Mad. Here's the word 'chef.' I missed it because it's in this Viking range ad. I wasn't looking at the ads before. And here's the word 'edition' in the Audi ad. And here's 'institute.' I can't believe this. Someone has clearly highlighted the words that make up the title of this cookbook. Why?"

"I'm not sure. Let's do some more."

"Okay. I'll read them off. 'The . . . professional . . . chef . . . seven . . . th . . . edition . . . culinary . . . institute . . . of . . . america . . . two . . . zero . . .' "

"Hey, what are those numbers?" I asked, looking up from the pad.

"I don't know. Page numbers?"

I grabbed the book and opened it to page twenty.

"What is it?" Wes asked.

"Pretty boring, actually. The section on creating standardized recipes for professional kitchens. And there's a picture of a food scale. The caption says, 'Cutting meat into portions ensures that customers get consistent value . . .' yadda, yadda, yadda."

"Very uninspiring," Wes agreed. "Let's see what else is highlighted. It looks like single letters. Take these down: 'n . . . o . . . b . . .' "

" 'Nob?' "

"Wait. And 'u,' then there's "the . . . cookbook . . . one . . . nine . . . eight . . .""

"That's '*Nobu: The Cookbook.*' We have that one, too." I got it down from my bookcase and quickly turned to page 198. "Hm. It's just the book's index," I said, puzzled.

"This is strange."

"I know. It's a code. Do you think Tim made this up? Or do you think someone else put it into the magazine and then passed it to Tim? Or did Tim even know about this magazine or even that secret room? This is all just too spy versus spy."

"Well put. It's pretty neat, though."

"You know what? These book titles in the code must refer to the books in the *Food Freak* library, don't you think? I'll have to check these out tomorrow. Wait!"

"What?" Wes looked up from the magazine. He had already gone on to find more highlighted words and he'd taken the pad and pen and begun writing them all down.

"This could be why Tim's office was searched."

"Because someone was hunting for this hidden copy of *Gourmet* magazine with its code?"

"I don't know, Wes. Maybe these certain books mean something. Without this highlighted guide, the intruder had to just pick books at random." I was warming to this idea. "That's the part of Greta's theory about contestants cheating that didn't make sense. I couldn't imagine why anyone searching an office to get an illegal look at the script would have pulled down so many cookbooks from the library shelves. Wesley, this could be why."

"Possibly," he said.

"But then why did they mess with all the old scripts? Oh, this is hurting my brain."

"Say, look at this." Wes had been working his way through the magazine, but stopped near the center where the "no postage necessary" subscriber postcards are stuck. "Did you notice that one of these cards is filled out?" Wes asked.

In the address section was written: "De Soto and Victory. Take El

Rancho Drive. Make first right and go to second building on right. 6 A.M. Thursday." The writing was in block letters in pencil.

"Oh my God, Wes. That's in just a few hours," I said, startled. Here we'd spent so much time mulling over highlighter marks and titles to obscure cookbooks when right before our noses was a disturbingly direct clue.

"There's no date. This note may be referring to *this* Thursday, to today," Wes said. "I don't know. This meeting could have taken place weeks ago."

He turned the card over. Written in pencil, just under the magazine's address, were the words: "Please help me, Tim. Monica and Heidi might have to die."

There it was again.

ONNETT had his arm on the back of my sofa, not actually touching my shoulders, but almost. It was just past two o'clock in the morning. At two, when the doorbell rang and it turned out to be Honnett, Wesley suddenly remembered that he had an early appointment and departed quickly. Alone, Honnett and I walked upstairs to the second floor, where I have my little apartment. At the top of the stairs, Honnett turned right, toward my small living room. Left would have taken him toward the bedroom. He knew that.

"You're working in television now." Honnett grinned. "You must be blowing everyone away with your talent and your charm."

"Oh, yes. Right."

"Come on. You know how to work your magic. You've worked it on me."

I smiled serenely and let him maintain that illusion.

"You know what I've been doing, what about you?" I asked.

"What about me," he repeated. "It's mostly been the job."

"Is everything you work on confidential and top secret or can you tell me about it?"

He smiled at that. "I've been on a case, a disturbing case. I'm pretty hung up on it right now. I don't know how much you want to hear. It's not romantic, let me put it that way."

"So, okay." I looked him over. "What would you like to talk about?"

"See?" he said, shaking his head. "I'm pretty hopeless. When I get working on a big case, I don't have much else on my mind."

"Really? And why did you come over here so late?"

"So we could talk."

"Chuck. Back in Studio City. Were you thinking only about crime?"

"Well," he said, chuckling like a bad boy who doesn't mind all that much getting caught. "I'm long past getting involved with some woman just because she's beautiful. Long past. But I missed you."

Relationships! I hate talking about them. Not with the guy in question and certainly not with some shrink. I've not had the best luck with men, it's true, but I don't want to go to some analyst and talk endlessly about my past pain. I know all about my past pain. Men, boys, have slipped away. I came home from fifth grade on the first bus with my little brother, Reggie. Simon was older. He was staying late to work on his sixth-grade art project. When he didn't come home on the last bus, my parents went out to search. I don't need to pay a couple hundred bucks an hour to talk about it.

"So you want to hear about this case?" Honnett asked, checking me out.

"Whatever you want," I said, turning to face him. "Talking's good."

He pushed a strand of hair behind my ear and said, "Okay, then. Five weeks ago, we had a homicide. It looked like it was a hit on a drug runner. Nothing strange about that."

"What a world," I murmured. To Honnett, there was nothing all that strange about men killing each other over drugs and territories. This was the part of himself he didn't want to show me and maybe, even, I didn't want to see.

"We had good reason to believe the victim was a coke importer and we figured he'd gotten greedy or whatever they do to piss one another off. Tom Reed and I caught the case, and we were working it. No leads. Looked like a professional hit. Then the next week, I happened to look at the sheet and saw another fellow had been taken out. Different deal. The first guy was shot in the head in his bathtub. The second one was beaten to death in his apartment in South-Central. But there were similarities. Both men had connections to the same gang, a gang that had been getting pushy and moving dope in neighborhoods controlled by other gangs. Both of the victims had been in prison at the same time. And both of their bodies were discovered on Wednesday nights."

"Is it a gang war?" I asked.

"Not exactly. But to me it seemed like a couple of homicides with too much in common to ignore. I brought it up at a meeting that we should see what happened on the following Wednesday night. That got a laugh."

"Then what?"

"Wednesday night comes and another Latino guy got wasted. Shot in front of his house. No witnesses. But this guy wasn't in any gang that we can tell. His wife said he was a peaceful man. He was the manager of a liquor store in Pacoima. She didn't know what sort of people he was involved with at work. But it seemed like we might make it fit. Kids had been dealing drugs near his corner. Maybe he took them on."

"So did the department begin to take your theory more seriously?"

"Well, who knows?" Honnett said with a smile that masked his feelings well. "Maybe. But then the following Wednesday night we got nothing. The only murder that came across our desk that night was some older woman."

"And she didn't fit the profile."

"Profile, huh? You've been watching too many cop shows."

"Get off my case, Honnett." I punched him and he grabbed my fist and pulled me toward him. We got lost for a moment, him pulling me back on the sofa on top of him. When we stopped kissing and touching, I pushed him away and sat up. How were we supposed to have a serious talk if we were just going to give in to lust? "Come back here and tell me about the old woman."

"You mean," he teased me, "if she fit the profile?" He stood up then and smiled at me. "She didn't. She was a white woman in her sixties. A physical therapist."

"A much-loved physical therapist?"

"Actually, no. She was a retired PT with a history of pissing off every patient she'd ever treated. The kind of physical therapist who was into 'tough love,' you know? She gave new meaning to the concept 'no pain, no gain.' But her patients seemed to recover in record time and worker's comp loved her. So no, she didn't fit our profile." He reached out and took my hand. As he spoke, he gently pulled me up. "She had no gang connections. She'd never even been in the neighborhoods we're talking about. Still, her body was found inside her home, which has been part of the pattern. She was found Thursday morning, with the time of death fixed as Wednesday night. There were no witnesses and no suspects, other than those dozens of poor folks she'd exercised to death recovering from busted ankles over the years. But what can we make of the fact that she was shot in the head in bed? No rape. Nothing stolen. More like an execution."

"There are so many ugly things going on all around us, all the time. In your job, you can't look away, can you?"

"Don't worry about me," he said. "I get angry when I don't have a case locked down. I was pretty sure there was a pattern. I felt like we were getting close. But then, the old lady."

"Can you stay here tonight?" I asked, disturbed that I wanted him so badly, and relieved when I saw him nod. Perhaps this is the way our bodies compensate, react to primal fears. Talk about death, and we need to hold on to someone, chest to chest feel his heart pounding, be physically reminded that we are still alive. Talk about the bogeyman out there in the dark waiting to get us some random Wednesday, and we need to find some good man to sleep beside until he does. I reached for my near empty glass of wine. "Was that physical therapy woman killed *last* Wednesday?"

"Two weeks ago." As we walked out of the living room and down the hall, he reached up to turn out the lights. "Last Wednesday night," he said, "there was another murder. Another possible drug hit. This guy owed a lot of money to some very bad people. His death was an example."

"So maybe your theory is right, after all."

"Is it?" Honnett asked. I turned on the lamp next to my bed as he tugged back my quilt and sheets with one long pull. "Aren't you tired of all this talk about crime, Maddie?"

"Honnett," I said, stopping his hand before he could distract me again. "This stuff, this string of killings you're working on, it's bad. But we live in a big city where those things happen. This is Los Angeles. If you need to talk—"

"You're a tough chick, huh?"

I smiled at his fond sarcasm, but I kept on. "Is this what's really bothering you? Or is there something else?" I sat down on the bed and waited.

"Your friend Stock." Honnett began pulling off his boots, but he watched my face as he mentioned Tim's name. "He got himself killed last night."

"I know." My voice became very quiet.

"It was a Wednesday night."

"Wait, now." Suddenly I wondered if I had drunk too much wine. I put my hand up to my face. "Are you saying Tim Stock's death is part of your pattern? Was it some kind of contract killing?"

"I don't know. The fire could have been a cover-up, Maddie. The coroner will tell us what he can. I wouldn't bet that we'll get a whole lot considering . . . Sorry. I knew I shouldn't tell you this stuff. You were a friend of his."

"Well, no. Not really a friend," I said slowly, watching Honnett's deep blue eyes as I spoke. I told him, then, what I knew about Tim Stock and what I didn't know. I admitted that my relationship was with Tim's office, rather than Tim himself.

"So," Honnett said, stretching out in his jeans and T-shirt on the bed next to where I was sitting, propping his lean body up on one elbow, "Stock didn't show up for work all week. He didn't answer his pager for days. Did anyone report the guy missing?"

"I don't know. Do you think his going missing makes him fit your series of crimes?"

"Maybe he got himself in trouble and crossed someone dangerous. Maybe he was trying to lay low. It's hard to say." Honnett began to tug at my hand and pull me down, fully clothed, beside him, and I let him. "Maybe Stock is part of the pattern," he continued, "maybe he isn't. Did this guy have a reputation for being a drug user, did you hear?"

"No. I don't know. I could ask around at the office, if you think it would help."

"I'll be getting to that myself."

Honnett conducting a homicide investigation around the office at

Food Freak, now that could only add to everyone's stress load. My face must have betrayed my thoughts.

"So, Maddie," he said, whispering into my hair, holding me close, "that's what I've been doing all month." It felt good to be in his arms again. I looked up, getting a close view of his profile.

"I think I should tell you some other things." I told him about what had happened earlier in the evening, when I'd been knocked out and placed on the sofa, and later when Holly and I found the magazine hidden in the secret room. "Do you think the clues left in the magazine could have something to do with Tim's death?" I asked.

He thought it over and then said, in a kind voice, "Some notes about cookbook pages?"

"Sounds frivolous compared to the high-level serial-killer case you've been working on."

"Well, I think you should have reported that assault. And I don't want you working in that office building alone at night. Got it?"

I nodded against his chest.

"But I can't really see any connection to what we're after. It doesn't fit the pattern, see?"

"Ah," I said. "The pattern."

"I mean to say, whoever killed Stock knew exactly where to find him. They nailed him in his garage. My killer wouldn't have been messing around at Tim Stock's office. The killings have always been professional-style hits."

"So that hidden room? And that magazine? And those highlighted words that Wes found?"

"I think some old, long-ago studio executive used to fool around with his secretary in the hidden bedroom, once upon a time, and those cookbook titles were probably some kind of code Stock used to keep the game-show material secure. That's not the work of my hit man, Madeline," Honnett said, smiling.

"And the note on the subscription card? The meeting near De Soto and Victory in a few hours?"

"You think that's important?" he asked.

"Yes."

"Seriously? But you don't have a clue as to when that note was written. Honey, it's all just too flimsy. Besides, it doesn't figure. Either Stock is part of my pattern, in which case he's got some connection to the drug gangs and we'll uncover that, or he was just a poor son of a bitch who got caught in a house fire. Either way, that note doesn't fit into my case."

"Uh-huh. But aren't you worried about Heidi and Monica? They're in danger."

Honnett looked at me. His eyes were amused. "Heidi and Monica who? That note isn't part of my pattern either. And if the department sent a detective out every time a Hollywood writer made a note about murder, we'd be swamped."

"Even a Hollywood writer who ended up being killed?" I asked.

"It's too little to go on, Maddie. You don't even know the date."

"Okay. Okay."

"You going out there anyway?"

"I might."

"You are so stubborn."

I bit his shoulder until he yelled "Ouch!"

"I know," I said. "So where is De Soto and Victory, anyway?"

He chuckled. "The deep Valley, darling. A ways out there." He was trying to dissuade me.

"So I'll take my cell phone," I said, "and if there's anything there to report, I can call you."

It was nearly three A.M. and the world outside the windows was quiet. We lay in the lamp-lit bedroom, silently thinking our thoughts. Honnett's case didn't seem to connect to what I'd known about Tim.

"What are you thinking about?" Honnett asked.

"Tim Stock. He was a guy who drove a fancy car and dated pretty women. He read Shakespeare. He wrote game shows. I don't think he'd be involved with serious criminals like the ones you are tracking."

"You may be right. Stock could just be another poor sucker who happened to die on a Wednesday night."

"And that's bad enough," I said.

Honnett got up and turned out the light. I heard him pulling off his jeans in the dark and then he climbed back into my bed. He pulled me closer to his body and I responded to the warmth of his breath against my neck. I felt uneasy, in bed with him like that, thinking about love and death. But it's an odd thing, hormones.

"Honnett?" I reached out my hand and felt for him.

"You want me to help you out of your clothes?"

"Thanks."

ON only one hour of sleep, nobody looks too good. That's my story and I'm sticking to it. I moved Holly's VW and pulled the Jeep out into traffic, awake only but for the curative powers of a hot shower, eyedrops, and a can of Diet Coke. Unfortunately, my old Grand Wagoneer is from the days before cup holders were a standard feature. I propped the soda can between the gearshift and my purse and tried to keep the car steady so the can wouldn't tip.

If I had been fully awake, I might have marveled at the almost complete lack of traffic on the Hollywood Freeway where it transitioned to the 101 North. Five A.M. was one hell of a good time to drive. I'd have to remember that.

Mile after mile I zoomed into the western reaches of the San Fernando Valley, as the sun rose from behind my car, turning the chilly, misty, overcast morning a brighter shade of gray by the minute. It's what native Angelenos call "the marine layer," the condition that requires us all to leave the house in sweaters on days that will end up in the eighties. I pulled my pink sweater a little tighter and checked the sky. The thick, low-level clouds seemed to go on forever, forming a lumpy ceiling over the Valley. I knew they'd burn off around noon.

Having checked the map book, I had learned that De Soto Avenue intersected Victory Boulevard out in Woodland Hills. It was approximately 16.4 miles from my house and, at the speed I was able to drive at this hour, I would be there in less than fifteen minutes.

I pulled off the freeway and turned north onto De Soto, cruising through the intersection at Oxnard, a Zippy-Lube next to a taco stand on the left. With only a diet soda for breakfast, I confess I eyed the taco stand, but then remembered my errand. On the right, I saw the campus of Los Angeles Pierce College, a two-year school whose bucolic acreage harkened back to the time in the twenties when this part of the Valley had all been ranch land and orange groves. Now, those former fields surrounding the school were filled with so-called ranch-style homes, built mostly in the fifties and sixties, each on its own small grassy lot. The college, however, was over two hundred acres and much of it was still open fields. I slowed down and reread my directions. Up on the right, I saw the entrance I was looking for, the turnoff onto El Rancho Drive. I was now on the Pierce campus, driving slowly, looking at pastureland.

On the left was an equestrian arena, with a barn farther off next to a park. Driving less than fifteen miles an hour, I passed the agriculture science building, but classes wouldn't start for another few hours at least and there were no students to been seen anywhere. The poultry unit next door was equally devoid of human activity. If Tim Stock or any of his associates were looking for a remote location within twenty minutes of the KTLA studio, they had found it. I scanned the hay-colored fields in the misty morning, making sure I didn't miss the first right turn. In my map book, this tiny path was called Pepper Tree Lane, but there was no street sign to be found that marked it as such. I made the right turn, hoping I wasn't lost already.

To my right was a complex of feed barns. This was not simple. The note instructed the second building on the right. Did they mean to include these separate barns as one building? I decided to keep going and check things out farther down the lane. When I came to the next structure on the right, I was glad my truck had four-wheel drive. I pulled in over the dried, rutted mud and looked for someplace to hide the Jeep.

As it turned out, this place was clean out of hiding spots. The parking area was there along the road. The fields all around the barn were pastureland. Not only was this site remote, but it also provided a great defensive position. No one could easily wait in ambush. I slid out of my truck and walked over to the nearest building, a rustic-looking wooden enclosure. My wristwatch said 5:30. If today was the day for some important meeting, and if I hadn't managed to get the directions completely fouled up, I had about thirty minutes to look around.

It was a wonderfully quiet morning, with only the music of a dozen birds noisily waking up and discussing this odd stranger walking around the mud in that crazy little skirt and those insane little tan suede boots. This, they were clearly tweeting, was no kind of ag student they'd ever seen.

I stepped carefully over the straw and the soft spots in the muddy field, watching out for the stones and small gullies that would guarantee me a one-way trip to the orthopedic wing of the nearest hospital. At the door of the barn, I looked back around. I could see the long stretch of the lane that had brought me here. No cars moved. An old truck was parked about a block away, but it was so bird speckled and rusted, it might have been there permanently.

I tried the door to the barn and it wouldn't budge. I was such a city girl. Did barns have locks? I looked for one and was treated to the sight of a large metal latch that had only to be thrown back to unhitch the hinged door. Well, duh.

With the door open, I proceeded to enter the dark enclosure. I heard the sound of rustling and I looked to my left. That's when I realized I was not, indeed, alone. Squealing ensued. Here in this barn there were row upon row of fenced-off pens, each one holding a nice, fat pig. A sign on each pen announced its occupant's name.

"Sadie and Lou," read one sign. I saw only one pig.

"Are you Sadie or Lou?" I asked quietly. She ignored me.

Another sign read: "Dumpling." Another: "Gladiola." I walked down the row and looked at the animals. On the ground, I picked up a mud-splattered copy of *The Journal of Swine Health and Production*, which billed itself as "the only refereed, swine-focused journal currently being published in North America." And I supposed I would now have to give up that dream to be the first to produce such a journal. Life can be cruel.

At the end of the row, there seemed to erupt a commotion of squeals and shoving. I walked down the aisle and found five adorable pink piglets squirming for attention. The pen was marked "4-week-old weaned pigs, 10 kg, hybrid." I couldn't help myself. I had to pick one of these cuties up and say hello.

"Say there. You lookin' for someone?"

I jumped. Standing at the door to the pig enclosure was a man, silhouetted against the bright outdoor light. I carefully set the happy little piglet back down among her brothers and sisters.

"Hello," I said, straightening up.

"You're not a student," the man said, without a shadow of a doubt in his tone of voice.

"No. I'm not." I tried to walk without losing my balance on the slatted wooden floor to meet him, but the one-inch heels on my boots were so narrow they kept slipping through the cracks. As I neared the door, I saw he was a trim fellow, maybe early to mid-thirties, dressed in dusty dark denim pants and a navy uniform shirt, with the cuffs rolled back and the name "Karl" stitched over the pocket. "Are you Karl?" I tried.

"Well, you may not be a student here," he said with a chuckle, "but at least you can read."

Drat. That always used to work for Charlie's angels. I might not have disarmed Karl with my wits, but at least the guy had a sense of humor.

"I was supposed to meet someone here," I said. "I may have gotten the wrong address."

"Address?" Karl looked at me funny. "You got a date for early morning lattes in the swine barn?"

"Well, not exactly. No." Karl backed up and ushered me out into the bright morning waiting outside.

"So who are you?" he asked. Karl wore a red feed cap on his head, its bill rounded in the deep curve that was currently in fashion. He was pretty nice looking for a farm boy. I wondered if he worked out in a gym or if that was the kind of body one got from lifting bales of hay all day long.

"I'm Madeline Bean," I said. I pulled out one of my business cards, one that says: "MAD BEAN EVENTS, Special Events, Parties, Catering," with my name and my phone number in the lower corner.

Karl read it over and smirked. I noticed he had a small scar across his right eyebrow. "You scouting locations for a hay ride, Madeline?"

"No. Just meeting friends."

"This is school property, and while I don't think you were planning to steal one of our prize pigs, there, it still doesn't do to have strangers at large on the farm. Know what I mean?"

"Sure. I won't be in the way, though. And I'm not a stranger, now. I mean, you have my card and you know how to reach me. If anything goes missing, you can send the cops out to arrest me. But what I mean is, nothing will go missing. I was just saying hello—"

"You can't wait for your friends inside this barn." Karl gave me a direct look. Now Karl was not an easy man to sweet-talk.

"Okay, then." What else could I say? It was five minutes until six and I wasn't sure anyone would show up there, anyway. I wasn't even sure I was in the right barn.

"So who is this friend of yours?" Karl asked as he escorted me back to my Grand Wagoneer parked on the lane out in front.

"Friends," I said. "Heidi and Monica. Do you know them?"

He stared at me. "Heidi and Monica?"

I nodded.

"Well, maybe you are all turned around. I think you might find those two up over there." Karl pointed up the lane to the last building on the right.

"Inside there?"

"Well, either inside or out back."

"Thanks," I said, giving Karl my warmest smile, and then I got into my truck and drove the quarter mile or so until I reached the next building. While I had been inside the swine barn, there had been some subtle changes outside. I saw a few more SUVs and trucks parked here and there. The Pierce College farm was beginning to see some activity.

I parked next to the only vehicle close to the building I was heading for. It was an older blue Honda CR-V. Like everything around here, it was pretty well splashed with mud. As I walked past it, a sticker near the back window caught my eye: KTLA PARKING PERMIT 011.

My head swiveled back, riveted to the words. Someone who worked at the studio was here. Someone who rated a parking permit on the lot. Someone, that is, besides me.

I stepped carefully across an open yard over to a barn, which was almost identical to the one Karl had kicked me out of. This time I knew about the latch and I pulled it open like a pro and walked in. Here, as in the previous farm enclosure, I moved out of the daylight and into a vast dark room. The only difference was that the fence sections forming the pens were taller. This barn held Pierce College's sheep population. I looked around for any women, students perhaps, that Karl had led me to believe might be working here. However, no one was there except us sheep.

I let my eyes adjust to the light. The sheep were actually quite cute. They were larger and quieter than the pigs, but there were slight rustlings and creakings as they pulled on hay or walked across their wood-slat floors.

I decided to wait here. After all, the note said "6:00 A.M. Thursday." My watch told me it was just a few minutes past six now.

I looked into some of the stalls. There were several different breeds, each with different characteristics and fleece color. Some were white, but others were straw-colored, and one was even black. I was surprised by how full their fleece was and suspected they were prize examples kept by the school's agriculture department for showing. A sign on the wall described the merino breed:

The long, unbroken line of breeding extending back for more than twelve hundred years of sheep bred for one specific purpose, the production of the best wool in the world, make the merino the best all-around breed the world has ever known. No other wool can compare with the wool of the merino in its color, uniformity, strength, density, and fineness. Fleece should be from 2.5 inches to 4 inches long in one year's growth. It should be fine enough to grade from 64s in spinning count to as high as 80s.

Frankly, I had had no idea that sheep people could get quite so passionate over their animals. I patted the head of one ewe standing quietly in her pen nearby. Her sign read: "Meryl Sheep." Hmm. The next pen contained "Dan Merino." Whoever named these sheep was my kind of shepherdess. Next to Dan was "Dances with Wool." I let out a giggle.

I took out the note. I reread the light pencil marks that told the time and the directions. I turned it over once more and read the worrisome comment on the bottom. "Please help me, Tim. Monica and Heidi might have to die." Something about those two names had always bothered me.

It didn't take me long to find the pen I was after. Just down the aisle and over to the left. There, in a double enclosure, were the objects of my search. Two beautiful plump sheep. The sign on the pen read: MONICA EWEINSKY AND HEIDI FLEECE.

16

THE sound of dogs barking in the distance didn't seem to faze Monica and Heidi the least little bit, but as the barking became louder and nearer, I was beginning to think about becoming alarmed. I glanced back and noticed I'd left the barn door open. Oops. Now I knew how boys felt. The barking grew even louder and then three large animals burst into the sheep barn. Three German shepherd dogs, their dark fur flying toward me. And yet, they looked familiar. Three German . . .

I stood up and drew a breath.

"Come back here, you!" Behind the dogs came their owner, trying to get them to mind.

"Susan!" I was stunned. It was Susan Anderson. I'd seen a group photo of the three beautiful dogs, each with his own distinctive coloring, on her desk at *Food Freak*. One mostly black, that was Niko, she had told me. One a beautiful golden color with a small patch of black, that was Thorn. The baby was Khailo. But he didn't look like much of a baby now.

Susan Anderson called out in a singing voice, like an affectionate if exasperated mother, "Khailo! Niko! Thorn! Out of here. Scoot."

Niko, the leader, turned for the door and the other two followed him as they heeded their mistress and reversed course.

"My goodness. Madeline. What are you doing here?" Susan asked, standing in the doorway and shooing her mischievous boys outside.

"Susan." I was really almost at a loss for words. Me. "I came here looking for Heidi and Monica," I finished. How to explain.

"*My* Heidi and Monica?" she asked. "Heidi Fleece and Monica Eweinsky? Really? I didn't know you were interested in sheep." There was more barking coming from just past the door. "Come outside a minute and we can talk. I want to keep an eye on the boys."

Susan Anderson was the head production assistant on *Food Freak*, but what else did I really know about her? Certainly nothing about her early mornings at Pierce College. And nothing about sheep.

The tailgate to her Honda was down and she beckoned me over to sit with her. "Really," she said when I joined her, "did you come all the way out here this morning looking for me?"

"I was looking for Tim Stock," I said, sitting next to her. "I found this note in a magazine near his office." I brought out the folded postcard and smoothed it against the tailgate. Susan looked at it and sighed. "You know about this?" I asked.

Susan looked at me and became thoughtful. One of her boys, Niko, jumped up, putting two paws on her lap. She sat there, rubbing his thick black neck absently, not quite ready to talk.

Susan had a sweet nature, a bubbly sense of humor, and a little shyness mixed in. She was a nurturer. I'd watched her on *Food Freak* taking care of everyone, from the producer to the director to her young assistant PAs. She was the one you turned to for advice or a Motrin or an extra pen.

I looked at her now, away from the artificial environment of the studio, and she seemed less hunched over out here. Susan was maybe three inches taller than me, I'd guess around five foot eight. She was slender, with a nice figure, but she tended to dress down. Today she was wearing Wrangler jeans and a tucked-in T-shirt that displayed the face of *Love Connection* host Chuck Woollery. I got the joke and smiled at her.

"I've got another one I'm wearing tomorrow," she said, noticing my smile. "It's a picture of Bob Ewebanks." Again, she dimpled. She had a beautiful soft smile and pretty gray-green eyes, which were partly hidden behind tiny wire-rimmed glasses. It was hard to gauge her age, but not yet forty, I'd guess. She could look a lot younger if she tried. Her skin showed not a trace of makeup and her full curly crop of hair had begun to show a few strands of gray among the chestnut brown.

"I take it you know about this note, then," I said.

"Oh, yes. I wrote it."

"You did?"

"But you can see, Tim's not here." Susan looked around the yard and we were still the only two humans near the sheep enclosure.

"So this meeting was supposed to be today?" I asked. "I wasn't sure."

"I don't know if I should tell you any more, Madeline. Some of this stuff is Tim's private business and he made me promise not to talk about it to anyone. I'm sorry."

"Oh, Susan." How could I tell her Tim Stock was dead? "You and Tim were good friends, then?"

"We are very, very close," she said warmly. Her voice betrayed the lightest of East Coast accents, like a touch of New York, but not as strong. "He's just the greatest guy. I forgot you don't really know him."

"I have some very difficult news, then," I said carefully.

"What news?"

"Last night, after I found one of Tim's magazines, I went out to see if he might be home. Everyone's been so worried about him. Greta was going crazy."

"Was she?" Susan asked, her face a blank.

"Yes. So I drove out to his house, not knowing what I'd find. But when I got there, there had been a fire."

"At Tim's house? In Studio City?" Susan looked concerned.

"Yes. In the garage, actually. And he was hurt. The police told me they found his body there, Susan."

"What?" She looked at me as if it wasn't possible. "Maddie, what are you telling me?"

"Tim died last night. They don't know what to make of it. The police are wondering if his death might be connected to some other drug slayings."

"That's ridiculous! Tim doesn't use drugs. You must have gotten this all mixed up. Tim isn't like that at all."

I looked at her as she patted her dog's neck and smoothed down his thick fur. Susan Anderson was taking the news of her close friend's death with an eerie calm.

"I apologize," she said softly. "You must think I'm not paying attention. I guess I am not able to talk about this right now."

"I know. I'm sorry to be the one to bring you such terrible news."

"That's okay. Don't feel bad," she said, and reached out to give my arm a reassuring squeeze. "I'm sure there's some mistake. Tim isn't dead. He can't be."

"But, Susan, haven't you noticed that things have been going wrong at the office? Lots of things don't make sense. I found a secret door in Tim's office . . ." Susan looked up at me and nodded. ". . . and a hidden bedroom. You know about that!"

"Tim wanted to get away and he thought the easiest way would be to stay in that side bedroom for a couple of weeks. Isn't it a tricky little hideaway? We figured it must have quite a Hollywood history, that bedroom. But then Tim thought our production schedule was over. It would have been if the network hadn't come up with this last-minute special. Tim never imagined Greta would hire another writer. And even when she did, he couldn't have guessed she'd put you in his private office."

"Are you saying that all the time Greta and Artie and everyone has been worried about him, Tim Stock has been living right there behind the bookcase in his old office at *Food Freak?*"

"Oh, please. Don't be mad."

"I don't know what to think. Why was he doing it?"

"I can't really explain. Something to do with his personal life, I think. He never told me what was behind it all. I brought him food and did his laundry and little things. He knows the studio and knows where he can hide. He stayed away in the daytime and only came back after everyone left work."

"Everyone except for you," I said, thinking it over. I had marveled at how late Susan had stayed at the studio each night, how she could possibly have any private life if she gave so many hours to her job. "But why would he hide out like that, Susan? That's the strangest thing I've ever heard."

"Tim has had some things pile up, personal things, like I said, and he just needed some time to think things through. Look, Maddie, I don't know anything and I can't talk about Tim anymore."

"Okay. I understand," I said. Finally, someone who might have some idea what the hell is going on, and of course she would never tell me. "Can you at least explain to me about all this?" I spread my hand to encompass the yard and the Pierce College sheep barn and the pastureland behind us. "This is the most un-L.A. place in the entire San Fernando Valley. How did you come to take care of sheep?"

"Oh, my gosh," she said, flushing. "You really want to hear about me?"

"Do you mind? I'm blown away."

Susan continued to blush, obviously much more used to staying in the background as able assistant than stepping forward onto center stage. She was terribly cute in her self-effacing way. "It's a funny story, if you really want to hear it. Just a second." She whistled and her dogs came running. They quickly jumped up into the back of her car and settled themselves down. She told me again each of her boys' names. Thorn lay in the backseat and raised a black eyebrow at us, as if letting us know what an intelligent guy he was. The other two, Niko and Khailo got comfortable in the rear storage area of the SUV where they would have the best view out of the back. Susan pulled the tailgate up and beckoned me to walk with her. We settled on a primitive wooden bench under the wispy tree in front of the barn.

"So, tell me," I asked, "how did you get into sheep? Do you come from farm people way back?"

She burst out laughing. "Oh, no. Nothing like that. My parents still live in Queens. I went to college in Manhattan. I never saw a farm in my life, I don't think."

"Then how?"

"Okay, you want the whole story? Here it is. I had been working in production for a lot of years. I was getting a lot of PA work but I was trying to move up. It's very hard. The goal is to get into the Directors'

Guild, to become an AD. You have to work at the same company for a long time before they give you that kind of break. The problem is, most production companies hire you for a show, but they don't always have a hit. Then you have to work for another company. It's hard to get someone to sponsor you, you know?"

I nodded.

"And I needed the benefits. The health insurance. I mean, I'm not married. I had to look after my career."

"So why are you still working as a PA?"

"Well, that's a whole 'nother story," Susan said, her eyes twinkling. "But let me tell you what happened that got me into the guild."

"And that leads to the sheep?"

"Yes, it does. See, I was working for Artie at the time. This was about five years ago. He had that *Great Escapes* show, do you remember it? It was on for two seasons."

"I think so. Where celebrities went on safari?"

"They went everywhere exotic, yes. And Tim was the head writer and Greta was the AD and I was the first PA."

"All the same people who are working on *Food Freak*."

"Right. Usually, when a team of people works well together, the executive producer keeps hiring us all from show to show. It's easier for everyone. We know we work well together. Anyway, Artie can be pretty difficult. You know that, right?"

"No."

"Oh, yes," she said, laughing a dry little chuckle. "He can be very difficult. You haven't seen that side of him yet, but believe me he can. A lot of these guys are like big babies. They want everything their way, and when they get it, they're still not happy.

"Well, I'd worked for Artie before. He'd blown up at me before. Every other time I just took it. I just stood there and let him scream at me. And the next day, he'd always apologize. He usually gave me some big generous gift and begged me to forgive him. He can be extremely sweet, as I'm sure you know. And it's like he has these temper tantrums and then when they're over, they're over."

"I am just amazed, here," I said.

"So anyway, we were in Mexico, I remember. We were getting set to shoot an episode where the woman who starred in *Touched by an Angel* and her family were going to visit the Aztec pyramids outside Mexico City, in Teotihuacán. So we're out on a scouting day with the director and the art director and the lighting director, so Artie can pick the exterior locations, and he's furious. These aren't majestic pyramids. They're dusty little broken-down ruins. It was hot, and we didn't have the time to select another location. We were having budget problems, but then Artie is always worried about money no matter how rich he is. And he just lost it."

"What did he do?"

"Typical Artie Herman tantrum. He couldn't yell at his good buddy the director. And he couldn't yell at his art director or his lead camera guy or his lighting director, so he turned to me and screamed that it was all my fault."

"Oh, Susan."

"This had all happened before, Madeline. I'd heard him blow up many times before. Only this time, it felt different. This time I was hot, too, and we were in a foreign country, and I had no way to just go to my room. I had to ride back in a van with all these guys who had just stood there listening to Artie fire me."

"He fired you?"

"Oh, yes," she said, smiling. "He fired me. I think he's fired me at least five times in the past eight years."

"Oh my God, Susan." She seemed so sanguine and unruffled, but this story was grotesque.

"Anyway, when I finally, finally got back to the hotel that night, I kind of lost it. I went to the bar to buy the biggest bottle of tequila I could to take to my room. I didn't know what to do. Artie was furious with me. I didn't have my return ticket. I didn't even have my passport—the hotel had it, I think. I didn't have any money. And I was crushed. I had counted on my salary at *Great Escapes* to make payments on my car, and to cover the months when I wasn't able to find work. Plus, I wasn't in the union at that time, so I was paying for all my own health insurance. It was just a terribly scary time for me to be out of a job. So I went to the hotel bar and ordered a bottle of tequila."

"And then what?"

"And then I saw Tim. He was at the bar. He hadn't been out on the location scout and he hadn't heard about me getting fired. I told him. We had known each other pretty well before, but this night I was hysterical. He took me back to his room and mixed me tequila and fresh-squeezed orange juice and just listened to me. I usually have such good control over myself, but that night I really lost it."

I shook my head, trying to imagine a younger Susan, scared about losing her job, working in such insane conditions. She was such a kind soul, it just made no sense.

"Then what? Did Tim help you get your plane ticket?"

"Not exactly. He did something better. He stayed up with me all night and we talked about what we really wanted to be doing with our lives. I mean, his point was so true. Did we really want to make some game show or some vacation travel show the most meaningful thing we would ever do? Tim told me he had a secret dream. He said the only reason he continued to work for Artie was to save enough money to buy his dream."

"What was his dream?"

"He wants to write historical fiction."

"Really?"

She nodded, smiling. "He is a really talented guy. He was a history major at Columbia."

"Tim Stock?"

"Yes. He just needs the money to get to his dream. He wants to buy a house free and clear so he won't need to make any more payments. He wants to travel to London to do historical research. He needs to save enough money to take five years off and write the novel he's always wanted to write."

"Wow. That could take a lot of money, five years and a house."

"That's Tim's dream. He's been making pretty good money writing television, but it isn't the big money that sitcom writers get. Nothing like that. And Tim has to have a new car and he likes to date expensive women. But still, he's been saving little by little. And he told me that night back in Mexico to do what he was doing. Think of my PA work as just a job. Turn it into a way to earn enough to bankroll my dream."

"What's your dream?" I looked at Susan, wondering why I never noticed before how serene she was, how positive and peaceful. Maybe she only felt that way outside the studio.

"That was the difficult part, Maddie," she said, laughing at herself again. "I had no dream. All I wanted was to get into the Directors' Guild to get my medical insurance covered. Pretty pathetic dream, right? So Tim kept pouring us tequila and orange juice and I tried to concentrate on what my dream should be. And I was still so tense, from my day out on location, I couldn't stop crying about not having a dream. Finally, Tim told me to close my eyes and imagine the most peaceful place I could think of. And from out of nowhere popped this image of a pasture and a flock of sheep."

"You're kidding! That is so weird."

"It's bizarre, isn't it? I mean, I'm a New Yorker. I knew absolutely nothing about sheep. I'd never been on a farm. And you know what, right then and there I told Tim I was going to buy myself a ranch someday and raise sheep."

"In your peaceful, tequila haze, you were Little Bo Peep," I said, in awe. "Amazing."

"I know! But whatever that vision was, whether it was the booze or my nervous breakdown or what, it made me feel incredibly happy to think about buying those sheep."

"And then what happened?"

"The next morning I couldn't even wake up. But I didn't care. I was fired anyway. I wasn't in my hotel room all night, so Artie couldn't find me and do his typical apology with a huge gift. So you'll never believe what happened. Artie started to panic. He had Greta searching everywhere."

"Because Artie really felt ashamed after he came down from his raging?"

"Yes. He felt bad. He always felt bad. He was the same guy he always was. But I had changed, Madeline. I was no longer sniffling in my room, cowering, waiting for the other shoe to drop. I was sleeping off a night of tequila sunrises in Tim Stock's bed."

"So," I asked delicately, "were you and Tim . . . ?"

"No," Susan said, laughing again. "No, he let me sleep in the bed.

He's such a great friend. And while I'm sure you have heard that Tim has slept with a lot of women, we never had that in our relationship."

"So what did Artie do when he couldn't find you?"

"He went ballistic. I mean, he was in Mexico. Where was he going to find another English-speaking PA. What had he been thinking when he fired me, anyway?" She shook her head. "So Tim was out in the lobby, listening to Artie going nuts and watching Greta come back with her field reports that I wasn't at the pool and I wasn't in the restaurant and I hadn't been in my bed the previous night, that sort of thing. And finally, Tim tells Artie, 'I know where Susan is.' And Artie is ready to kill him and Tim says, 'But I won't tell you until you agree to make Susan the AD, pay for her to join the Directors' Guild, and buy her six sheep.' "

"This is too much. And Artie said 'Okay'?"

"Yep. And that was the start of my flock. I went back to work and when we got home, I found out that Pierce lets some of its students keep their livestock here at the college. I had Artie lined up to pay for them, so I decided to get started right away. I took a course here in sheep."

"They have courses in sheep?"

"They do. And I took the course and was allowed to bring my sheep here. That was five years ago. To this day, I've been saving my money for my dream. And I'm almost there."

"I'm amazed." I looked at her and smiled. "I've known you at the office, but I had no idea about all of this."

"It's funny about people, isn't it? We all have so many layers. We're not what you expect."

"Especially you," I said, admiring the way Susan had found her own freedom. "And yet, you still work for Artie Herman?"

"Yes, I do. And you know what, he's never blown up at me after that time. I don't know if it was how scared he got the next morning when he probably thought he had driven me to suicide, or if it is how much damn money he has to pay every year to keep my flock in feed and to pay for shearing."

"Artie still pays?"

"Oh, yes. Tim hammered out the details and Artie was happy to sign. He can really be a generous guy at times. Temperamental. But most creative guys are. Only a few days ago, Artie walked into my office and told me his stock portfolio was in trouble. He said he wouldn't be able to pay for the sheep this quarter. I don't know if I believe him, so I wrote that note to Tim. Maybe Artie has just kept paying all these years because he was afraid to cross Tim. Now that Tim is gone, maybe Artie figured he could renege on our deal. And if I don't pay for my sheep, the school can't let me keep them here. I've worked out the numbers, but I would have to let two of them go."

"How can you be so easygoing and forgiving?" I asked. My temper runs way too hot to be able to forgive and forget.

"It's the time I spend with my animals," she said, smiling. "I love my dogs and I love coming out here. Three mornings a week, I come out and tend to my little flock. Then I drive back into town and work on the show."

"So I guess *Food Freak* will never feature a recipe for mutton."

"Maddie!" Susan's eyes twinkled, or at least her wire-rimmed glasses did. "Let's not go there," she said. "You're ba-a-a-d."

I couldn't groan. I deserved that

NORMALLY, most of *Freak*'s office staff arrive at work sometime between nine-thirty and ten. Some go-getters are in earlier. They, and the one or two individuals who draw excellent paychecks but have come to discover that their positions serve no earthly purpose on the show, tend to arrive just a hair before nine, the better to impress Artie, who usually pulls his Cadillac onto the lot a few minutes later. At seven-thirty, however, even the most insecure production executive is at home in bed. At this hour of the morning, our side of the studio was a ghost town.

I used my key to unlock the glass door to *Food Freak*'s reception area, and then, once inside, to lock myself in again. No reason to take chances. I turned on the lights and Chef Howie was everywhere, smiling down at me. Chef Howie frying bacon. Chef Howie flipping flapjacks. Chef Howie frappéing a banana smoothie. Gigantic framed posters of Chef Howie filled three walls. As it had been left by the hardworking contestant department the previous night, everything in this room was in readiness for that department's great daily quest, to sift through hundreds of amateur chefs and find for the show just the right talented home cooks with just the right telegenic personalities to make it on the air.

I walked past a credenza where an instant camera and ten boxes of film were staged near a section of plain white wall. Pictures would be taken of every hopeful *Freak* contestant, to be attached to his or her application. Across from a large reception desk were rows of black plastic seats with wide arms on one side like college desks. Aspiring contestants were seated here, in groups of thirty, to fill out forms.

I walked across the empty room to one of the stairwells located on either side of the open reception area. Again, I flipped a light switch and this time illuminated the staircase. I had never been the earliest one in the office before, and with each of these steps, I began to wake up the building.

Up on the second-floor landing, I tried a few switches until I found the one that lit up the hallway, and as the fluorescent fixtures buzzed into brilliance, I listened for a moment to the slight tickings and faint hummings that make up the silence in a silent and empty office suite. I walked down the hall, watchful, careful, and thought about Honnett's directive of not being alone in the building. I hadn't meant to. I had agreed to never again stay at work after-hours, not alone. But for some reason, maybe from lack of sleep or lack of some basic talent for paranoia, I had forgotten to consider how deserted this floor was likely to be at this early morning hour. Rooting around in my bag, my fingers identified my cell phone by touch, and I grabbed it. I punched the numbers—911—and held the instrument in my left hand like a weapon, my thumb over the Call button, ready to shoot off an instant distress signal should an emergency arise. I looked quickly behind me. No one. Of course not. Damn Honnett.

I pulled the tricky maneuver of unlocking Tim Stock's office door while keeping the phone in play, alternately glancing over my shoulder into a perfectly deserted hallway and feeling like a perfect fool. I hated this. Always nervous, always second-guessing. But just as I managed to jiggle the old lock and open the office door, I was instantly alert. The overhead lights had been left on. And before I could recall whether I might have left them burning all night, I discovered I had a visitor.

Fate Finkelberg was sitting on a beautiful new rose-colored sofa. Chef Howie's wife, lying in wait, upon my reward piece of furniture, the ugly brown Herculon monster that clearly figured into my ugly bump-on-the-head memory of the previous night.

"Fate." What else could one say?

"Oh, Madeline, dear." She turned to me and smiled. When she used that expression, her thin lips almost disappeared, but the tight line they made did curve upward. "I am so relieved you are an early bird. I had expected to be here for hours before we could chat. I let myself in Tim's office. I thought I'd get a bit of work done."

"You have a key?"

"I have all the keys. I'm executive producer."

"I thought Artie . . ."

"Well, yes, Arthur has that title, too." She smiled again. Really, I had been treated to 200 percent more affability in the past minute than in all our previous encounters. "We're partners, really, Arthur and I. He provides the studio and production staff and so on and so on, and then sells the show and deals with the network assholes, and I provide the star."

"I see."

"You should watch the show's credits, sometime. You'd find them fascinating. I think I may even have them . . ." Fate deftly flipped open a mammoth-sized three-ring binder that contained about thirty colorful dividers. She quickly came to a page and turned the binder to face me. The paper showed the order of the crawl, that moving list of names that rolls over the final seconds of *Food Freak* each week.

I read the names and noticed the order of importance:

FOOD FREAK

Starring
Chef Howie Finkelberg

Executive Producers
Fate Finkelberg
Arthur Herman

Produced by
Greta Greene

Directed by
Peter Steele

Head Writer
Timothy Stock

Written by
Madeline Bean
Neal Herman
Jennifer Klein
Quentin Shore

"Hey, they put my name in." I looked up at Fate. "So soon."

"Susan is very efficient," Fate said, pulling the large binder back to face herself. "I'll give her that." Something in Fate's voice got colder.

"But, wait, who is Neal Herman? Artie's son?"

"Um-hmm."

"I'm so out of it. I've never even heard that Artie has a son or that he's a writer here, too."

"That's not all that surprising."

"Oh?" With Fate Finkelberg, one had to be prepared to measure the depth of sarcasm, drip by drip. "You mean," I suggested, "Neal Herman doesn't make his presence felt?"

"Well put," Fate said, giving me another tight-lipped grin. "He's on the payroll but I don't think he's ever made it to the studio. The good news is, he'll never get in your way, right?"

Fate had such a dog-eat-dog way of looking at the world. I perched on the desk chair and studied her, watching her recross her thin legs in her gold Capri pants, dangling one foot. The foot, like its partner, had been perfectly pedicured in blood-red lacquer and was shod in a gold wedgie sandal, tied up her calf like the ones worn by Roman gladiators. The woman took fashion way past the limit, to be kind about it.

"Did you want to see me, Fate? Or were you just at the studio early and thought you'd use Tim's empty office?"

Fate arched an almost completely plucked brow. Whatever coloring that brow had originally been blessed with was now a faint memory. A narrow line of dark-blond pencil marked the spot. "We need to talk, sweetie. I need an ally and you're it."

"That's intriguing."

"Good. This is personal, so I don't want anything I'm about to tell you to get around. Not even a scent. Do you understand me?"

"Of course."

"I know you're one of Greta's little friends, but I particularly don't want Greta to get any of this information. Am I clear?"

"Yes."

"If she does find out, I'll know it came from you. And then, Madeline, you can kiss good-bye any chance of working in television again."

I was amazed. They really do say that. How quaint.

"Well, come on," I said, remembering how tough I needed to be. "Do yourself a favor. Don't tell me anything at all, Fate. I'm not breaking into your office at seven-thirty in the morning to have a nice private chat."

"True," she said, smiling her smile. "Well, here's the nasty little business. My husband is having an affair with someone at work. I'm not stupid. I know. And I will kill whoever she is. Make no mistake."

"Fate, hold on." There was no way I wanted to be hearing this. No way.

"You are about the only one who is safe, Madeline. Howie has been carrying on for at least a month. You've only been here a week. Do the math."

I hate that phrase.

Fate stared at me, expecting me to react to her bombshell of a news flash, but I guess I wasn't fast enough. She said, "Well? You're certainly not shocked. Is it that easy to see why Howie would make a fool of me?" Tears literally sprang into Fate's green eyes.

"Fate, I hardly know you and Chef Howie. Actually, I *don't* know you and Chef Howie. I mean, I'm sorry for you if it's true. But why are you telling me this?"

"Not to get your pity, doll," she said, dabbing her eyes with a tissue she grabbed off the desk. "I just have to find out who he's sleeping with. I have to."

"You don't know for sure, then," I said. "Maybe . . ."

"Maybe dogs sing and pigs fly," Fate said bitterly. "I know. I know. How can I tell? Well, he's much happier, for one thing. All of a sudden he got happy."

Ah, that's a problem all right. When the husband gets happy, that's definitely something to worry about. This was the sort of thing that could make a girl glad she wasn't married. Fate kept her unhappy eyes on me. She needed some reassurance, perhaps. "Maybe he's just happy about something else. Like he's enjoying how popular *Freak* has become. His star is rising."

"Oh, right," she said, miserably. "Right. He's a star. And who made him a star? That would be me. I'm such a damned fool, Madeline. I worked and worked to make Chef Howie a household name. Did I tell you we just signed a huge deal with Target for a line of Chef Howie kitchen cleanser? And now he'll leave me and what have I got left?"

Ten percent of the cleanser money? I couldn't, of course, say that aloud. Instead I tried to seem interested in her anxiety. "You must have more evidence than Chef Howie's recent joie de vivre," I said. "You're too hardheaded to make all this up over a mood swing."

"He's been lying," she admitted. "I've caught him a dozen times. What kind of idiot does he think I am? He knows he is an atrocious liar. I always find out."

"What sort of lies?"

Her voice got much softer. "He went away for the weekend. To Santa Barbara. He was going to visit some friends, a chef who just opened a restaurant in Montecito. He knew I couldn't go because I had already told him I had to fly to New York with Arthur for the network affiliates meeting. When I tried to reach him at the hotel in Santa Barbara, he was never in. They took messages. And then he'd call me back ten minutes later."

"That's it?"

"I called him seventeen times, Madeline. Seventeen messages were taken by the desk clerk. Seventeen times Howie returned my call within ten minutes. Don't you get it? He had paid the hotel desk to hold all his calls. He didn't want to be interrupted while he was catting around in some fabulous hotel suite with his . . ." Tears sprang into her eyes once more, and as she dabbed at them, she calmed her voice down. ". . . with his mistress. I don't think I can stand this."

"I'm so sorry," I said. I wasn't sure what was going on between Howie and Fate, but she was probably right.

"The thing is, I want to find out exactly who the little bitch is and I want her head on a platter. I am still the executive producer of this show and Howie is bound to his contract for seven years. Until he comes to his senses and crawls back to me, I will be damned if I will allow his little concubine to work in these offices."

"Who do you think it is?"

"Susan Anderson."

"What?" I was shocked. "Susan doesn't seem like—"

"Like what?" Fate interrupted, her eyes angry. "She's a woman, isn't she? She's so sweet and self-effacing I could kill her. What's with those bizarre T-shirts she wears? And those dogs! She has never worn lipstick in all the days I've known her. She's just all wrong."

"Well, I think she's very pretty," I said, "but I know what you mean. She's got a more natural kind of look."

Fate glared at me. She and Susan Anderson could not have been more dissimilar. Could that be a turn-on for Howie? Was Fate even thinking straight? Susan Anderson having an affair with Chef Howie? I didn't think so. "You must be wrong about this," I said.

"You think?" she asked. "The weekend Howie disappeared up in Santa Barbara, Susan was supposed to come to New York with Arthur and me. At the last minute, she told us she had a cold and canceled."

"That could be a—"

"You want more?" Fate cut in. "I was getting worried, as I told you. I kept calling the Four Seasons and I could never get through directly to Howie. Then on Sunday morning, when Arthur and I were at breakfast, I asked him a question I knew he wouldn't know. He had to call up Susan. He used his cell phone and dialed her right there at the table. It was nine A.M. in New York, which is six A.M. in L.A. And Susan didn't answer. She wasn't at home in her nice warm bed nursing a cold. She was in Santa Barbara having a romantic tryst with Chef Howie!"

I wasn't so sure. At six A.M., it was a good bet that Susan Anderson and her dogs were out on the farm at Pierce College, communing with her flock. But what did I know? These were private issues and I had no reason to get involved.

"Anyway," Fate said, "I just want you to keep your eyes open. If you should see anything going on between the two of them, let me know. I've hired a detective, would you believe it? But so far he's turned up absolutely nothing. It's a huge waste of money. But he's still following Howie. I have to know the truth, Madeline."

"I understand," I said. "But it may be nothing, Fate. You don't have that much to go on, after all."

"There's more. How can I convince you? It's little things. He's happy all the time. And he started doing this goofy little sign-off at the end of each episode of the show. He gives the camera two winks. It's awful. I've told him now a dozen times, it makes him look like he's got some sort of twitching disease. But he insists on it. Can you imagine that? He's listened to my advice every second of every day since we fell in love, and now suddenly he comes up with his own gimmick? He winks? I can't stand it."

"Oh, Fate . . ."

Her voice grew more stressed. "I'm convinced he's sending a signal to some woman. He's sending her a message of"—she stood up and tossed the bunched-up tissue into the wastebasket—"a message of love. So." She gathered up her books and binders and briefcase. "That's why I need an ally. If it's not Susan Anderson, it is probably that obnoxious Greta Greene. And I honestly don't know which of them I hate more. You help me find out, Madeline. You help me and I'll help you, okay?"

I wouldn't say yes and yet I couldn't bring myself to say no to a woman so clearly in pain, so I said nothing.

"Thank you, Madeline. You know I love him, don't you? Chef Howie is my whole world. I am willing to forgive him if he'll come to me and apologize and promise me he won't act crazy again. I just want us to go on."

"I know," I said. So lame.

"And if there's anything I can do for you," Fate said, "just say the word."

I looked at the sofa she had just been sitting on.

"What? Name it."

"Do you think you could help me move the sofa over against that wall?"

"You want to . . . ?"

"Yeah. I'm thinking I'd like to push something heavy against that wall of bookcases right over there. And that sofa would be perfect." I figured Fate was talking about offering me job security, but I had another kind of security on my mind.

"Against the bookcases? Are you sure?"

And after the two of us shoved the sofa across the room, I had had enough of being a gracious hostess. "If you'll excuse me, I have some work to do. It's why I came in early."

"Work?"

"Research, actually." I had to hunt down Tim Stock's copy of *The Professional Chef*, and check page 20. I had to find *Nobu: The Cookbook*, and check page 198.

"You are a great find for *Food Freak*, Madeline," Fate said, and then she caught me off guard and hugged me. "Even if Greta Greene is the one who found you."

"Thanks."

"I'm so glad we've become best friends," she said. And then Fate Finkelberg kissed me on the cheek.

18

WHAT'S NEW?"

"Well," I said, "I spent the night with Honnett, I learned all about merino sheep, and I made a new best friend. But not all together. You?"

"What?" Holly's pale face was made up with a lot of black around her eyes, emphasizing their wide-open reaction.

"There's more. Tim Stock may be dead, I have been thinking about getting a German shepherd puppy, and I just found two thousand dollars in cash taped in some cookbooks in the *Food Freak* library."

"Maddie, what gives? Tim Stock isn't dead, he's missing."

"There was a fire at his house last night."

"Oh, man," Holly said, nodding her head in recollection. "Those sirens. And Donald said there was a fire."

"And a body was found in Tim Stock's burnt-out garage next to his melted BMW."

"Ew."

"But as to whether it's Tim who's dead or not, I am having some doubts."

Holly was reclining on the new rose sofa in my office with one of her long legs flung over the rolled arm. "How come?"

"Something about the way Susan Anderson reacted to the news. It was odd. She told me a long story this morning and it sounded like she and Tim have been very tight. But she seemed to dismiss the idea he'd been hurt in the fire."

"It's such a sudden and horrible thing to happen, Mad. Maybe Susan just couldn't accept that Tim had died that way. She's in denial. I would be if one of my very best friends . . ." Holly began to tear up. She looked at me funny.

"Oh, please," I said, handing the second woman in as many hours the office box of Kleenex. "Let's get a grip."

"Fine," Holly sniffled. "But Susan could be in shock. News like that, about a friend you love, it's too tough to take."

"Maybe."

"And all that other stuff you were talking about, whew! I just can't keep up with current events."

"Did you stop by my house and get the magazine?"

"Yes. I got your message. Donald dropped me off there an hour ago."

"Was Honnett still there?"

"No," Holly said. "Are we going to have a discussion about why we are back with the guys who done us wrong?"

"No," I answered. "We're going on a treasure hunt, instead."

"Thank goodness," Holly said, sitting up on the sofa. "I found the *Gourmet* magazine on the kitchen island. It's got Tim Stock's address label on it so I figured it's the one." She reached into her backpack and brought it out. "And there was a page of notes in Wesley's handwriting. This what you wanted?"

I reached out and read through the list of cookbook titles Wesley had decoded. "Perfect. Now we're going to have to hunt for some of these books."

"Is this how you found the money?" Holly asked.

I opened the top drawer of Tim Stock's desk. Since Holly and I had spent much of the previous evening cleaning up the office, the drawer was now tidy and organized. In the center was a neat stack of $100 bills, held together by a paper clip.

"Wow. Okay, read off the book titles and let's get moving."

We spent the next forty minutes finding an extraordinary quantity of hundred-dollar bills, each cookbook holding anywhere from four to twelve. They were taped neatly onto the pages that had been indicated in code.

"How much?" Holly asked.

I had bundled the money we found into stacks of fifty hundred-dollar bills each. "I've got"—I had already finished the count but had decided to count them over just to be sure—"ten stacks here."

"And there is, like, five thousand dollars in every stack?"

I nodded.

"Wow. Fifty thousand dollars," Holly said.

"In cash."

We sat there, pretty dazed.

"Well," Holly said. "I guess this could explain why everyone seems to want to break into this office. I wonder who knew the money was hidden here?"

"I wonder. It also might explain why Tim Stock was so keen on living in the little bedroom right next door," I said.

"He was?"

"I just found out from Susan. Maybe he didn't want to get too far away from his cash. I wonder what he planned to do?"

"And where all that money came from. Do you think this could be his life's savings?"

"Maybe. But wouldn't it have made more sense to park these hundreds in a nice safe money market account? Susan told me that Tim had a dream and he needed a lot of money. But something is wrong about all this cash, Holly."

"Cash," Holly said, as her leg hanging over the sofa arm tapped a mindless rhythm. "It's untraceable, Madeline. People don't hide this much cash unless they are worried about making big deposits in their banks because then it could be traced, right? I'll bet this cash has something to do with money laundering! Of course, I don't have a clue what laundering money means. It's not really washing the money, I know that."

I threw Hol an affectionate look. "Very good."

"Maybe it's drug money," she riffed on. "Or from a bank robbery?"

Drug money. I wondered. Could Honnett's theory be right? I considered his suggestion that there had been a series of murders taking place each week and the targets had been involved in some way with the illegal drug trade. I set the ten stacks of bills like the spokes of a wheel, aligning them so they were perfectly arranged on the desktop. What if Tim Stock's hidden cash was drug money?

"What do you want to do?" Holly asked.

"We've got to get the money out of here," I said, "and locked up for the time being, until we can figure all this out."

"Where?"

"Take it over to Wesley's house, the one he's selling on Chiselhurst. Ask him to put it in the safe in the bedroom floor and not tell anyone it's there."

"Okay."

I was scribbling a note and stuffing it into an envelope. "And do me another favor. Mail this letter for me."

Holly looked at the address. "You're mailing a letter to Tim Stock? But I thought he was . . ."

"Maybe he is. But it's a way to show our honest intent. We found his money and we're keeping it safe until he can claim it. If nothing else, the letter will get to one of his heirs . . ."

"Right."

". . . and I'll feel a lot safer. I'll let it be known that we found some money in the office and have put it in a safe place off-site. It might dissuade anyone else from thinking of banging me over the head and trying to search this damn room."

"Okay," Holly said, as she finished stuffing the last packet of hundreds into her large black backpack. "I'll see you later."

"Be careful."

"Careful?" Greta Greene asked, from the doorway. Holly and I both looked up and saw Greta standing there, calm and cool in a tan pantsuit. "Hi, Holly," she said. "I need a moment with Maddie, but you can stay."

"That's okay. I was just leaving." Holly gave me a quick wave and left the room.

"Do you like your new sofa?" Greta asked when we were alone. She seemed pleased with herself.

"You sent it?"

"Didn't I promise you? You both did a wonderful job of cleaning that mess in here last night. By the way, I stopped back to say thank you but you and Holly must have already gone home. I was worried about you fainting. Are you sure you're okay?"

"I'm fine."

"You're sure? Well, we've got to get started on writing a new final-episode script immediately," Greta said. "I hate to pile more work on you, Madeline, but I just saw Jennifer in her office and I've called a meeting for ten o'clock. That's in fifteen minutes. Are you all right with that?"

I nodded, and then changed the subject. "Do you have a second?"

"Maybe one," she said, smiling.

"It's just some office gossip. But it's interesting."

"Well, for gossip I have two seconds," she said, pushing her hand through her short blond hair and sitting down.

"It's about Chef Howie."

"Tell me."

"Do you know anything about Chef Howie hooking up with anyone on the staff?"

Greta looked even more interested. "Have you heard something?"

If she was hiding her own involvement, she was one smooth actress. "What do you make of Fate? They aren't the most likely pair."

"She hates me, you know. She fought hard to get my ass kicked off the show."

"Why?"

"I don't know. She has this raging-jealousy thing going. She seems to hate every woman who works within ten feet of her husband, so watch yourself. She's older than he is and I think she's so insecure she's half crazy."

"But, you and Howie . . . ?"

"Never. Come on! I have better taste than that! Are you serious? Besides, I've already got a guy."

"I didn't know," I said. "Is he someone on the show?"

"That wouldn't be very smart, would it?" she asked. "He's a great guy."

"Cuter than Howie?"

"Well, I go for a different type, Maddie."

"So you think Fate is just insecure."

"Howie seems to tolerate her pretty damn well, considering she does everything but cut his steak for him."

"What do you know about Artie?" I asked. "Has he always been a sweet guy around you?"

"Why?" Greta asked, then quickly changed her tone. "Everyone loves Artie. Artie's wonderful. He's a doll. They don't make executive producers like Arthur Herman anymore."

"Do you remember something happening a long time ago down in Mexico?" Greta didn't seem to get what I was referring to. "In Mexico. With Susan Anderson?"

"Oh, that." Greta got up and closed the door. When she returned to the sofa, she scooted over so I could join her there. "This is a very sad story, really, but it goes to show what a prince of a guy Artie Herman is."

"Really?" I sat next to Greta on the sofa.

"We were working on a show called *Great Escapes*. Different celebrities would get a free vacation to some exotic location in exchange for letting our crew come along and shoot a lot of footage. As a matter of fact, Tim Stock was the writer on that show. It was a fabulous job to land. We all loved it. We'd get to travel to all these romantic destinations and stay in the best hotels, and everything was comped. Well, Susan was the PA on the show. Artie always hired her. He's so loyal. And here's the sad part. I'm not sure if you are aware of it, but Susan had a very serious drinking problem."

"What?"

"Yes. And on that particular trip, she got totally out of control. It got so bad that she disappeared one night and drank an entire bottle of tequila or something. We were frantic. Artie couldn't find her. I couldn't find her. And remember, we had a show to shoot. Roma Downey was waiting in the makeup trailer and Artie couldn't even find the script."

"I heard this story a little differently," I said slowly.

"Really? Well, no one could forget how trashed Susan was that next morning when we finally found her."

"Where had she been?"

"Poor Tim," Greta said. "When Susan was wasted, she'd go to bed with any man who'd buy her a drink."

"Are you saying that Susan and Tim were together?"

"Tim was genuinely fond of Susan, I'm sure. But I'm afraid she was just in a downward spiral. Under the circumstances, Artie should have shot her. But not Artie. He was magnificent. He talked Susan into getting help. He gave her a promotion so she'd get health insurance, which could help pay for her to sober up. And he even talked her into starting a hobby. He came up with the neatest idea. He bought Susan some pet sheep. And now, everything has been going so well for her. She loves those animals. Just talk to Susan. She'll tell you what a sweetheart Artie is. He saved her life."

Oh, man. Which version of the story was correct? It *might* have happened that way. But perhaps someone had devised a very clever cover story that accounted for most of the facts and made Arthur Herman look noble in the bargain?

Greta stood up and checked her watch. "We're having our meeting in less than five minutes. I'd better get going."

"Greta," I said, stopping her at the door. "Look, there's something you might not know yet. Have you heard anything about Tim?"

"Tim?" she said, turning back quickly. "Did Tim finally get in touch with somebody? Do you think he'll come in today? That would be perfect."

"This is difficult news. I thought you might have already been informed by the police."

Greta looked pale. "What is it?"

"There was a fire at his house last night. And the police found a body. They think it's Tim."

Greta opened her mouth to say something, but not a word came out.

19

BY ten o'clock, the sun was a pure white globe hanging behind a thin gray scrim. That globe had burned, by now,
through most of the thick morning haze, and had almost
conquered the chill. In thirty minutes, the city would be warm. Its cit-
izens would begin to relax. In Los Angeles, the sunshine was soothing,
forgiving, and free, making it even better than Xanax. With an entire
city eagerly basking in the generous sun, where no one wants to check
in dark corners, I began to wonder if it might be easier here for evil to
hide its secrets.

I squinted at the parked cars, picking out the spot where I'd left my
black Jeep. I'd be late for Greta's ten o'clock writers' meeting, but I had
left my notebook computer in my car and I would need it to take notes.
I didn't rate one of the few prime parking spots located right next to our
office building—they were reserved for the biggest moguls on the lot—
but I didn't mind. As I'd walked the couple of blocks across the KTLA
studio compound, I'd checked the thinning cloud cover above and felt
reassured. We'd have clear, blue skies by ten-thirty. Another sunny day.

The computer had slipped under the passenger seat. Figures. After quickly relocking the car door, I made a slight detour. A shortcut around the broadcast building would allow me to make better time.

The more I thought it over, the more convinced I became that Tim Stock might still be alive. His death was just speculation, after all. Until the body was identified, it was nothing more than a conclusion to which the officials would naturally jump—guy's garage burns down, body is found in garage, ergo: body = guy. But if someone had wanted to make it look like Tim had died, they might have tried to pull off something like that fire. Of course, that would require a dead body available to be sacrificed in the scam. That was a tricky and disturbing thought. And who would want to make it look like Tim was dead?

I turned up a narrow alley between soundstages. Up here, there was a lot of activity. Prop guys were running power saws in the street. A huge sign, which would be used as part of a stage set, was being freshened; the curly letters of the title *Let's Make a Deal* were in the process of being reoutlined in new gold paint. I had to smile. I remembered that old game show. Perhaps they were doing a pilot for yet another re-make. Or perhaps some sort of anniversary special.

I went back to my thoughts. Let's say Tim was in some kind of trouble. That could explain his recent behavior. He had tried to lay low— not returning messages, staying away from work, living in the hidden bedroom on the lot. Perhaps he still felt in danger. Could he have faked his own death in order to convince whoever might have been after him to give up? And what did it have to do with the $50,000 in cash he had hidden away in an assortment of old cookbooks? It all seemed slightly unreal and theatrical and over the top. With what sort of danger had Tim Stock gotten himself entangled that could possibly necessitate literally playing dead? How the hell had a game-show writer with a dream of doing historical research in London and a fondness for Broadway musicals earned himself such serious enemies?

I turned the corner and stopped. Thoughts of Tim Stock and deadly plots and cover-up fires flew out of my head. Standing twenty feet ahead of me was a lion. A yawning lion. On a leash. The leash was held by a short man who was looking off in another direction. The lion, however, was looking directly at me.

Quick panic question: If a 400-pound lion, on a leash, decides to pounce and attack and maul and eat a 118-pound caterer, how much freaking good is that leash going to do? Even though it might be made out of a nice sturdy chain, how much freaking use could it be considering it was being held loosely by a bored, 130-pound guy who gets paid roughly the same amount they pay kids to ask if you want to super-size that?

I stopped breathing. Perhaps some primitive instinct suggested I wouldn't seem too noticeable if I wasn't moving a muscle. The natural camouflage afforded by my bright pink sweater and short tan skirt was minimal. My tan suede boots probably just pissed Mr. Lion off.

I was afraid to move. Where could I go? Forward, I'd be rushing into the jaws of death. Backward, I'd just look like a little elk (clothed in a Prada sweater) fleeing into the woods. I would be pulling hard on the lion's "chase" trigger. Flying after me would be the jaws of death.

Why, I wondered, hadn't I given more money to the World Wildlife Fund? Why hadn't I more vigorously protested the use of lions in circuses? Why hadn't I sent a thank-you note to Siegfried & Roy for all their good work? I stood still and prayed. Please, dear God, let the attendant, the sleepy little fellow at the end of Mr. Lion's chain, turn his bored little head. Please, let him just look my way. If he did, dear God, and if he had a compassionate bone in his body, he might offer up a suggestion. What, if anything, was a good way to extract myself from the role of "soon to be dead meat" in our little live scenario?

"*Señora!*"

He saw me. He was talking to me. Heaven was not indifferent. I would have to join a church or temple tomorrow.

"*Señora.* Maybe go back," he suggested.

Why hadn't I thought of that? Oh, I did, but I was frozen in "I'll be prey" anxiety.

I walked backward, slowly. It was only a few feet until the corner. I kept eye contact with the beast on the chain—by that I did *not* mean to disparage my 130-pound Hispanic savior in any way—and calmly, calmly got my butt out of there.

What the hell was that? Why were lions just hanging around in the street? When any zoo in America would have six different cages and moats and metal bars and posted signs between a wild animal and a civilian, the studio lot had a live lion out for a stroll on a leash? A live, mane-embellished, SAG-card-carrying lion, I should point out, who was likely being staged for a few minutes off to the side before he would be used as a freaking "Zonk!" on a freaking game show, for crying out loud. My breathing came back with a vengeance, hyperventilation all over the place. While I have always been one to argue against the prejudice that one should "know one's place," I had just this second discovered that at least some stuffy rules were really worth upholding. Starting with: keep huge lions in Africa. I'm absolutely certain the lion would back me on this one.

As the charged-adrenaline high began to wear off, I realized how late I was now sure to be to Greta's meeting. But, I mean, who cares? I was just this very second *not* eaten by a lion. The rest of the world would have to wait. I took a moment to listen to the birdies chirp. Life was good.

Come to think of it, Greta had seemed less gung ho about starting her writers' meeting after she heard about the fire at Tim's house. She hadn't looked all that good when I left. And, of course, that brought me back to thinking about Tim Stock. Tim and Greta had worked together on many of Artie's shows over the years. What was their relationship like? Perhaps Jennifer Klein might know.

I opened the main door to our building and entered the front reception area. The place was bustling. The chairs, which had been empty only three hours earlier, were now filled with an assortment of aspiring *Food Freak* contestants, chatting or joking or milling about. The show uses teams of adults in any combination of relations or friends, but they all have to be avid amateur cooks. Teams were usually made up of siblings, coworkers, spouses, and college roommates. There were often mother/daughter or mother/son combinations. For some wacky reason, the people who had come in to audition together seemed to be dressed in matching outfits. One chubby couple had on bright red polo shirts with their own shish kabob logos and their names embroidered above the heart: "Sheree" and "Lloyd." A male three-some who might work at any big eight accounting firm, so Brooks Brothers was each of their suits, sported matching navy blue aprons embellished with sequins. Most of the groups were filling out applications. Two senior ladies were standing by the white wall next to the credenza. Their unnaturally red hair was teased into up-flung styles that made each of their heads seem aflame. Nellie called out, "Say Provolone!" and snapped their picture.

"Hi, there. You're the new writer, right?" asked the young, pretty woman sitting at the reception desk.

"That's right. I'm Madeline Bean. Hi."

"I'm Dawn Weiss. We haven't actually been introduced." Dawn had big brown eyes and a cheerleader's smile.

"Nice to meet you."

"I should be forwarding calls to you," Dawn said, looking at her phone list, "only no one told me your extension. Sorry."

"I'm only here for the week. I've been using my cell phone to get calls."

"Well, it's no problem," Dawn said. "Where did they put you?"

"I'm in Tim Stock's office."

"Oh. Tim. Have you heard about what happened?" Dawn lowered her voice, mindful of the ears of the contestant pool sitting not far away.

"Yes, I have."

"It's so sad," she said. Her heart-shaped face was perfectly framed in long, dark hair. "And did you hear? Quentin Shore quit."

"What?"

"That's what I was told. Frankly, I wouldn't be surprised if he got fired." Dawn looked up at the couple that had just arrived. "May I help you?"

"I'm Lois Hirt, dental hygienist, and I'm here with my favorite cooking dentist, Dr. Hy Gennaro?" Lois was a trim, attractive blonde. She wore a pale green dental smock, which perfectly matched Dr. Gennaro's scrubs. They each wore equally green chefs' hats.

Dawn looked up from the master list of that day's contestant interviewees and their appointment times. "I have checked off your names so we know you are here. Please take a seat, go over these forms, and make sure you answer all the questions. We really need as many phone numbers as you have, so give us your work numbers, cell phone numbers, pagers, everything. When we need to reach you, we *really* need to reach you. You might get a call to be on the show and if you miss it, that would be a shame."

"No problem," Lois said in her cheery, spit-please lilt. "And we know we're going to get that call. We have created some terrific dental-licious recipes. Dr. G. and I only prepare food that is good for your teeth."

"That's wonderful," Dawn said, her voice full of enthusiasm. "Fill out these forms first, and then you'll get to talk with Stella and Nellie, okay?"

Dr. G. and Lois said thank you and went to find a pair of chairs.

"Dawn . . ." I was too curious to leave, no matter how late I was going to be to the meeting. "What do you mean, Quentin quit? When did Quentin quit?"

"I just got the word. Frankly, it will make my whole job much easier."

"Really?"

"I do a lot of the odd jobs on the show. I answer the main phone lines. I keep track of contestant interview times. I sit here in reception. I also help out with the show correspondence. I answer all of Chef Howie's fan mail."

"You do? How funny. Does he get love notes?"

"You can't even imagine," Dawn said, stifling a laugh. "He gets hundreds of letters a day. Some of them are really wicked. I send the nude photos of housewives to Kenny upstairs. He enjoys them. Mrs. Finkelberg got really pissed at me when I used to give those to Chef Howie."

"Do you have to answer every letter?"

"No, no," Dawn said, smiling. "Just send off a signed photo of Chef Howie. And guess who signs them?"

"You?"

"I am actually quite good at doing his signature. Anyway, I also have to answer the general fan mail for the show. We get lots of people who want to find out how to be contestants, and I send them the standard packet. And we always get hundreds of letters after each episode airs if there have been any mistakes, or if people at home think there have been mistakes. Sometimes, people are so nuts. You would think they would wake up and get a life, but no, they spend their nights sitting by their television sets looking for mistakes and then they spend their days writing to us about it."

"Wow. So you have to write back?"

"We can't ignore our loyal fans. We usually send them a correction and an apology. It's a standard thing."

"I didn't know that. What sort of mistakes are we talking about?"

"Nothing that really affects the game part of the show. If we made those kinds of mistakes, like not accepting the correct answer to a question, we would have to bring back the contestants and give them another chance on the show. The only errors that ever get made on *Food Freak* are in the stupid little recipes that go in the bumper."

"I see," I said. She smiled at me. "Um, what exactly is that?"

"The bumper?" Dawn asked. "It's the fifteen seconds or so of infotainment that comes right before the commercial. You know, like, 'How do you make macaroni and cheese for a crowd of forty hungry tots? Just use seven sixteen-ounce packages of dry macaroni,' and so on and so on. 'Come back for more *Food Freak* in a moment.' We bump out to commercial. That's the sort of thing."

"Oh, thanks."

"Or if they say, 'Want to know how to make the most decadent chocolate mousse? Chef Howie will show you, when we come back.' That's a tease."

I shook my head. "I am so new."

"Don't worry. You'll get the hang of it. The bumpers on *Freak* are really sort of lame. They don't add anything to the show at all. But presenting pithy little recipes was originally Artie's idea, cheesy though they are. I guess that's why they stay in. The problem is, they gave all the bumpers to Quentin to write, and the guy always gets something wrong."

"Wrong?"

"I mean it. Every week we get a thousand letters telling us you can't possibly cook seven sixteen-ounce packages of dry macaroni in two cups of water, or something stupid like that. So I have to mail out a thousand letters with the corrected recipe and say thanks for watching *Food Freak*."

"I had no idea. I wonder what Tim thought of that."

"He and I used to joke about Quentin all the time," Dawn said, sighing. "Tim was a great guy. We went out a few times, you know."

"You did?"

She nodded.

"Dawn, just take it as a given that I know absolutely nothing about anything here."

"You are so funny," Dawn said. "But Tim and I, we kept it pretty low-key around the office. Not too many people knew."

"That must make this whole situation about Tim very difficult for you."

"I know. It's creepy. Tim and I had stopped going out around Christmas. Anyway, it had never been anything serious. Just a good time. Like he took me to New York, which was so hot. We saw *The Producers.*"

"So much of what goes on around here amazes me. Why do you think Tim put up with Quentin, if Quentin was screwing up so much?"

"Tim said Quentin was a really sweet guy who just needed a break."

That deserved a reaction, and I threw one at Dawn. She laughed. "I agree," she said. "I couldn't see it, either, but then maybe I haven't been that impartial. Frankly," she said, lowering her already low voice, "I've been trying to get a job as a writer here from the day I started. I had no experience, so they put me out here. I think I'd do a much better job than Quentin Shore ever did."

This was getting to be rather awkward. "Oh, Dawn. You must hate me," I said.

"I do," Dawn said, with a smile.

"How can you stand it? Instead of moving you up, they brought me in at the very last second. How annoying."

"That's okay, Madeline. Hey, it's not your fault Hollywood is screwed. You're old friends with Greta, right?"

I nodded.

"Thought so. I don't think Greta is all that wild about me. Look, if Tim had been here and one of the other writers had gone missing, I might have had a chance. It doesn't matter. Things are changing fast. Now that Quentin has left, I have another shot at getting the promotion. Artie likes me, and that counts for a lot."

"I would imagine it does." First Tim, and then Artie. Dawn had her own way of working the system.

"You think I'm too ambitious, don't you?"

"No."

"Yes you do. I'm ready to be discovered in the chorus and given my shot at being a star, what can I say? But don't worry, Madeline. I can wait my turn. I've got time. I'm a lot younger than you are." She smiled at me and I couldn't help but gasp.

I threw Dawn a look. "But you're sure you're old enough to work?"

She laughed out loud. "I graduated from Hastings Law School last May. I passed the bar in September. And I figure I'm about to move up here pretty soon."

"You could be practicing law, but instead you are answering phones at *Food Freak*?"

"You have to start somewhere, Madeline. I'm paying dues. I remind contestants to give us their cell phone numbers. You probably spent years slaving over a hot stove somewhere to earn your chef stripes. I have no problem with learning the ropes and doing a bit of grunt work. But what I really want to do is write," she said earnestly.

"Thanks for all the scoop, Dawn, and also the tip. If I am asked to write up recipes for the bumpers, I'll watch the measurements and ingredients."

"Don't sweat it," she said. "It's just part of my job. The more I handle down here, the more chance Artie might notice. And so far, Artie has been very impressed."

Was there any limit to how far the adorable Ms. Dawn Weiss was willing to go? My guess was, not really. She flashed me another bright smile, a smile of such whiteness I was sure contestant applicants Lois and Dr. G. would certainly approve. Nothing would stop Dawn. If there was a current Mrs. Arthur Herman out there somewhere, I was getting the distinct impression she should be calling her lawyer to overturn the prenup before it was too late. It's not that I'm against a girl having a goal, but didn't anybody around here realize they were not, for instance, vying for a Nobel Prize? Cancer was not being cured here. *THIS IS A SIMPLE FREAKING GAME SHOW.* Perhaps, in the interest of mental health, they needed to put that sentiment in a large frame in each office in the building.

"And, Madeline, here's another tip for you," Dawn said. "Don't ever keep Artie waiting. He hates that. He's fired writers for less. And don't you forget, there's someone sitting right here who is determined to join the writing staff for next season." She smiled a perfectly happy little smile.

"Th-thanks. And since you've been so helpful, here's a tip for you," I offered, as I turned to leave. "There is an adorable cat outside and down the left alley. He's being used in a TV spot and you've got to see him."

"Cute?"

"The cat is to die for."

According to the clock on the wall above Dawn's tidy glass-topped desk, it was nearly ten-thirty. Damn. The writers' meeting. I said "Later," and as I left I checked my back nonchalantly for any daggers. Dawn was scary. But then, so was the last twenty-four hours in Game-Showville. With Tim Stock's presumed death and Quentin Shore's resignation and Dawn Weiss's determination, I was beginning to suspect that the life span of a game-show writer might not be all that long.

"Madeline?"

I looked back at Dawn, who was just replacing the receiver on her desk telephone.

"That was just Artie," she said. "It seems everyone is looking all over the place for you. He said to tell you to come quick. It's an emergency."

DARLING girl," Artie said, looking up. "Madeline, doll-face. You are here. Good. Good. Marvelous. Let's call Jennifer and get started."

I stood at the door to Artie's third-floor office. The huge old-fashioned skylight reminded me of a retro-style New York loft apartment, the bright expanse of industrial glass covered by a grid of wire hexagons. Artie's furniture was of a boxy fifties style that was currently the rage, but I suspected it had all been with Artie pretty much from way back then.

"We were concerned, you know, about where you were," Artie said, getting up from behind his desk and coming to see if I was really okay. "So much I don't understand," he murmured. "So much going on. And we have a script to write, you know."

"I'm sorry," I said. "I—"

"No, not a word. No bother at all. I'm just happy to see you. Sit down. Sit down. Find a comfortable spot. I just called Jennifer and Susan. They should be up here any minute. So, would you like something to drink? I have a little fridge here, so I don't have to go downstairs to the kitchen. I'm spoiled, aren't I? I know I should get the exercise. That would be good for me. But what's the point of being a big shot if you can't have a fridge if you want one?"

Artie guided me to a love seat with big, block-style cushions that were upholstered in orange leather. He offered me a choice of bottled waters and soft drinks. As he went off to get me a soda, Speedy Alka-Seltzer, from his dominant framed position on the wall behind Artie's desk, winked at me. But then, he was always in midwink, so I tried not to make too much of it. Artie insisted on pulling the tab on my can of Diet Coke. I had to laugh at him, he was fussing over me so. Was this the man who raged and screamed and humiliated Susan Anderson five years ago in a snit over some Aztec ruins?

"We're here," said Jennifer, coming through the door. "Again. Oh, Maddie. We didn't know what happened to you."

"Hi there," Susan Anderson said. "We thought maybe you went home, too."

"I had to get my laptop out of my car," I explained.

"Well, let's get started," Artie said.

"Where's Greta?" I whispered across to Jennifer, but Artie heard me.

"Ah, Greta. Yes. We have had to accept her resignation. Can you believe that? Just what we need right now, more staff changes." Artie was very serious and choosing his words slowly. "Tim Stock . . . well, Tim is gone. And I was informed in a most insulting manner that Quentin Shore will not be at work today. Can you believe that? Mrs. Finkelberg, of all people, got a message from Quentin earlier this morning. Well, if he can't make it to work, he's out of a job. And now—I hate this like poison—Greta Greene has left us as well. So. So. Here we are then. I have never in all my years in television seen anything quite so irresponsible and unprofessional. But I'm washing my hands of them, all of them. They chose to leave us. They have lost out. That's all I'm going to say. They could have carried on here and finished one final episode, but . . . But, well, they didn't. Okay. We'll go on. We only have the one final show to do, right?"

Susan nodded.

I was stunned. Greta had left the show. What on earth had happened?

"But we can't waste a second. Not a second," Artie continued. "And here's the good news. Here's the emergency. We're going to shoot the final episode of *Food Freak* in five days. Live."

"What?" Jennifer asked, startled.

"Live?" Susan stopped scribbling notes and looked up, eyes round.

"Why not?" Artie asked. "We're in a pickle, my dears. The facts are the facts. By delaying yesterday's taping, we lost our window. We don't have enough time left to make it up. How can we tape a new show and edit it in postproduction at this late date? This is exactly what I told Greta, but she refused to see it. Without enough lead time to edit the show and deliver it for broadcast this coming Wednesday night, what else can we do?"

"But a cooking show, *live?*" Susan said, looking horrified.

"We'll be fine. We'll be fine." Artie sounded amused. "We'll use some pre-cooking tricks like they use for the morning shows. Live is exciting, ladies. That's the way we did all our television programs a few years ago, chickadees. It was a hoot. Of course, you are all much too young to remember those days. And did I tell you about the network? Oh boy. The kids who are running the network absolutely love the idea. They are hog wild over it. They think everyone in America will be glued to their sets. And they will. Of course. Just think of the added suspense: Will Chef Howie flub a line? Will some contestant freeze under the pressure? Will a dozen eggs hit the floor? Heh-heh!"

"Good questions," I whispered to Susan, and, luckily, Artie did not overhear my comment this time.

"So, we are doing the show live," Artie finished triumphantly. "Next Wednesday. And, Madeline, tell your partner to reschedule the wrap party. We'll have our wrap party on the set, after the show on Wednesday night."

"This coming Wednesday," Susan repeated, sounding stunned.

"Okay," Jennifer Klein said, thinking it all over. "But the show will look so different. I mean, our regular format isn't . . . I mean . . ."

"Format, shmormat. We'll do a different show," Artie said, preaching hard to the doubtful. "Look, who says *Food Freak* has to be the same old thing all the time? Why not give *Freak* a new zetz of life?"

"A new 'zetz,' " Jennifer repeated, her face absolutely straight.

"But," Susan interrupted, still not sure that Artie comprehended the massive production difficulties ahead, "who's going to direct it? Live is completely different from tape. And what about contestants?"

"Here's the beauty part," Artie said, his faded blue eyes twinkling. "We need our best contestants to pull this off, right? Listen to this. We'll make it a battle of the alumni chefs! Our first one ever. We'll end the season with a showdown cook-off between this past season's two biggest winning teams. Don't you see? We'll bring back every-one's favorite contestants and give them an even bigger jackpot to compete for."

"More than the half million dollars they have already won?" Susan asked, incredulous.

"What do you think of this?" Artie reached over to the side of his desk and held up a matted eleven-by-fourteen photograph showing a château in France. "They get this."

"That castle?" Jennifer asked.

"Yes. Thirty minutes outside Paris."

"Oh, Artie," I said, almost drooling. The limestone-fronted mansion looked like a fairy tale. It even had a turret and a moat.

"With the current exchange rate, real estate in France is a bargain," he said. "And that's not all. The winners will get to design their very own dream kitchen. Everything they want, they get. It's part of the prize package. The network boys are going to start the on-air promos tonight."

"Oh," Jennifer said, "I like that. That's good. This whole idea could be fun."

"You catching on? Good," Artie said, turning to her. "Now, imagine the fun Chef Howie can have with our two returning champion teams. It's a battle, yes? It's conflict. It's rivals with a grudge. It's a race to see who is going to win this magnificent palace near Paris, France, outfit-ted for the most discriminating chef. Now, that's great television."

"Who are the returning champs?" I asked. I had been a pretty faith-ful viewer for most of the season, but I couldn't count myself as a true *Freak* freak. I didn't have an official *Freak* spatula or a poster of Chef Howie pinned up on my bedroom wall. I never kept track of all the past players nor did I memorize the details of their personal lives like some of the show's most avid fans. I'd heard there were Websites that featured contestant bios, which were devoted to describing the homes and families of the show's biggest winners and most popular amateur chefs. I'd never visited any of the Websites, but I had been just as fascinated by the players as the rest of the country. I'd tuned in to see a few of my own favorite *Food Freak* winners do a cooking segment with Regis or be interviewed by Jay Leno. I had to admit it. Artie's idea did have a certain . . . zetz.

"Our champs? They're wonderful, Madeline. You will love them," Artie said. "I've already got Nellie and Stella working on my plan. They were told to dismiss all the auditions for today and get right on to our new agenda. We have got to book the champs immediately."

Susan looked at a file and read off the names to us. "Marley, Sydney, and Emily Baker, the sisters," she read.

"They are dolls," Artie said, abuzz with excitement. "Pure gold."

"And then we've got the divorced team of Bruce Holtz and his ex-wife, Belinda," Susan added and looked up at us. "Now, they were hysterical."

"Oh, Bruce and Belinda," I said, with real enthusiasm. "I loved them. I just knew those Baker sisters had made the best wedding cake."

"See? Madeline gets it. Everyone in America loves those girls."

I was becoming excited, once again. *Food Freak* was a lot of fun. And now I was getting to write recipes for the show that would be seen by millions. And here we were, talking about some of the coolest people on reality TV. And it looked like I'd be getting to meet some of them on Wednesday.

"See?" Artie crowed. "It's a winner of an idea. The best of the best. It's magic."

"So, we'll bring back those two teams for an encore," Susan said as she wrote it down in her book.

"It's like that whatchamacallit on *Jeopardy!* that they do all the time when they run out of good new contestants," Artie said, still upbeat, still pitching.

"Tournament of champions," Jennifer answered.

"Yes, Jennifer. Yes. That's it. That's exactly what we need. But with a better title. Something much more alive and fun than that. How about this? We could call our grand finale show '*Food Freak*'s Kool Kitchen Kook-Off!' We use all *K*s."

Susan made a face dismissing Artie's *K*s, and I could see a lightbulb go off over her head. She said, "What about: 'War of the Cooks'? No, that's not good. 'Cook-Off Face-Off.' No." She burst into laughter at herself. "See why I am not a writer?"

" 'Grub Match'?" I tried. "You know, like a play on words for 'Grudge Match'?"

"Maddie, Tim always used to say, if you have to explain it, it stops being funny," Susan said. We all giggled.

"Or," Jennifer suggested, "how about: '*Food Freak* Revenge: The Final Food Fight.' "

"Ooh!" Susan said. "Great."

I joined the laughter and said, "I love it!"

"What?" Artie sounded slightly put out. "You like 'Food Fight' better than 'Kitchen Kook-Off' with the *K*s? Maybe you can't visualize what cool graphics we can make with those *K*s on the Avid."

The room became quiet. One should be careful when dismissing the boss's suggestion but, then again, I wasn't planning on working here more than a couple of days longer, anyway. "Well, if you're asking, Artie, I think 'Food Fight' is cooler," I said.

"It's fun, Artie," Susan agreed. "You want this to be fun, right?"

"Yes, sure, sure. Make it '*Food Freak* Revenge: The Final Food Fight.' Okay."

Susan took quick notes, and we proceeded to work out the menus for the special show. As usual, the format of the basic game was simple. Two teams would be challenged to answer two rounds of food and cooking trivia questions. For each round they won, that team could select extra ingredients to use in the final cook-off. The most exciting part of the show was when the amateur chefs donned their aprons and met in the show's "Kitchen Arena." Under hot lights and against a background of driving hard-rock music, they vied for culinary dominance and half a million dollars in cash in the set's identical back-to-back kitchens.

Each cook-off team is given identical ingredients but they must select their additional items, if they've won them, right then and there, before they know what they'll have to cook. After all that buildup, Chef Howie finally reveals exactly what kind of recipe they will be challenged to prepare. The announcement of the night's recipe was always a great moment on the show, a big surprise. If the leading team selected their bonus ingredients unwisely, they might not have any advantage at all. In one great episode, a team of Philadelphia Main Line matrons asked for jumbo prawns and curry powder as their extra ingredients, only to discover later that they were to prepare ice cream sundaes for their final challenge. Those women ended up bickering for the rest of the show and lost the cook-off to a down-to-earth father/son team from Arkansas, with their own plumbing business, who hadn't answered one culinary question correctly. Score one for the working guys.

The mix of contestants was critical to *Freak*'s success, and Artie had a talent for mixing the right types together. Their reactions under pressure made the show unpredictable. Any home cook could relate to the stress of discovering a forgotten pan of popovers by the smell of the smoke. There have actually been fires on the set. Once the contestants are in the Kitchen Arena, anything can happen. Chef Howie calls out, "Five-four-three-two-one, blastoff!" and off the two teams scramble to make the most original, complex, and delicious dishes they can create in the time allowed. Contestants are permitted to modify the show's recipes in any way they choose, and originality is key. Assembling the final dish and its dramatic presentation are also big components of the judging, and let's not forget to consider how good the thing actually tastes. Celebrity judges perform the final sipping and nibbling and then the awards are presented.

"What about talent? Who is going to judge?" Susan asked, looking up from her notebook.

"The best," Artie said, smiling. "We've got Tom Hanks, Liza Minelli, and Pink."

"Locked in?" Susan asked hopefully.

"Just about. Just about," Artie said quickly. "It will be a wonderful, wonderful show, I'm telling you. And live! Now just write me a terrific game, you two," he said, looking at Jennifer and me. "Jennifer, you are now the head writer, okay, my dear? You have the seniority here."

"Really?" Jennifer looked astonished. "Thank you, Artie."

"It's a long time coming," he said. "You deserve it. Now, I've got to meet some network boys for a lunch. Would you believe it? I told them we were too busy. It was crazy. I couldn't leave the office. But they have ideas for a new opening for next season's shows, so I can't say no. You girls stay here. Help yourselves to anything you want from the fridge. I'll be back as soon as I can."

"Okay, Artie," Jennifer said. "Don't worry. We'll be fine."

"I hope so," he said, looking a little more worried than he had previously let show. "I hope so. Tim isn't here, which is a real, real shame. And then Greta left us. So now we must move ahead, yes? Okay, now. I have to go to lunch." He looked at us and smiled. "You'll do well. And, Susan, get the finished script to me by five, will you, honey? We've got to send it to Pete Steele right away. He's having a conniption fit." And with that final instruction, Artie Herman was just about to leave us.

"I still can't believe Greta would walk out on the show," I said before he got to the door.

Susan and Jennifer became quiet instantly. Perhaps this wasn't a comment I should have made within earshot of Artie.

"Greta has worked for me for a lot of years," Artie said, turning back to us from the door, "but never again. Sure, the police with their questions can upset a person. 'What happened to Tim? When did you last see him,' and so forth. I don't want to think that anything terrible might have happened to our Tim any more than Greta does. But did I rush home and have to lie down?"

My stomach sank. Greta had run out.

"No," Artie answered his own question. "I stayed. I talked. The policemen were out of here in five minutes flat."

"The detectives were here?" My voice was small.

"That's what I've been saying," Artie said. "I told the guard, 'Sure, go ahead and send the cops right on up here.' Why not? I didn't have time to see them, of course. I'm trying my hardest here to save our show from disaster, as you three know. So I told Greta to handle it. That's her job. But Greta had a headache. A headache. I told her, 'If you walk out now, don't you ever come back.' " Artie kept his voice even, but we could all tell he had to work at it as he finished his story. "You see how much Greta cared about my show? Don't get me wrong, ladies. The thing with Tim Stock, it's terrible. No one wants to hear bad news. No one wants to think maybe one of our dear friends might be dead."

Jennifer gasped. This was clearly news to her.

"Yes, I can see that Greta would be very upset. But . . . but . . . Hell, what's the phrase I'm looking for?"

" 'The show must go on'?" I said.

"The show must go on! Where the hell are people's priorities anymore? Where are their values? Hell, people die every second of every day. That's part of life. But how many times in the history of the world do we have a chance to create a game show as perfect as *Food Freak?*"

HE good news was, nothing at all was out of place in Tim Stock's office when I returned. The bad news was imagining why Greta Greene would leave the show that meant more to her than anything in her life, rather than talk to the cops about Tim Stock's death. I wasn't going to jump to conclusions, though. There could be some simple explanation, after all. I dialed Greta's home number and got her machine. Perhaps she just wasn't picking up. Perhaps she was lying down. Perhaps she was at the doctor's. Perhaps she was just about to cross the border from San Diego to Tijuana. I hung up.

Just because Greta got a headache at a weird point in time didn't necessarily mean she was avoiding the cops, did it? There had to be other reasons for her having fled. Maybe Greta had known more about Tim's disappearance than she'd let on. Perhaps she knew he had been hiding out. Hiding from what, I still couldn't figure, but Greta could have known Tim was in danger. Perhaps she was afraid of the same men who were after Tim.

Or maybe Greta was more involved with the fire at Tim Stock's garage last night than I'd ever suspected. I swallowed hard. That grim possibility was shocking, but could I ignore it any longer? What if instead of worrying about Tim, all this time Greta had been the one who was after Tim and wanted to see him dead? I had witnessed her manipulate situations to her own advantage before, with no one the wiser. Had she manipulated everyone again this time? Even me? Wasn't it possible? Maybe Greta had sent an accomplice to search Tim's office and then feigned shock when we discovered the room had been vandalized. Maybe they were searching for signs of where Tim might have been hiding. And here I'd been, helping her cover up evidence, tidying the room, throwing away papers. Helping her keep secrets. What did that make me? Some sort of idiot, obviously. Damnit. How did I get into this?

The phone on my desk rang. I looked at it, wondering if it could be Greta, calling me back, full of simple explanations rather than an intricate web of lies.

"Tim Stock's office," I said into the receiver.

"Madeline? Is that you?"

"Honnett?"

"Yeah," he said, his voice warm. "I must have missed you earlier this morning."

"At the house," I said, recalling how I had quietly crawled out of bed, leaving him to sleep longer than the hour I'd managed to catch. "You knew I had to go out early."

"So what happened with that? Wild-goose chase out to Woodland Hills, or what?" Honnett had a deep, gravelly voice and it sounded wonderful, even as he teased me.

"I learned a few things," I said.

"Oh, yeah? Like what?"

"Well, I did find those girls I was looking for. Heidi and Monica. The ones the note said might have to die, remember? And they are just fine, if you were worried about them."

"You did? No kidding. So, who are they?"

"Well," I said, trying not to admit defeat too easily, "they're livestock."

"What?"

"Sheep, actually, but the point is, they were fine. Not dead. Nothing like that."

"Sheep, did you say?"

"Okay. Yes. They were sheep in a barn out at Pierce College's school farm. But the good news is, they have not been harmed. So we don't need to worry."

He let out a soft laugh. "You are too much, Maddie," he said. "And you were too much for me last night, too."

"Don't start with me, Honnett. I don't think I can handle any sexy talk after the morning I've had."

"What's going on?"

"I'm not sure. That's the problem."

"Tell me about it," Honnett offered. He was taking me seriously and for that I was grateful.

"The body that was found last night? I can't shake the feeling that it wasn't really Tim Stock. Everything about that fire seems suspicious, doesn't it? It seems like an awfully convenient way to disfigure a body beyond recognition."

"Why do you think someone would want to do that?"

"I had this notion, based on how hard Tim had been trying to disappear last week, that it might have been helpful if some people believed Tim was dead. I have tried to ask around here and I've gotten exactly nowhere. No one wants to tell me anything." I knew I sounded angry.

"That's usually the way it is, Maddie," Honnett said in his soothing tone. "I was out at your office this morning, by the way. I asked a few questions. But I got nothing. That's the way it works."

"So I'm left with this hunch," I said, "but there's really no way to prove the fire victim wasn't Stock since all the evidence was conveniently destroyed in the fire."

"Not necessarily," Honnett said. I heard him pause.

"What's that?"

"Here's the thing about a fire," Honnett said. "Some folks would think you could have a body in a fire and there'd be nothing left to identify, like after a cremation. But that's not exactly true. It's got to do with the temperature of the fire. A simple garage or house fire would

likely leave behind a great deal. Teeth, bones, even tissue and clothing. The kindling temperature of wood is low enough that the body
may not be completely consumed by the time the fuel is exhausted.
Also, if the structure collapsed, as is often the case, pockets where there
is less fire damage might occur. If the body were in such an area, the
ME might be left with a great deal of evidence. Unfortunately for us,
that wasn't the case in Tim Stock's garage."

"Damnit."

"Hold on. We can also learn a lot by just how much damage we find.
Too much damage to that little garage, and we start asking new questions."

"Like what?" I asked, intrigued.

"One way to assure that as little as possible of the victim remains
after a fire would be to use an accelerant such as gasoline, rocket fuel,
almost any highly flammable substance. That means the fire is delib-
erate, and whether the fire causes the death or is only meant to be a
cover-up, you've got a crime."

"Did the fire investigators find traces of an accelerant at Stock's fire?"

"Gasoline," Honnett answered.

"Really? So that proves it was arson."

"Yep. Whoever set it, guess he figured like you did that everything
burns up. But that's not exactly true. Even if the body was completely
consumed by the fire and no clothing or tissue was left, the teeth and
bones are almost always found in the debris. As it happens, bones were
recovered that gave us general height information, and teeth were
found in good enough condition to make a match."

"And you tried matching them to Tim's dental records? And they
didn't match?"

"Whoa. Slow down. It's only been about sixteen hours, okay? Nobody works that fast except maybe Superman."

"But I thought you *were* Superman," I said into the phone, "last
night."

"Now, don't get me started, Maddie."

I liked to yank his chain, but I turned my mind back to considering
Honnett's news. "So what you are saying in your infinitely slow way is
that the body could still turn out to be somebody *other* than Tim
Stock."

"More than that. I think it's *likely* that our victim is not Stock, yes," Honnett said.

"You do?" I was stunned. "Because of my theories?"

"Well, don't take this wrong, Madeline, but no. It's not your theories. It seems that the man who got torched there was mid-thirties or a little older, like Stock. But our victim's teeth couldn't have been Stock's. Our victim had been wearing braces. The metal and plastic were melted, but they were still there.

Braces.

"The thing is, we can try to match these teeth we found with the dental records of Tim Stock, but if they come up negative, like we think they will, we are kind of stumped. We'll check missing persons reports and other databases to see if anyone missing might fit the general size and sex of the corpse. Then we've got to check the teeth we recovered against any dental records available for the missing persons. Of course, if the victim has no dental records, or hasn't been reported missing, this will obviously be a fruitless search."

"I see," I said. "You know, I have an idea."

"Shoot," Honnett said.

"There's a guy who worked here. Quentin Shore."

"Yeah?"

"He didn't show up at work today."

"Well, I'm sure we could find a thousand guys in L.A. who didn't show up at work, Maddie."

"Yeah. That's true," I said. "But Quentin Shore was a thirty-eight-year-old guy. And I'm pretty sure he wore braces."

"That so?"

"I think."

"Well, I'll check on it. We'll go out and see if we can find him. If not, we'll look for his dental charts. It takes time, but I'll get on it."

"Good. Have you had to give up on your drug-world contract-killings theory yet?"

"Naw. Just a new wrinkle, that's all. A matter of sifting out the deaths that belong in the pattern and those that don't. Even if we do make a positive ID with Quentin Shore, we still have a lot of questions to answer."

"I see."

"But as long as we're talking, you wouldn't have any idea why Shore might have got himself killed over in Tim Stock's garage, now would you?"

"Not yet." My speculation meant nothing to Honnett, obviously. He'd said as much. Without the sort of hard evidence he dealt with on a regular basis, like identifying traces of accelerants and matching teeth to dental records, my notions were of no use at all. The ponderings of the lion down the alley would probably hold more credibility.

I saw no point in sharing my concern that Tim might have tried the ultimate way to keep pursuers at bay, by playing dead. And if it turned out to be Quentin who had died in the garage, did that make Tim the killer? Was Susan's buddy and Artie's head writer and Dawn's former date the kind of guy who would kill a coworker just to cover his own tracks?

"So, now, what are you going to do?" Honnett asked.

"Me? I'm working. I'm slaving away in the game-show salt mines," I said. "I'm writing questions for our next show."

"Try some out on me," Honnett said, making small talk.

"I would. But if I told you any of my new questions before they air, I'm afraid I'd have to kill you."

There was a pause on the other end of the phone. Not perhaps the most prudent joke to make to a homicide detective.

"I won't take that as a threat," he answered calmly.

Lucky for me, cops have a pretty dark sense of humor, too. And as he hung up, I thought back to the last time I'd seen Quentin Shore, the previous morning out at Chef Howie's trailer. At the time, of course, the man had had little reason to smile. I recalled using a few strong words. But still, I was almost positive he was wearing braces.

22

USAN Anderson popped her head into my office. "Hi, Madeline. Do you have a minute?"

"Sure. Come on in."

"Sorry to disturb you. Here's some copy. It's a recipe for one of the bumpers," she said, and then kindly explained, "A bumper is the part of the show—"

"I do know what a bumper is, Susan," I said, with a hint of dignity in my voice.

"Oh, of course. Good." She handed me a few sheets of paper. "You'll need to rewrite that a bit. We need about forty seconds for this one."

"So, I write something, and then read it out loud, and time myself?"

"I think so. I always heard Quentin talking to himself, so I guess that's what he was up to. I think Tim used to give some recipe ideas to Quentin, and then Quentin wrote the bumpers and I put them in the scripts. But now, without either of them here or . . . Well, whatever you come up with will be fine."

I glanced at the pages. It was a simple enough recipe for guacamole. Susan turned to leave.

"Susan?" I called after her. "You know he isn't dead, don't you?"

Susan turned back around with an almost guilty expression on her sweet face.

I looked her over. "You knew it all along, didn't you?"

"I'm not good at keeping secrets." A resigned look crept into Susan's eyes. "Even when I was a kid, I would warn everybody in my neighborhood not to tell me anything."

"That sounds promising," I said, smiling at her. "Have a seat."

Susan, in her Chuck Woollery T-shirt, stared at the large rose-colored sofa in disbelief. "Where did that come from? Where's Tim's old sofa?"

"I hope they took it out and chopped it up for toothpicks," I said. "It was pretty gross."

"Oh, damn," Susan said. She looked like she might start to cry.

"What? What's the matter?"

"I had given Tim a gift. It's a long, long story. As sort of a joke, Tim kept it under one of the sofa cushions. Anyway, it cost over fifteen hundred dollars and I bet it was still there." She sighed a big sigh. "Never mind."

I opened one of the deeper side drawers in Tim's desk and extracted a knitted woolen vest in a bright turquoise blue.

"You found it!" she shouted. "Oh my gosh! I just can't tell you how much that vest means to me. Maddie, how can I thank you for rescuing it?"

"Well," I said, patting the sofa cushion on the brand-new sofa, "let's get back to the part where you aren't very good at keeping secrets."

"You want some more answers."

"Start with this vest. It's very nice," I said, "but . . . fifteen hundred dollars?"

Susan nodded.

"And just why are you giving Tim gifts that cost fifteen hundred dollars?"

"It's a long story," she said, sitting down and shaking her head. Her brown curls jiggled.

"About Tim?"

"Well, yes and no. It's about money."

"Cash money?" I asked. This discussion had suddenly become much more fascinating.

"Did you find some?" she asked, hope in her voice.

"As a matter of fact, I did."

"Oh, thank goodness! It's mine," Susan said.

That stopped me cold. "It's your money? All of it?"

"Tim helped me sell something pretty valuable and he got the money in cash. He was keeping it for me. That's why he was meeting me at Pierce this morning, Maddie. He was going to give me the money. To save my sheep."

"Tim was going to give you fifty thousand dollars in cash," I said. "For your sheep?"

"Maddie, what are you talking about?"

"Fifty thousand dollars in one-hundred-dollar bills."

"Are you crazy? No. Tim owed me five hundred."

It was my turn to stare.

"Five hundred might not sound like that much, but it is enough to keep Heidi and Monica in feed for three more months at least."

"I think we're talking about two entirely different things," I said, and sighed, "but money is money. Where did Tim come up with the five hundred?"

"I told you. I had something kind of special and Tim knew how to find the right kind of buyer."

"Are you talking about drugs?" I asked, keeping my voice steady.

"Are you crazy?" Susan almost shouted. "What kind of person do you think I am? Tim and I are game-show people, Maddie. That's bad enough. But don't make us out to be druggies."

"Sorry," I quickly apologized. "I'm sorry. Someone kind of put that idea into my head and I had to ask. So, what did he sell for five hundred dollars?"

"A packet of Kool-Aid."

"I'm sorry?"

"Berry Blue."

"A packet of Berry Blue flavor Kool-Aid?"

"Yes."

"For five hundred dollars?"

"Yes."

"And there were no drugs of any kind in the packet of—"

"No! Of course not." Susan giggled. "It was a very old packet. Rare."

I groaned. "Don't tell me there are Kool-Aid aficionados out there somewhere who appreciate the rare vintages. Don't tell me that, please," I begged her.

"I know these people sound strange . . ."

"Strange? I know strange people! I count many honest-to-gosh strange people among my dearest friends, Susan. But I can't say I know any who yearn for a good packet of aged fruit-drink powder. I must be slipping."

She giggled again.

"Go ahead. Tell me about them."

"There are these collectors . . . ," Susan said.

"You're deadly serious, aren't you?"

"They call themselves Koollectors, spelled K-O-O-L—"

I groaned again.

"I'm not making this up," she said, smiling. "They buy and trade all the different flavors of Kool-Aid. I think it's just a hobby."

"Why not?" I offered. "Not any weirder than collecting stamps, I guess."

"Right."

"But," I muttered, "at least stamp collectors stop short of calling themselves stampectors."

"Well, yes, but probably because it doesn't sound as cute."

I looked at Susan and appreciated her simple perspective. "Okay, vintage Kool-Aid traders. Tell me more."

"Honestly, Maddie, I only learned about these Koollectors recently myself. Primarily, I know about Kool-Aid from the dyers who are just crazy to get their hands on the great bright colors. The old Berry Blue 'Smiley,' that's the packet with the smiling frosted pitcher, makes a great dye. Kool-Aid hasn't produced Berry Blue since 1988 and any original packets marked P-5139 are extremely rare."

All of a sudden, I had the crazy impression I'd recently seen just such a Berry Blue "Smiley." I pulled open the center drawer in Tim's desk and found the paper I had left there. A Xerox copy of an old packet of Kool-Aid, a Berry Blue Smiley packet marked P-5139. Bingo.

"Tell me again. You said something about dyers?"

"Yes. You know I'm into sheep, but you probably don't know I'm also into wool. Most of us sheep women are. We spin it and dye it and knit it. All of that stuff."

"And where does the Berry Blue Kool-Aid come in?"

"That vest you're holding was dyed with Berry Blue. It makes a beautiful dye color, don't you think? I made that vest for Tim using the fleece of one of my favorite sheep, Dances with Wool."

That stopped my train of thought like a, well, a fluffy white sheep in the middle of the tracks. "Susan, where do you get your names?"

"My friends think them up," she said with a smile. "Tim named Dances and as a reward, I spun some of Dances's wool and dyed it this special color for the vest. Of course, not everyone can appreciate a color this bright. Tim didn't wear it much."

"But I still don't quite get it," I said. "You use *Kool-Aid* to dye your wool? Why not just use real dye?"

"It's part of the fun, really. You can use lots of things to dye wool. You'd be surprised. Every year I have a group from my spinners club who come to my house and we do up a bunch of different dye batches in the backyard. It's so much fun. We drink beer and talk. We have to watch it, because all the minerals and chemicals we use can get pretty toxic if you aren't careful. For instance, we boil a big cauldron of water and add some copper to it, to make up our own mordant. But sometimes buying this chemical called alum in the store works best. And there's always vinegar, of course."

"Wait. What's a 'mordant'?"

"If you use something to help the wool accept the dye, it will make the colors brighter. That's what the mordant does. Anyway, then we usually gather all sorts of natural materials to dye the wool. You get a cool reddish brown by using onion skins. And alfalfa leaves and stems leave the wool a nice baby yellow. But unfortunately you just can't get a good blue using all natural materials."

"So you use Kool-Aid?"

"Kool-Aid makes for a terribly effective dye. Didn't you ever dye something using Kool-Aid when you were a kid, Maddie?"

"I wasn't that kind of kid, Susan, no."

"You have to try Kool-Aid dyeing! You don't need a separate set of utensils. If you hate the color, you can drink it. It makes the kitchen smell terrific. It works without any mordants. The colors are a stitch. And if the baby gets in it, you don't have to worry about poison."

"Thanks. I'll keep that all in mind," I said, awonder at the myriad weaving-arts expertise developed over the millennia, none of which I possessed, except this new Kool-Aid trick. "So you like to dye with Kool-Aid."

"Well, I actually prefer the natural colors, myself. But for folks who have got a craving for that clear aqua blue . . ."

I caught on. "They need to find a packet of discontinued Berry Blue," I said.

"Right."

"Only they can't get any more because it's so rare," I finished.

"Right. For a while, Kraft was making this flavor they called Great Bluedini, but now that's been discontinued, too. It made a nice turquoise-color dye, but my spinners are sticklers for the Berry Blue. I've got this friend Lenny who came up with a great discovery of Berry Blue Kool-Aid last year. Her aunt found an old display case filled with it at a yard sale in Maine, of all the weird things. Anyway, for holiday gifts, Lenny gave everyone in our spinning group four packets."

"How cool!" I was enjoying Susan's tale of found treasure.

"It was. I used three packets to dye the wool for Tim's vest."

"So then what?"

"Then, as I told you before, I had this trouble with money. Artie wasn't going to keep paying my sheep's bills, and I was pretty depressed. Tim and I tried to figure out if I had anything of value to sell. That's when he found out about the Koollectors on the Internet, and how much they would pay for a rare Smiley packet in perfect condition. And I had one packet left over."

"I can't believe it. Who would know something like that?" I asked, marveling.

"Tim is a professional game-show writer, Maddie," she said, quite matter-of-fact. "He knows everything, and anything he doesn't, he can research in about three seconds."

I had an instant flush of unworthiness. I was not fit to wear the crown . . . But I got over it, fast. "So he sold your Kool-Aid. How?"

"I think he used eBay," she said.

Just like Holly, Tim had been mining the odd tastes of the buying public by putting up an unusual item for auction. It was a great way to connect with just the right buyer, and if you were trying to unload an old packet of drink powder, I suspected that right buyer might have to find you.

"Tim took care of everything. When he told me it brought in five hundred dollars, I nearly fainted. Just think. I used up three packets to dye Tim's vest."

"So that's why you said this vest is worth fifteen hundred dollars."

"And," she whispered, "he didn't even like the vest."

We both looked at the bright-turquoise woolen garment.

"Only then Tim had to leave so quickly . . ." She shook her head at the recent memory. "And then he was hiding out next door. He planned to meet me at Pierce today and I slipped him that note about what time we should meet. You know the rest."

"Do you know where Tim is right now?" I asked.

"Of course not." Her eyes were wide. "And now, I really have to get the scripts collated."

"Susan, finding Tim is pretty important."

She ran her hand through her shaggy hair, the curls twisting through her fingers. "I wish I could tell you more," she said.

It was infuriating. I could get only so much, and then she clammed up. "I'm frustrated," I told her simply. "In the week or so I've been here, I've been insulted, flirted with, frightened, bullied, praised, hit on the head, mocked, underestimated, stalked by a lion, kissed, barked at, locked in the dark, off on a wild-goose chase, introduced to sheep, yelled at, befriended, confided in, overworked, and lied to. And now, what I'd really like is to know what's going on with Tim Stock."

"Look, Madeline, okay. I'll tell you. But please understand, I am scared. Really, really scared. Tim won't tell me any details. That's the truth. I swear. But he says he's sure someone is going to kill him."

"Who would want to kill him?"

"He absolutely wouldn't tell me. Maybe he was just trying to protect me, I don't know. But here's the thing. Tim and I had a long talk about two weeks ago. That's when everything turned upside down."

"Tell me," I said.

"Tim said he was finally ready to start on his dream. Somehow, he'd come into a lot more money than he was expecting. I don't know where it came from, he wouldn't say. But maybe it was the money you told me you found. He said he had taken on this extra assignment this season, and it paid very well."

"What else?"

"You remember when Tim and I had that talk a long time ago, and he told me he was only working on game shows to finance his big dream?"

I nodded.

"Tim said he was ready. He had the money now. He could go to London and do research for his novel."

"And you must have been happy for him. You have been friends such a long time."

"I was. Of course. And I told Tim I had saved just about enough money after this season of *Food Freak* to buy some land up near Eugene and start my sheep ranch. And you know what? I realized right then, when Tim and I were talking, that I didn't want to move to Oregon."

"You didn't? You don't?"

She shook her head. "And Tim said he didn't really want to move to England. See, we realized sort of all at once that we would be too far away from each other."

"You and Tim? You mean, romantically?"

"We suddenly realized what we really wanted was to get married," Susan explained, looking quite pretty in a dazed way. "We might have never figured it out, if it hadn't been for this trouble he got himself into. He was always a guy who liked to date around but never wanted to settle down. I am pretty much the opposite type. I don't think I've had a date in two years. But then, things changed. He's been under this incredible stress. He's had time to think. He said he's probably loved me all along."

"Oh, Susan."

"And he loves my dogs."

"Oh, Susan."

"But it's horrible, Maddie. Now that we know what our big dream really is, and I love him and he loves me, Tim may have disappeared for real. I'm afraid they may catch him soon and kill him. And I don't know what to do, so I'm here, working my tail off to keep my mind off what I can't do anything about, and hoping for a miracle for Tim and me."

"I had no idea," I said. "And you really don't know what extra job he took on or who is after him?"

"I promise and I swear," Susan said. "If you can help us, Madeline — you may find something here in the office, or you might hear something. I don't know — but if you can possibly save Tim, I'd do anything. Say the word. I'd owe you."

"Would you knit me a vest?" I asked her, trying to keep it light.

"I'd even dye it Berry Blue," she said and rushed over to give me a hug.

"I'll keep my eyes open, Susan."

"You're the best," she said and, checking the watch she wore around her neck on a chain, hurried out the door.

Tim Stock and Susan Anderson. I suppose even the worst predicaments bring with them a spark of enlightenment. I told myself to remember that the next time I was in a jam.

But just what kind of trouble had Tim found while earning extra income? I thought over all that Susan had told me and kept coming back to Berry Blue Kool-Aid. I pulled the Xerox copy out of the desk drawer again, and smoothed it on the desktop. Could Tim have raised $50,000 in Kool-Aid sales? One hundred Berry Blue packets at $500 a pop would do it. And lacking the real deal, had Tim indulged in a little phony Kool-Aid fraud?

I reviewed the facts. Tim knew he could get $500 for a packet of the rare drink mix. Susan said Tim had found a way to make a lot of extra money recently. Had Tim found a way to make some "creative" sales? On the road to riches, had Tim Stock unwittingly cheated the wrong guy? Was there some incredibly vicious Koollector out there right now — set up by the promise he could own a "Smiley," and then bitterly disappointed and scammed — lurking in the shadows, out for un-sweetened revenge?

FIVE days passed, and getting ready for *"Food Freak* Revenge: The Final Food Fight" kept us all busy. On such a short schedule, the preproduction staff simply had no time to relax. Just like in the catering business, the traditional hours of business were not observed. Everyone was at his or her desk, working, every minute of every day. No one in the office remarked as Saturday and then Sunday flew past. No one even looked up at the clock each evening as the windows in our office went from bright to black. Everyone who worked on *Food Freak*, from the question-writing staff to the PAs, was focused on getting the script in order and the production team coordinated. Script changes were rushed out to Chef Howie's house in Beverly Hills by runners. Shopping lists were filled by the PAs. Contestants were treated like stars, with the contestant staff ordering limos to pick up each of the returning champs and guarantee their safe and prompt arrival at the studio. Time was a fixed commodity. We had to be ready by Wednesday at six.

"You got it, sweetie?" Wes asked Holly, patiently, as the three of us representing Mad Bean Events had a final meeting to lock down details for *Food Freak*'s rescheduled wrap party.

"Yes," she said. "Everything except the time thingie."

Taking into consideration the country's four time zones, and the TV scheduling quirk of prime time starting at eight P.M. everywhere in the country except the Midwest, where, for some early-to-bed reason, it starts at seven P.M., broadcasting a live one-hour program in key viewing time across the nation was not altogether possible. Therefore, the final *Freak* was going to be broadcast live only to the East Coast and Midwest, at nine P.M. and eight P.M. respectively. The show would be taped and rebroadcast to the West Coast three hours later, airing at nine P.M. here. It meant that even though our "live" show was being produced in California, it wouldn't be viewed in this time zone live. But, of course, it was more complicated than that. Any folks who had satellite hookups, and could figure out the hieroglyphics in their program guide, could view the East Coast feed, which meant they could actually watch *Freak* live at six P.M. Wes and I had to explain this mathematical insanity to Holly several times, and she still looked uncertain.

"See, Holly. It's airing at nine P.M. here. That's all you need to remember," I said, trying again.

"But you're shooting the show at six. And it's live, right?"

"Yes," I said kindly, "but not live to the West Coast."

"Oh," she said. "I see."

I looked at Holly. Her white-blond hair was artfully gelled into asymmetrical peaks and spikes. The low-cut V of her skinny black tank dress was covered at the moment by a bulky magenta ski parka. The studio was kept extra cold to offset the heat of the lights. When the full stage lights weren't on, it was like a meat locker. Holly's lips were slightly blue and her brow was furrowed.

"Don't worry, Hol," I said. "We'll tell you when it's on so you can watch it."

"At nine?"

"Right."

"So we'll be able to watch the final episode at the wrap party," Wesley explained to her once again. Some of us have a talent for time, but Holly clearly had that timeless quality.

"And that's why we needed to rent giant-screen TVs," she said. "So the crew can watch the show as it airs here in L.A. Got it."

The three of us were seated in the empty Kitchen Arena on *Food Freak*'s soundstage. The set for the program was a giant in-the-round theater. Audience seating was designed in a full circle around the stage, extending upward in tiered levels. On this Wednesday morning, the three of us sat huddled together in the semidark in the front row. Wes and Holly would be directing our catering staff to load in the party tables and chairs immediately after the live broadcast was finished.

"How much time will we have for setup? We've got to roll in ten tables and eighty chairs, and load in the bar and three buffet tables." Wes was checking his yellow notepad.

"And we need time to decorate." Holly was using a stylus on her little electronic notebook Palm device.

"You can't take more than an hour," I suggested. "Less if possible. We can ask the cast and crew to hang around outside. Maybe get a bar set up out there?"

"Good idea," Holly said, tapping the screen on her PalmPilot. "The waiters can pass hors d'oeuvres outside, too, so no one has to starve." She looked around the stage below us and made a broad gesture. "Do you think we need to dress up the stage here?"

"No," I said. "But the stage crew will be cleaning up the kitchen sets while you are doing your thing with the tables and buffet. After the final cook-off, these kitchens are a mess."

"Good point," Wes said. "But with the set as our backdrop and the professional lighting already in place, decorating for the party will be simple. The table linens. The flowers. The centerpieces. The gift bags. It's done."

As centerpieces, Wes had found neon-colored DVD racks and had filled them with dozens of the latest movies on DVD as well as the hottest new video games. As gifts, Artie had approved those video-game consoles that double as DVD players. Boxes of them were wrapped by our crew and would be in place at every seat. We'd also ordered special *Food Freak* T-shirts and baseball caps for all the show's staff as well as our own party crew. Wes was wearing his. The T-shirt had the slogan IF YOU CAN'T STAND THE HEAT on the front, and on the back, GET OUT OF THE KITCHEN ARENA!

"Is the mobile kitchen up and running?" I asked. Wes was supervising construction of a temporary kitchen and grill that were being built outside on the street next to soundstage 9. An orange-and-white-striped tent was going up at the moment, which would allow our eight chefs a place to work on last-minute dishes. The fresh-baked items and desserts, as well as all the prep work, like marinating and chopping and making sauces and salads, happened at my kitchen, only five minutes away.

"We seem to be on schedule," Wes said. "No worries. So, how are things going with the show? We've hardly seen you all week."

"I know," I said, pulling my sweater tighter. I had learned to keep an old sweater at the office for those times when I had to come onto the freezing set. "It's been frantic around here, but no one is losing it. I think we would have had a much easier week if we hadn't lost so many key people."

"And if you weren't under so much pressure, what with shooting a live show, with no margin for any slipups," Holly added. "Except that it's not really going to be 'live,' is it? So I don't know why everyone is in such a fuss."

Wes and I let that one go.

"I better go. I've got to get back," I said.

"See you later," Holly said, head still bent over her electronic planner.

I left the two of them to finish up the party schedule, feeling that awkward feeling like when you graduate from sixth grade. All of a sudden you realize you don't belong to that old school. I wasn't the party planner today. I was responsible for writing a game show.

I opened the heavy stage door to the outside and walked into another brilliantly sunny day. Yet today I wasn't warmed. I couldn't shake the feeling I was stepping away from my comfortable old life and walking into some new disaster.

In the five days that had passed, the police had kept a tight lid on the information they were gathering on the previous Wednesday night's death at 12226 Lemon Grove Drive, in Studio City. At the *Freak* offices, no one spoke about it. It was still assumed that Tim Stock had died in that fire. But I got a few updates from Honnett along the way. By Tuesday, the identity of the dead man had been confirmed. As I'd suspected, the victim turned out to be Quentin Shore. But Quentin hadn't been killed by the fire. The coroner determined the cause of death as blunt-trauma injury to the head. The fire damage had occurred after death. Honnett reminded me not to discuss this information with anyone on the staff, so as the days wore on, I felt even more detached from the people I worked with at *Food Freak.*

As I walked down the block, I made a quick decision to talk to Chef Howie. His star trailer was parked up ahead, its chrome accents gleaming in the sunlight.

"Hey, Madeline. Come in," Chef Howie said, answering his own door. "Good to see you."

"Thanks." I stepped into the RV and noticed that Chef Howie was barefoot. It was much too early for him to change into the clothes he wore on camera. He had on a tight black T-shirt that said, "Greengrocer from Hell," and a pair of running shorts. The show wasn't due to shoot for another few hours, so he had plenty of time to get into his Chef Howie gear, the famous silver lamé chef's jacket, tight black jeans, and cowboy boots. I looked around the trailer and noticed we were alone. "Where's Fate?"

"She's over at the office building meeting with Artie, I think," he said. "Sit down a minute. I've been working on my lines." Howie had been seated on the white leather love seat, and a mass of script pages and note cards littered the white marble coffee table that was attached to the floor. "I'm really not sure about doing the show live," he mumbled.

"Really?" I hadn't realized that Chef Howie was nervous. "It should be fine. Almost the same format you always do, right?"

"But there's no chance to stop and start again," he said, laughing. "I'm out there all alone. It's pretty intense, when you think about it."

"You'll be great," I said.

"Here's hoping," he said, and he drained a long-neck beer. As I observed more closely, Howie didn't seem all that great. His face was worn out, haggard, beat. At the moment, his not-quite-shaved beard gave him a look that was closer to hobo than rock 'n' roll.

"You okay?" I asked. "I just wanted to see if there was anything you needed. I know this has been an unusual week." Talk about your understatements.

"Tim's dead," Chef Howie said, scratching at his long sideburns. "I still can't believe it. That guy was a prince. He was a hell-raiser when he was out drinking, but he was a real good guy. Did you know him?"

I shook my head no.

"That's too bad," Howie said. "He was a great guy, Madeline. I don't get why God makes one guy dead and not another." He shook his handsome head and after a moment of reflection looked up, noticing me again. "Hey, sorry if I'm getting too heavy. I have this spiritual side to me. Fate doesn't always think I do, but I do."

"The death of a friend can be devastating," I said, trying to be helpful.

"You can say that again," he said. "I'm all torn up. Tim Stock was my buddy. That guy looked out for me so the scripts made me look good. The world is gonna miss that guy. I'm gonna miss him." He opened another bottle of beer and took a long swig.

I sat there wondering what I should say. It was awkward listening to this eulogy for a guy I knew wasn't actually dead. And Howie was so broken up about Tim he was drinking pretty hard. He was knocking back beers with a recklessness I was sure Fate would have stopped had she been there. It was maddening. Some folks enjoy secrets, but I find withholding the truth almost too hard to bear. I figured this did not make me a great cop candidate.

I stood up and cleared my throat. "Well, I had better get—"

"Stay a minute, Madeline. It's good to have someone to grieve with, you know?"

I sat back down slowly.

"Say," he said, looking nervous, "have you heard from any of the others?"

"Who?"

"From Greta or from Quentin?"

"Greta is suffering from exhaustion."

"Oh, really? I hadn't heard. So is she, like, in a hospital?"

Greta had checked into a rehab clinic to fight an addiction to painkillers. Now, it had never been established that she actually had such an addiction. Apparently no one who knew her had suspected such a thing. No intervention had been performed by anyone on the *Food Freak* staff. However, after Artie fired her, she dropped out of sight. Next thing we heard, she was out in Palm Desert fighting a painkiller problem.

"I think she's in a hospital, yes," I said.

"Pills?" Howie asked, looking concerned. "Booze?"

"I don't know," I answered truthfully.

"Think she's really out there getting a lift?" he asked.

"A face-lift?"

He nodded, as if any of those things—pills, booze, face-lifts—were the sort of occupational hazards for which television producers might be sidelined.

"I really don't know."

"What about Quentin?" he asked, changing the subject and looking into my eyes. That interested me. If Fate Finkelberg's visions of her husband cheating on her were true, I doubted Chef Howie was having an affair with Greta. His reaction was just the right unstudied mix of being out of the loop and of low-level interest.

"Oh, I wonder if you could do me a favor," I asked suddenly. "Do you think you could give me Susan Anderson's home number? I told her I'd bring over some toys for the boys."

"Does Susan have children?" Howie asked. "I didn't know that. I know she has sheep. She knitted me a chef's hat out of some special wool. It was incredibly sweet of her, not to mention weird as bat poop."

I laughed at that. "No, she doesn't have kids. She has three gorgeous dogs. She calls them her 'boys.' "

"That so? Susan is a nice gal, but I had to tell her I couldn't wear her knitted chef's hat on the air. It gave me a rash."

Fate Finkelberg was paranoid. Susan was not the object of Chef Howie's affections, either. Susan had just found love with Tim Stock. And Howie showed no special interest in Susan. He didn't recognize "the boys," and what was more, he was allergic to wool! I felt foolish even considering Fate's charges.

I supposed Fate had been working herself up over nothing in a fit of control-mania. She couldn't stand Howie making up his own special sign-off signal. Rather than accept the fact that her husband wanted a little autonomy, she had to manufacture some deeper betrayal—like an affair at work.

"So where's Quentin?" Howie said, getting back to his initial question.

"Quentin?"

"It's got me pretty worried," Howie said.

Now, as a rule, I like honesty. I try to resist lying when asked a direct question. But Honnett had warned me to keep all the information he'd given me quiet. I thought about the art of vagueness and sidestepping.

"I'll let you in on something, Madeline," Chef Howie said, holding significant eye contact, "I helped Quentin get his job on this show. I can't believe he'd run out."

"Ah. Well, Artie doesn't tell me everything. I'm so new."

"That's right," he said, as if just remembering that I'd been on the staff only a couple of weeks. His stress was real and it was making him a little forgetful.

"You knew Quentin before *Food Freak?*" I asked.

"Well," Howie said, shuffling the papers on the coffee table. "We were acquainted, that's all. Nothing unusual there. Only, do me a favor? Don't tell Fate I asked about him, would you? No reason to talk about it, right?"

"Okay," I agreed. Hm. Howie wasn't concerned about Fate hearing we'd talked about Greta. He didn't warn me not to tell Fate we'd been discussing Susan. But Quentin worried him.

Now what was this about? The more I thought it over, the more I figured Jennifer Klein might know something that could be important. She'd worked closely with Quentin and Tim and Greta. And I decided right then to go see if Jennifer might enlighten me.

WALKED across the studio lot quickly. For five days, I'd come to
work hoping I'd find Tim Stock back in hiding in the secret bedroom next to his office. For five days, I'd pushed the rose-colored
sofa away from the wall of bookcases, and opened the swinging case.
For five days, I'd come up empty-handed. No sign that Tim had ever
returned.

For five days, Susan had become more and more unsettled. She
couldn't understand why Tim never again contacted her. Even if he
still felt threatened somehow, he should have called to let her know
he was all right. I didn't want to suggest that Tim might have a new
reason for running, now. It might be that Tim was responsible for the
fire at his own garage. Yet, I still couldn't believe that was true. It
made no sense at all that Tim would kill Quentin Shore. Did it?

I knocked on Jennifer's office door and heard her call out, "Enter."

"Hi," I said. "Got a minute?"

"Sure. Sit down."

Jennifer looked up from her computer monitor and smiled at me as

I walked into her office. Jennifer's office was smaller than Tim's, and it had none of the charming two-story library atmosphere, either. It was a plain room with a desk and a few chairs. It did, however, possess a large floor-to-ceiling mirror about three feet wide, located on one wall. I had peeled off my sweater on the walk across the lot, as the heat of the day had quickly made it unnecessary. Now, I smoothed my shirt and straightened my jeans.

"You look like a real writer," Jennifer said, still smiling.

"You mean a little sloppy?"

"I prefer to call it 'casual,' " Jennifer answered. She was a comfortable-looking woman, always dressed in denim. Her dark hair fell over her forehead in deep bangs. A dimpled chin gave her face a heart shape.

As I turned away from the mirror, something odd caught my eye. There seemed to be a line in the wall along the edge of the mirror. For a moment I stood there, startled. Behind that wall, I knew, was the hidden bedroom. And I was willing to bet that behind the wall mirror, there was a second hidden door into that room. Funny, Holly and I hadn't noticed it when we were in the bedroom, but we hadn't spent a lot of time investigating after we found the trapdoor that led us downstairs and outside.

"Madeline?" Jennifer said. I got the feeling she had asked me something and I'd missed it entirely. I turned around quickly.

"Sorry, what?"

"I said, watch your behind today. Fate Finkelberg is charging around the office as if she wants to shoot someone."

"Thanks for the warning. Tell me, Jennifer, you've known her longer than I have. What is wrong with her?"

"Now there's a question that could inspire a serious discussion," Jennifer said, chuckling. "Unfortunately, we don't have the time to even scratch the surface."

"Can you give me a hint? Act it out? How many syllables?"

"She's one of those people who isn't particularly desirable to a town like this. I mean, her greatest talent is her ambition," Jennifer said, folding her hands on her desk. I pulled up a chair. "And so she's found someone who can be her meal ticket. Chef Howie has got the right looks and personality for television. He's still a young enough guy and he's getting hotter and hotter since *Food Freak* has become so popular."

"He's not terribly . . ." How should I phrase it? ". . . bright, though, is he?" I asked.

"To get into Hollywood, no report cards are examined." Jennifer smiled at me. "That's why they need us writers."

"I see."

"But Chef Howie is smart enough. He may not be a genius, but he knows that Fate has made all this possible for him. She does the massive amount of work with the agents and the lawyers and the producers and the network. All Howie has to do is show up. It seems to be a relationship that works. Why?"

"Fate came to see me last week. She wanted to be friends."

"Uh-oh." Jennifer leaned forward, hoping I'd tell her more.

"She was worried about what extracurricular adventures Howie might be getting into. It turns out it was all nonsense. The women she was worried about couldn't possibly have been involved with him."

"I'll say," Jennifer said, smiling to herself.

"How's that?" It seemed an odd comment, considering I hadn't even mentioned who the suspects might have been. I looked at Jennifer more closely. She looked more padded and practical than the type of woman I would have imagined Howie might tumble for, but one could never tell. "Do you know who Howie is involved with?"

"We'll have to talk about all of this later," Jennifer said, sighing. "Right now I'm swamped. I've had to take on a lot of the work Tim and Quentin used to do. Not to mention Greta. Would you mind helping me out? Can we go over some of the script material?"

"Of course." There was no time to think around here. I had to help get the show on the air.

Jennifer handed me a copy of the latest version of the show script and we settled into the task of reading the pages aloud. She and I found a few typos and one question that might have two possible answers. Instead of doing a lot of last-minute research, she decided to substitute another question instead. Then we had to read through all the material to make sure the new question didn't sound too similar to anything else in the script.

"This is what Tim was so good at," Jennifer said, sighing. "I really miss him." She picked up her telephone and called Susan to give her the last-minute substitution. Then she called Chef Howie, out in his trailer, and asked if he could come over so we could review the material. Normally, one of the writers went to him, but today we were just too shorthanded.

While we waited, I went over the bumper material I had written for the show, reciting the recipe for a simple guacamole.

" 'Want to take a smooth trip south of the border? Say olé with a lovely guacamole dip. The ingredients are simple, and so are the steps:

GUACAMOLE INGREDIENTS
3 ripe avocados
1 vine-ripe tomato, diced
4 small onions, minced
2 tablespoons fresh cilantro, chopped

" 'With requests for second helpings from all of your guests, you'll be so glad you served this delightful guacamole dip, you'll soon be thanking San Gabriel!' "

I stopped and looked up at Jennifer, who was deep in thought, reworking her own material. "Jenn? I have a question. I wrote up the guacamole recipe exactly as it was given to me."

"Tell me about it," Jennifer said. "Artie likes those to be written in a style that is so corny and 1950s, it kills me. Their kitsch charm completely eludes me, but the audience doesn't seem to notice how lame they are. Go figure. This show is camp for a reason."

"I know. I'm not complaining about all those 'olés' and 'second helpings.' I just think the recipe itself is questionable. I'd never make guacamole like this."

"Well, my advice is, don't second-guess it, Madeline. The show likes to keep these recipes simple. They don't believe America can cook anything, so they make it like 'Avocado for Dummies.' My advice is to just go with it."

"I understand your point. And I don't want you to think I'm trying to be difficult. But I think there must have been a typo in the recipe I received. Take a look. Page nine."

Jennifer fluttered through the bound script and read the recipe. "You mean all those onions?"

"That is a seriously inedible dip," I said. "Not to mention, it would really be better with some lemon juice to keep the thing from turning horrendously brown and disgusting."

"You take your food seriously," Jennifer said. "And I can tell that you've succumbed to the writer's disease."

"Which is?"

"You know this is just a stupid game show. And you know you shouldn't take it seriously. But you don't want to put your name on something that is an ounce more dreck-filled than it absolutely has to be."

I smiled, aware that she had nailed it.

"Well," Jennifer said, "caring is a good thing. It means you're willing to fight for your material, regardless of how ridiculous it might be."

"Thanks." I chuckled. So true.

"I'm not the food writer on this show. That was Tim and Howie. If you say it is inedible, what does it need to fix it?"

"I'd take it down to one small onion. And maybe add the lemon juice?"

"Tell you what—when Chef Howie gets here, I'll run it past him. If he approves, you can change it."

"Okay," I said.

"And it's not because I don't trust you, Madeline. It's because I want to cover your butt. This way, if anyone gets agitated that there was a change, we'll just say that Chef Howie approved it."

"Excellent."

The door to Jennifer's office flew open and in the doorway stood Chef Howie himself, and right behind him, his wife, Fate.

"Come on in," Jennifer called out. "We're just talking about a few tiny script changes. Always like this just before a taping."

"Yes, but really." Chef Howie sounded concerned. "I hate to mention it, but this is a 'live' event. I've just about memorized the script you gave me. Any changes and I'm not sure I can promise I'll get it right."

"Nonsense," Fate said, cutting Chef Howie off. "We've got every confidence in your abilities, my dear. Besides, all of this will be on cue cards, won't it, Jennifer?" Before Jennifer could respond, Fate asked, "What are the changes?"

Jennifer walked right past Chef Howie to confer with Fate. Howie had long ago learned to just shut up. While Jennifer was showing Fate the new material we were adding to the question round, I showed Chef Howie the recipe for guacamole and my suggested change. He was nervous, he said, to make too many changes, but he did agree that four onions was impossible. He told me to change it to only one, but not to add the lemon juice.

"Are you sure?" I asked.

"Madeline, I don't give a gnat's ass what color the guacamole turns when all those millions of folks at home try to make this recipe. They should be grateful they aren't choking down four goddamned onions!"

I had to admit, while he may not have shown a missionary's zeal to lift the masses up to a higher gourmet plane, he did take pity on them. I made the quick revision, knocking four onions down to one and called Susan with the change. She told me she'd come down to Jennifer's office and pick it up.

A few minutes later, Susan arrived, out of breath.

"I've got some wonderful news," Susan said to the room at large. "The fire at Tim's house. The body they found wasn't Tim. It was just on the news."

We all looked at Susan. I noticed that each one of Tim's work friends seemed to take the news a little differently, but they all seemed to be relieved. Then she continued her report. "There is sad news, too. The police have identified the body. It was Quentin. They said it was murder."

Everyone in the room seemed stunned into silence. Then Chef Howie spoke up. "That's not true, is it?" His words slurred just the tiniest bit.

"Damn you," Fate said, looking right at Susan. "My Howie has to go before the cameras in an hour and you slap him with this? Why not just hit him over the head with a sauté pan?"

"Why I . . . ," Susan stuttered. "I thought he would be happy with the news about Tim. I thought Quentin . . ." She let the sentence hang in the air.

"No one understood him," Howie said, fiercely. "He had a poet's soul. He—"

I turned to look at Chef Howie and saw him in a whole new light. I am not exactly naive on this subject, just so nonjudgmental that I sometimes fail to notice the obvious. I'm willing to let everyone live his or her own life however they may. It doesn't strike me as odd that people should form close friendships, so I don't always imagine the next step such friends might take. But I suspected even at a time like this, when not a soul would dare speak ill of the dead, no one but a very special friend could see the poetry in Quentin Shore's soul.

Was that true? My head spun. Quentin Shore and Chef Howie Finkelberg? That stopped me cold. Had we all been looking at the whole puzzle from the wrong side?

25

ABOVE the twin, gleaming, high-tech kitchens on soundstage 9, an iron grid hung from chains. And from that grid, aimed down at the set, shone an array of brilliant stage lights. Each spotlight and Fresnel and Baby Fresnel and Tweenie Fresnel was focused on the Kitchen Arena below. Each light had been tested. Each colored filter gel had been checked and, if needed, replaced. On this late afternoon, inside this dark, cavernous building, each fellow pushed his wattage to the max, together on a joint mission to light up *Freak*'s final episode in a blaze of glory. All these expensive stage lights, soaking up a thousand dollars' worth of electric current, all carefully clustered, and aimed, and plugged into the central dimmer board, were necessary to make our star chef and his contestants look great on camera. Good lighting made a show's set look rich and its performers look beautiful. Bad lighting revealed the truth. It was no wonder actors made friends with the lighting director before they thought to meet their costars.

Here's the thing about intense light. So much light focused on one spot makes anyone standing in the glow feel washed with warmth and power. Even I felt it, and I was merely onstage for an errand, doing my own last-minute checks before *Freak* was to start. I squinted in the spotlight, facing the rows of in-the-round audience seats. All looked inky black. Just beyond the edges of the lit-up Kitchen Arena, the world seemed to stop. If I hadn't heard the sounds of talking and feet shuffling, I might not even realize the studio audience had been let in and were finding their seats, so little of that area only three yards from me could I see.

"Maddie, you know what to do?" repeated Jennifer, like a mantra. Who could blame her for feeling the pressure? She had been asked to replace three people, Greta, Tim, and Quentin, and had been handed a complete novice as her able right hand.

"I'm checking Randy's cards," I said, just to make her feel a little more in control. She needn't worry. I could follow instructions like a champ. Over at the edge of the Kitchen Arena, to one side of the back-to-back cook-off kitchens, I stood at the podium for the show's announcer, Randy East. He wasn't there yet, but his portion of the script was waiting on the podium. Susan's junior PA staff was in charge of the announcer's cards, and they were efficient. Since Randy's segments were mostly voice-overs, he was actually off camera when he read the material from the prepared five-by-seven index cards. Each little bundle was paper-clipped together and kept in order. I picked up the first packet and read it to myself:

"Good evening and welcome to . . . *FOOD FREAK!* — the cutthroat culinary competition that pits teams of the most daring amateur chefs against one another . . . in the Ultimate Battle of Good Food versus Bad! Join us for tonight's knife-sharp game in which even the ingredients can turn against you!"

So far, so good. I read on, almost unaware of the hyperbole in my pursuit of the misplaced comma.

"CHEF HOWIE FINKELBERG, the legendary chef at San Diego's POSH NOSH, will give us the play-by-play and lead us through the WAR ZONE in our Kitchen Arena! (Hold for applause.) We've got the hottest stoves and the coolest stars!! Like tonight's tasting judge SU-PERSTARS . . . We've got *Spider-man*'s awesome star arachnid,

TOBEY MAGUIRE! (Hold for applause.) We've got red-hot J.LO! and, baby, JENNIFER LOPEZ knows what sizzles! (Hold for applause.) And we've got JON "BOWZER" BAUMAN!—the leader of that oldies music sensation, Sha Na Na! So get ready! Tonight, for the first time ever, we are LIVE! (Hold for applause). It's gonna be RAUCOUS! It's the match of year!! As two battle-scarred teams of champion warrior food freaks come back in a no-holds-barred cook-off we like to call . . . '*FOOD FREAK* REVENGE: THE FINAL FOOD FIGHT'!"

"How's everything look?" Jennifer asked, checking the index cards over my shoulder.

"Fine. I think."

Jennifer looked up, worried. "What is it?"

"I have never seen so many exclamation points. Or capitalized words. Or sentence fragments."

Jennifer relaxed. "Yes. Artie loves them. It's game-showese."

Jennifer had written the opening copy, but I knew her words had gone under the editing pen of Artie, as he was the guy who had the final approval.

"Did Artie write this part?" I asked, pointing to one card. " '. . . *Spider-man's* awesome star arachnid TOBEY MAGUIRE.' "

"Of course. Do I think the word 'arachnid' is cute? For prime time? But try telling that to Artie. He finds the word 'arachnid' hilarious, despite all my objections."

"Don't you think it might sound better if we changed the word order just a little so it reads '. . . *Spider-man's* awesome arachnid star'. . . ?" I suggested.

"Yes, I do. But once Randy's cards are set down by the PAs, it's too late to make changes. It means we would have to find Artie and get his approval again, and get Susan to issue new script pages to all the production staff in the control booth. It isn't worth the pain and aggravation. We just don't bother for anything minor."

"Like making the language more precise or appealing?"

"Exactly. Ain't television writing fun?" Jennifer smiled and then dashed away, mumbling something about checking that the questions had been corrected on Chef Howie's cue cards.

I replaced the large paper clip on the index cards and moved to the next stack. As I reread them once more for typos or omissions, I wished I could instead be sent on an errand a little nearer the dressing rooms. Our celebrity judges would arrive soon and I longed for a peek. Artie hadn't booked Tom Hanks, but he'd gotten us Tobey Maguire. I was human. I wanted to look. I thought it might be nice if Mr. Maguire's invitation to the wrap party was delivered personally.

I daydreamed a bit about impossible romantic scenarios as I silently read through more of the announcer index cards. The next packet on Randy's podium contained the intro cards, the language used to introduce the teams of returning contestants and describe their previous victories, all of which would be read over videotape clips of their past appearances. The cards were typo-free and looked in good order. It's Nellie's responsibility to go over this set of cards and proof them with Susan, so I just glanced through.

My cell phone went off, beeping a little tune, the opening notes of "Stayin' Alive." It was Chuck Honnett, returning my call.

"What's up, Madeline? You okay?"

"Hi, you. Are you able to get over to the studio later?" I asked.

"That's right. The studio," his low voice drawled, making it sound sexy. "Say, I don't know. I'm going to be pretty busy tonight."

"Aren't you off at seven?"

"Technically. Yeah. But, you know."

"It might be fun. You might get a kick out of watching America's number one television series do its final show. You know, I wrote a few things in this one."

"That's terrific. You must be excited, huh?"

"And after the show, Wes and Hol and I are catering the wrap party. You should come for that part, at least. They're cooking up the hottest gumbo and all the fixings. I could show you off to my new friends here. And just think—you could use the social setting to interrogate everybody who knew Quentin Shore. Much more effective."

"Maddie," he said, sounding tired.

"Please?" I asked. "It's my first and probably last time writing on the staff of a TV show."

"I'd like to get there, but . . ." He let it hang. Honnett sounded on edge. And then I put it together.

"It's Wednesday night," I said. "You're expecting another one."

"I have a bad feeling, Madeline. I better go. Look, I'll try to stop by if things are quiet, okay?"

As I stood in the blinding glare of full stage lighting, clicking off my cell phone, I became aware that I wasn't alone. The audience was now, apparently, seated. Just beyond the blackness all around the stage, there was a perceptible charge to the air from the proximity of human beings. Their voices were subdued, but the constant shuffle of belongings, purses hitting the floor, throats being cleared began to make me feel self-conscious. Great. I had just been rebuffed and rejected in front of a full house. Perfect. My face grew hotter.

Making a big entrance, Randy East swept onto the stage. It was his job to warm up the audience before the show, just to get them roused and ready to scream and applaud. Randy had a big handsome jaw and hair that looked like it had been cut with a laser. He was speaking into a hand microphone, using his big voice to get the crowd excited. He was saying, "You know, folks, we really do give away half a million dollars every week to the team that wins! Of course, we don't give it all at once. Like the state lottery, we parcel it out over time. What is it now, Madeline?" he said, turning to address me, the only other human on the overlit stage. And then without waiting for my answer, he said, "Oh yes. We pay them fifty cents a year for a million years." The audience roared. "We don't do this for ourselves," he continued, milking the laugh. "You can imagine how much it lowers their taxes." The audience roared again. They seemed just as happy as I was that they now had something to amuse them other than my personal life. My flush began to fade.

As Randy moved into the audience to meet and cajole some nice individual named Pat Tracy from Kentucky, I got back to my task. The next packet of cards contained material I had helped write. An unaccustomed swell of pride made the tips of my fingers tingle and my brain feel hot and sweaty. In a good way. Actually, most of this material was written exactly the way I had been instructed to do it, leaving in most of the abominable clichés. Still, I felt pride in the one line I had changed and the corrections I'd made. I read to myself the bumper copy that leads into the first commercial:

"Want to take a smooth trip south of the border? Say olé! with a zesty guacamole dip. The ingredients are simple, and so are the steps.

"Start with:

3 ripe avocados
1 diced vine-ripe tomato
4 small onions, minced
2 tablespoons of chopped fresh cilantro

"Mash and stir it all together in a small bowl, then serve with tortilla chips. You'll be so glad you served this delightful guacamole dip, you'll soon be saying 'Gracias!' to San Gabriel! Stay with us . . . Next, Chef Howie shows us how far our teams will go to get their FOOD FREAK revenge when we return."

"That's odd," I said aloud. Somehow, the old ingredients with the mistake had remained in the script. Those excessive onions. I remembered going over the correction with Susan, but it never got corrected. Not her fault, I knew. It must be impossible for one woman to keep every single change straight. I took out a pen and quickly crossed out the "4" and replaced it with a "1."

Just then, Arthur Herman, wearing a blue-pin-striped sports jacket and red bow tie over his trademark khakis, walked onto the stage and over to me.

"So what's up, cookie? Everything check out?" Artie asked, his Brooklyn accent making him sound like a vaudeville straight man awaiting the punch line.

"It's looking good, Artie," I replied. "I found one small mistake, but it was just a typo. Everything else looks excellent."

"Do me a favor, doll-face," he said. "Could you go to my office and find me a seltzer?"

"Sure."

"Bring it to me in the booth," he instructed. "You'll find it in the little fridge behind my desk. I only like the New York kind, and down here they don't give me what I like."

"No problem," I said. It seemed anyone who was within shouting distance was called upon to run errands. Aside from my desire to check out the arriving celebs, I was perfectly willing to help in any way. Besides, getting a guy a drink felt like old home week for me.

Artie handed me his office key and I left him at the announcer's podium, taking his turn checking Randy East's announcer copy. Meanwhile, Randy's amplified voice was booming, "There he is, ladies and gentlemen! Our creator . . . our boss . . . our God! . . . Mr. Arthur B. Herman!"

By the time I'd jogged the five blocks back across the studio lot to our office building, I was slightly out of breath. The sun was making its late afternoon descent, until, about twenty miles to the west of our lot, it would once again take a graceful dive into the Pacific.

In the production office's lower lobby, our returning contestant teams were milling about. I recognized them from their star turns on past episodes and I was dying to meet them, but I was in a hurry. I took a side door, instead, and bolted up two flights of stairs.

On the executive level, all was silent. Here I was, alone in the building again. It made me nervous, thinking I might be running some risk, and then made me angry I couldn't fetch a simple bottle of seltzer without having to get paranoid. I shook off the jitters and tried the key in Artie's office-door lock. It opened easily. I flicked on the light switch and saluted my boy Speedy who, not surprisingly, was still winking.

Behind the desk was a small bar-size refrigerator, Artie's "fridge." I bent down and opened its door. Inside were the usual assortment of soft drinks and bottled waters. The entire top shelf contained Artie's favorite beverage. I took two short bottles, figuring it might be a long night and I'd be saving someone else the trip over, and placed them on Artie's desk.

Now that wasn't smart. Artie's desk was covered in correspondence and memos and stacks of papers. The condensation on the cold glass bottles might leave a wet spot on the documents. I quickly pulled them off and set them on the floor, finding a tissue and starting to dab the dampened paper.

It was a billing statement from Eagle Post, the postproduction house where *Freak* was edited. The ink had smeared and I glanced at it to make sure the important stuff was still legible. This particular bill itemized an extra voice-over session. Randy East had gone in to loop a few words, which were then edited into one of the finished programs. The job was for show number 10021. It seemed that *Food Freak* was being charged an additional fee of $400 for changing "2 ounces," to "1 pound." That particular fee was the minimum charged for recording-studio time. For the editor who worked on the session, the show was charged an additional $200 an hour, two-hour minimum. And the rush charge, another $200.

That seemed pretty expensive, even in Hollywood. In addition, the show would have to pay Randy to come in on his day off, at his guild's minimum. It probably cost Artie close to two thousand dollars just to change two words. Why would he bother? If it was to fix one of the bumper recipes, Dawn Weiss, current-receptionist-and-future-studio-president, had explained that the normal policy was to send out correction letters and be done with it.

I checked the airdate listed on the invoice against the large month-at-a-glance calendar blotter underneath the stacks of paperwork. Show number 10021 aired on Wednesday night, exactly three weeks ago. Nothing remarkable about that particular episode that I knew of.

This was indeed a mystery. Why had it been worth a couple thousand dollars to fix two words?

26

HOLLY, where are all those scuffed-up *Food Freak* script pages you were going to list on eBay? You didn't sell them yet?"

"Mad?" Holly's voice sounded puzzled on the phone. "Where are you?"

"I'm in Artie's office," I said, trying to stay calm. "Listen, do you still have any of them?"

"Sure. I have all of them."

"That's great! Where are they?"

"I hate to tell you."

"Holly, we don't have time. I need some quick answers."

Over the phone, I could hear Holly clearing her throat. "Look, we haven't talked much this past week. You've been working on *Freak* all the time and I've been . . . well, I've been busy getting back together with Donald."

I tried to contain my urge to scream. "Holly. Where are the scripts?"

"They've been in the backseat of my car all week."

"What?"

"I haven't been home yet."

"You haven't . . . Okay, look, never mind. You're still here, right? On the lot, in the tent kitchen, right?"

"Not exactly. I'm nearer the greenroom."

It figured. That's where J.Lo and Tobey Maguire would be hanging out when they finished with makeup.

"Where is your car parked? I need to see the scripts now."

"Well, the thing is, we needed to use my car to help carry junk over to the studio for the party. So I unloaded that huge pile of scripts a few hours ago."

"Okay, Holly. Give it to me all at once. Where the hell are the scripts?"

"I stashed them in that room next to your office. I didn't think you'd mind."

"You put them in the hidden room?" I think my voice squeaked. "That's just downstairs. That's brilliant. Look, can you meet me there? I may need help."

"Sure. Wes has everything covered out in the tent. And Tobey isn't out of wardrobe yet. But I think they are calling places on the stage. I just saw Emily Baker walk by and I nearly fainted. These contestants are so cool."

"Meet me as soon as you can."

"Rightio," Holly said.

I took the bottles of seltzer, and I grabbed the damp invoice, too, and charged my way out of Artie's office, remembering to shut the door and lock it. Down on the floor below, the hallway was deserted. All the production staff were surely down at the soundstage by this time, keyed up and ready to go into action. At the door of Tim Stock's office, on a hunch I tried Artie's key in the door. It worked. Apparently all the big bosses got the master key. Handy. It saved me the time of scrounging for my key ring. I shot across Tim's empty library/office, wasting no time. The job of pushing aside the large rose sofa was made more difficult because it sat on the carpet, but in a minute I had managed to shove it far enough away from the bookcases that I could open the hidden door.

The sound of the knock startled me. Being alone in Tim's office was not my favorite thing. Holly was at the door. Of course. And I was happy to get her inside and have her company as well as her help.

"What are you doing?" she asked. She had long ago shed the magenta-colored ski parka and was dressed in a long, slinky, black-knit dress with a V neckline that plunged far south of her bosom, revealing her white skin and the bone structure of her midchest. She was model tall and model thin, and on certain days, like when she expected to bump into young Hollywood dishes like Tobey Maguire, Holly worked it.

"Nice dress," I said, as the two of us entered the darkened bedroom next door. "New?"

"Donald didn't want me to go home, so he took me shopping, instead. Please don't tell me I'm bad."

I located the pull chain for the light easily this time. In the sudden brightness, I found myself staring at stacks of scripts, some bound, but many pages loose.

"Look," I said, "I want to find the bumper copy for show number 10021."

"Okay," Holly agreed. She was always eager to jump into any job. "What does a copy of a bumper look like?"

"It will just look like any other page here. Only the show number is typed in the upper-right corner on each script. The bumper copy is just the words the announcer reads before the commercial."

"Hey, that's cute," Holly said. "So I guess it would be a page like this one?" She had quickly flipped through the bound script on the top of the pile and held out the first page that showed a speech for Randy East.

"Yes. Only this section is the contestant intros. And this script," I said, checking the show number, "is show number 10023." But I flipped further ahead to show Holly what the bumper recipes looked like. "See here?" I read it to her aloud:

" 'RANDY EAST: Don't go to Rome when you have a craving for Caesar! Salad, that is! Just jot down this grocery list:

1 anchovy
2 heads of fresh romaine
2 cups of extra-virgin olive oil

2 cups of grated Parmesan cheese
6 squeezed lemons

" 'You can use an extra one, but you don't have to buy a lemon grove!' "

"If you ask me, that recipe sucks," Holly said flatly. "Who uses two cups of Parmesan in a recipe that small? And what's with the lemons?"

"Holly!" I felt dizzy, the words swimming in front of my eyes.

"What's wrong?"

"Read down the list of ingredients. Just the numbers."

"One-two-two-two-six. What is that?"

"And the last two words in his speech?"

She looked it over again and read, ". . . lemon grove." Holly looked up at me then, puzzled. "Why does that sound so familiar?"

"One-two-two-two-six Lemon Grove is Tim Stock's address."

"Oh my God!"

"And what was the airdate of show number 10023?" I asked her, my voice dropping out at the end.

Holly turned back to the cardboard cover. "Last week. It was the show that aired last Wednesday night."

"And that was the night . . ."

Holly just stared at me.

"Holly, find show number 10021."

The two of us attacked the pile. One by one, we discarded scripts from other weeks. When we had gotten down to the bottom of the stack of bound scripts, Holly cried, "Eureka!" In her hand was a slightly disheveled copy of the script for show number 10021. Its cover was missing, and so, by the looks of it, were several pages. I took it from her and raced through it. The page that held the bumper copy was missing.

"What does it mean?" she asked, disappointed.

"Help me go through these pages that have been torn out of the scripts," I said, resigned. "I don't think we'll find the page we want. I am beginning to suspect that page was torn out of its script for a reason. And maybe that reason was worth someone breaking into Tim's office in the first place."

"You mean," Holly said, thinking it all through, "somebody trashed that office just to cover up the fact that they ripped off one page from an old script?"

"I do. Something in that script had to be covered up, Holly. A show that watches every penny in its budget does not just frivolously shell out two grand to make a minor correction. I've got to see that recipe in the bumper. Tell you what. We can make it simpler. Greta told me she had backup copies of all the old scripts in her office."

"But it's locked and Greta's not here," Holly said, biting her lip. "It'll take time, but maybe we could try to track her down."

I just couldn't wait. We were finally going to get some answers. All along, we'd been running into codes, like the code in the magazine that led us to the cookbooks where Tim Stock's cash was hidden. And now it turned out that the mangled recipes might be some sort of code, too. "We can't waste any more time," I said to Holly.

"What else can we do?" she asked, ready to leap into action by my side.

And then I showed her Artie's master key.

27

A NEAT row of twenty-four scripts, each about thirty pages thick, each covered in pastel card stock, each fastened with brass brads, filled one shelf next to Greta Greene's desk. Holly and I had let ourselves into the quiet office without any trouble. It was five minutes before six o'clock. Five minutes to air. Down at the stage, the crew and contestants would be in their places. In the booth, the small control room, the director was by now at his seat in front of a bank of monitor screens, ready to call the show. The show's producers would be sitting in the row behind, watching the monitors, too, hoping for the best. Susan was sitting by the director's elbow, counting down the time until the final *Food Freak* episode would begin. It was her responsibility to make sure the live production stayed on time throughout its allotted hour. With everyone already in the booth or on the stage floor, the entire floor of production offices was empty.

I flipped on the television set on Greta's desk. The KTLA studio had their own private video feed. They picked up the live shots from each of the working soundstages and broadcast it in-house to all of the production offices on the lot. Sitting in your office, you could watch any of the shows that were taping at the facility in real time. I flipped a few channels, looking for the live feed from the *Food Freak* set. The first noncommercial station I came to displayed the slate for *Let's Make a Deal*. According to the schedule, *Deal* was on soundstage 2, but wouldn't begin taping until seven. I flipped a few more channels and found the video feed from soundstage 9. Because *Food Freak* had yet to begin taping, what we saw was a master shot of the stage from an untended camera that revealed the crew's last-minute activities. Randy East could be seen shuffling through his hand cards at his podium. Chef Howie walked over to the contestants and began chatting to help ease their nerves. Because his mike was live, we could hear him as they made small talk.

"Maddie," Holly said, "here it is. Show number 10021. Randy East's part. The recipe is for a Swiss Cheese Omelet."

I met her at the bookcase, where she had the script open, and read: " 'You'll need . . .

1 pound of Swiss cheese, grated
3 large eggs
1 tablespoon of butter

" 'This will taste as good the first time you make it as the twenty-first!' "
I stopped reading and shook my head.

Holly said, " 'One pound of Swiss cheese'? Get real."

I read down the numbers and the last words in the piece. "One-three-one twenty-first."

"Is that an address?" she asked.

I checked the invoice from Eagle Post. The words that had been edited out were "1 pound." The words that were looped in were "2 ounces."

"That's it," I said. "The recipe was fixed in post. Before they aired that show, someone had made the decision to change the quantity of Swiss to two ounces."

"I'm not sure I'm following you there. That would be more sensible, wouldn't it? To use two ounces of cheese?"

"Yes." I looked at the invoice again. At the bottom was a notation that explained who at the production company had placed the rush order. In that blank were typed the initials "T.S." I pointed it out to Holly.

"So you mean Tim Stock is the one who ordered the correction?"

"I think he did. And instead of the recipe code spelling out 131 Twenty-first, it must have been broadcast as 231 Twenty-first."

"But what does it mean?"

I put up a finger. "*Food Freak* Revenge: The Final Food Fight" had just begun taping. The opening music picked up and we both turned to watch. We heard the familiar raucous version of "Who Let the Chefs Out?" and then the full, hearty voice of Randy East. He was reading off the opening copy while we saw a fast-cut montage of different shots: contestants, the set, and Chef Howie. It was surreal to hear the words I had just proofread now being read live over the pulsing close-ups. It was Randy's talent to turn a card full of exclamation points and ellipses into something that sounded like spontaneous excitement.

I used my cell phone to call Honnett's cell phone, relieved when he answered his after the first ring. "I've got a strange question," I said, without waiting for a greeting. "Does the address 231 Twenty-first Street mean anything?"

There was a pause so long on the other end of the phone, I wondered if we had become disconnected. In the silence, Randy East's voice came booming from the office television monitor. He was introducing "*Spider-man*'s star arachnid" I watched Tobey Maguire waving from the judges' platform as the awkward wording was read aloud. That language should have been fixed.

"Honnett?" I said into the phone, impatient, worried.

"231 Twenty-first Street," he said slowly, "is the Burbank address of our female shooting victim three weeks ago. The physical therapist. Where'd you come up with that?"

"Look," I said, "I think something bizarre has been going on at *Food Freak*. We have to do something fast. Our final show has just this minute started taping. It's going out live to the East Coast. Anyone here in L.A. could be watching it right now if they have the satellite."

"Calm down, Maddie. Tell me what's going on."

"I think Tim Stock tried to correct a mistake on a recipe that was read on the show that aired three weeks ago, the night the physical therapist was killed. I think he accidentally altered the code. The address was supposed to be 131 Twenty-first Street, but Tim made it 231."

I told him the rest. It took awhile. Last week the recipe on the air had been a code for Tim's address. And a death occurred at that address, too. I read Honnett the code addresses from the last few weeks of shows as Holly kept handing me the open scripts she was sorting through. "It's your Wednesday night string of homicides. *Food Freak* is the king of Wednesday night. I'm pretty sure this show has been broadcasting a secret message that has sent contract killers out on the streets of Los Angeles."

"Do you hear what you are saying?" Honnett asked. "You're saying your game show is killing people."

"I told you it was bizarre," I said, keeping my voice steady. "But it all makes sense."

Honnett wasn't as convinced as I was, but he would send a police officer out immediately, to guard all the scripts. He'd get a search warrant, too, but that would take longer. He told me to stay with Holly.

I was just about to disconnect, but on the office monitor, the first segment of the show was concluding. A beautiful shot of Chef Howie preparing guacamole appeared on the screen. Randy East's voice could be heard over the shot as he read the bumper copy that led into the first commercial break:

" 'Want to take a smooth trip south of the border? Say olé! with a zesty guacamole dip. The ingredients are simple, and so are the steps.

" 'Start with:

3 ripe avocados
1 diced vine-ripe tomato
4 small onions, minced
2 tablespoons of chopped fresh cilantro

" 'Mash and stir it all together . . .' "

The recipe I had fixed at the very last minute had been un-fixed. As

Randy East read off the ingredients, I spoke quickly into the phone. "Wait a second, Chuck. Someone has to get over to 3142 San Gabriel. I'm not sure what part of the city that is, but that's the code address in tonight's recipe. They should get there fast. Someone in that house is not safe."

I pressed the End button on my cell phone and turned to Holly. "We're sticking together. Honnett's orders."

"Did he say we have to stay right here?"

"No. Let's go to the soundstage. This is my big break in show business, damnit, and if the cops are coming to shut this place down, I better make the most of being a glamorous TV writer while I still have the chance."

"Wow," Holly said, following me out of Greta's office. "When they say 'fifteen minutes of fame,' they aren't just joking around, are they?"

We walked across the lot together, Holly in her high-heeled sandals and long black dress, and me. I had changed earlier into my best new clothes, a low-slung olive-colored skirt and a short gauzy white top that left a tiny gap of skin exposed at the waistline when I raised my arms. Holly looked at me once again as we walked up to the *Food Freak* soundstage. "You have become bold, Maddie," she said approvingly. "It's the new Mad Bean."

"Stop it," I said, shushing her. The red light outside the heavy door of the soundstage began to pulsate, on and off. It warned that the show inside was taping and all needed to be extra quiet.

"Mad Goes Hollywood," she whispered in my ear, to annoy me. It worked.

We walked behind the set as quietly as possible, careful to step over cables on the floor, until we came to the back of the audience risers. Onstage, the Baker sisters were just answering their final question.

Chef Howie was standing next to the trio, reading expertly from his cue card, "Okay, we're playing 'Bad Recipes'! For the final point, and the round, remember you must replace the incorrect words in the following culinary statement. Just correct this silly recipe: '*Bullwinkle J.* mousse is made with eggs, butter, sugar, and cocoa.' " As Chef Howie read the words, they appeared in graphics on the lower portion of the screen on a large monitor that faced the audience.

Marley Baker looked at Sydney. Sydney said, "Chocolate?"

"Yes!" Chef Howie said, beaming. "*Chocolate* mousse is made with eggs, butter, sugar, and cocoa! You did it! You won the round!"

Holly and I stood to the side of the audience risers and noticed the "Applause" sign flash on. We saw Randy East, his full face smiling at the audience, cheering at us all, getting the audience to give it some more oomph! Without thinking, Holly and I began to applaud. Over the noise, I spoke into Holly's ear. "I wrote that question," I said.

"Awesome," she replied.

Chef Howie waited for the cheers to die down and turned to the contestants on the set. "Who are the hottest chefs competing here tonight? We'll find out in just a moment, when the Baker sisters take on Bruce and Belinda Holtz in the showdown of the year . . . Don't you dare leave your seats, friends!"

The show took a two-minute break for commercials, and the stagehands and gaffers began to attack the set. The contestants were moved into the Kitchen Arena section where they would do their thing, back to back.

"So can you tell me what you think?" Holly whispered.

"I'm not sure. Someone has deliberately planted those bumper recipes in the scripts to communicate a code over the air. That code has been addresses, Hol. I'm worried. Those addresses may connect to a series of homicides."

"Who would do something like that?"

I shook my head. "Only a few people had the influence with this show to get those recipes on the air."

"Like the head writer, Tim Stock?" she asked.

"Yes. But if Tim was behind the address code, why did he order that expensive looping session? I'm afraid, Holly, that by correcting that one recipe, some innocent woman in Burbank died."

"That's horrible." Holly looked ill.

"I know. And something else is bothering me. The very next week after Tim made the change in the recipe, he went into hiding. It seems like whoever is behind these deaths must have discovered what Tim had done."

"You think they threatened him and he ran?"

"Maybe Tim discovered what those recipes really meant. He could have noticed the Burbank woman's address in the newspaper, and started to figure it out. This code is not that sophisticated. Anyone who can cook would recognize that the quantities of those ingredients don't make sense. The fact that no one on the show stopped them from getting aired is the key here. I bet Tim freaked when he finally figured out the truth. Those recipes meant death. Maybe the people behind these killings decided Tim knew too much and had to be eliminated."

"So they put out a contract for Tim," Holly said, worried, "by putting Tim's own address in the show."

I kept thinking it over. Who could be behind such a string of killings, anyway? Honnett had told me the deaths looked like professional hits, but they didn't share the same methods, which made it much harder to prove they were linked. What the deaths had in common was the night of the week they occurred, the night *Food Freak* aired, and the suggestion that most of the victims had disputes with a certain drug gang. Perhaps the address going out on network television each week was like some macabre job posting. Any hitman out there could make a kill and pick up some money.

"It can't be true. We gotta be missing something," Holly said, worried. "Why would anyone on this show want to be involved with this? These people are game-show people."

I remembered that Susan had said much the same thing. Game-show people might be guilty of the sort of infractions that could get them pulled over to the side of the road by the culture police, but they were hardly organized criminals.

In front of us, the large letters spelling "Applause" lit up. The audience sitting on risers next to us began to yell and clap. The televised competition was about to resume.

Chef Howie told the contestants that the recipe they would have to prepare for the evening was a spicy and rich "Mumbo Gumbo."

Holly turned to me and grinned. "That's yours, isn't it? That recipe? Oh, Mad, you are famous now."

So this was fame.

FRENZY of slicing, dicing action was about to get under way in *Food Freak*'s Kitchen Arena and I wished I could just focus. The audience all around us was screaming for their favorite players. The band had begun to play "Let's Get This Party Started." It was my recipe for gumbo, after all, that these *über*-contestant chefs were about to modify for the final food fight, and I wanted to pay attention to the cooking mania ahead. But then, I was so close to understanding this recipe-address puzzle and it wouldn't leave me alone. The answer seemed right there, just beyond my reach. If I could figure out who had written those mangled recipes and gotten them in the script, I'd know it all.

Quentin Shore could have done it. He had access to the show material. He had been the primary writer responsible for the bumpers. But now Quentin was dead, and still the address code had made it into the current script. Quentin might have played a part in writing up the bumper copy, but he wasn't the only one involved.

Greta. I had to consider Greta. She was Tim's boss and as such she reviewed all the scripts. But that didn't work, either. Greta wasn't here this week and somebody here was involved. Somebody had changed the bumper copy back to its original numbers just a few minutes ago, after I'd tried to fix the guacamole recipe on Randy's script card one last time.

A shot rang out.

I looked up, startled, nervous. It was just the starting gun on the final *Food Freak* gonzo cook-off. The contestants, wearing their neon-colored aprons, rushing about in the Kitchen Arena, had begun cooking their gumbo. The show's band, The Freaks, moved on to another hard-rocking number and it was off-the-charts loud. Holly couldn't stop herself from bopping along with the beat. Neither, I noticed, could most of the audience members. This show was now in overdrive. The divorced couple, Bruce and Belinda, started fighting immediately over how much cayenne, if any, they were going to use. Chef Howie dashed over to their side of the kitchen set to interview the ex-wife, who was almost in tears. Her new boyfriend was sitting in the audience section a few feet away from where Holly and I stood. He was yelling at Bruce to lay off and let Belinda spice it up, goddamnit!

As the music pounded and the cooks raced around the Kitchen Arena, I kept wondering who else on the staff might have had control over the script. If I could eliminate all the people who couldn't have done it, I'd have an idea who did.

I considered the *Food Freak* people, one by one. Chef Howie Finkelberg and his wife, Fate, had relatively little access to the scripts. It was possible they might have proposed some recipes, but neither could make sure such mixed-up numbers as were actually aired made it to the final script. Too many others reviewed the content of the show for errors and would have fixed any mistakes that were found. I had to rule them out.

In the same way, the contestant coordinators, Nell and Stell, were out of the loop. They had no contact with the script material at all.

The announcer could have changed the recipes, I supposed, by reading it out his own way, but in the normal course of shooting this series, the shows were pretaped. He would have been stopped by the director and asked to redo it if he didn't follow the script. I could rule out Randy East. Our problem was with the script itself.

Jennifer Klein had more involvement with the scripts as they were being developed. As a staff writer, she had some input on changes. But Jennifer hadn't worked on the bumpers. And that left her out.

I considered the show's PAs. Kenny and Jackson were just too low on the totem pole to have any say. Too many people above them had the authority to change their work. But that didn't apply to their supervisor, Susan Anderson. Susan controlled production of the scripts. She typed them and made any updates and it was conceivable she could even alter their contents slightly, if no one else noticed. I thought that over and then had another uneasy thought. Susan had a lot of influence over the show's head writer. She could have fed Tim those bumper recipes, I supposed, and persuaded him to hand them off to Quentin to submit. It was true. Susan's position in Tim's life and her job supervising the scripts gave her just enough opportunity to get those recipes through. And then I had one more horrible thought. Susan had a lot of reasons to hate Artie Herman.

But Susan Anderson? The sheep lady? The girl who named one of her lambs Mutton Jeff and dyes her wool with Kool-Aid? No matter how much opportunity to tamper with the scripts she might have had, Susan could not possibly be involved in a scheme that dispatched killers. It's true, Susan might have hated Artie enough, with some hidden revenge in mind, to want to destroy his hit show. But aside from the complete improbability of Susan getting involved with a drug cartel, Susan was in love with Tim. Susan couldn't have knowingly typed a bumper recipe and placed it in the show's script that would have sent a killer straight to Tim's house.

The whole idea of Susan as the guilty party was completely impossible. Susan Anderson? I had gotten to know Susan. She was not even capable of talking back to her demented boss, much less of masterminding some gangland-style killings. I thought it over again. Could she really have added those recipes to the script? I changed my mind. Not really. Surely others would have noticed if the script was being typed "incorrectly" too often. Artie would have noticed.

And that's when I knew for sure. I remembered Jennifer telling me that any changes to the final script cards had to be shown to Artie for his approval. Artie had final say over the script. Artie was the last word. And Artie had been standing by the announcer's podium right after I'd tried to correct the bumper recipe. He'd had the chance to override that correction one last time.

But was Artie—that sweet little nebbish of an old man—capable of this sort of monstrous enterprise? Of sending killers out into the streets? I thought about it. I was inclined to believe Susan's version of what had happened in Mexico, the version where Artie came unglued and went ballistic, and then later repented and paid off Susan to forgive him. So, okay, yes, I could believe Artie had a terrible temper. Look at the way he got rid of Greta—Greta, who had worked for him for years. I believed Artie could blow. But why would he get mixed up with killers? He was an old ad man, a corny guy who made corny jokes. He was a guy who loved *alliteration*, for Pete's sake. And now, capping years of success in television, Artie Herman had the biggest hit series of all. *Food Freak* was number one. Would such a man at such a time in his life go into business with gangbangers and drug lords? Was he the kind of man who could order the deaths of so many people? It made absolutely no sense.

And yet, Artie was the one with the ultimate control over what script material stayed in or came out. Artie might have given the bumper recipe to Tim each week, telling Tim to make sure he didn't alter one ingredient. Tim must have seen immediately that some of the proportions of ingredients didn't make sense. Tim was stuck between doing what he was told by the man who owned the show, and his dignity as a game-show writer. I smiled. A month back, that would have been a concept I couldn't even imagine. But now I had walked a mile in Tim Stock's Gucci loafers.

Tim would have been angry. He would have passed off the bad recipes to Quentin. Quentin, of course, was struggling anyway. He had been hired because of his connection to Chef Howie. Quentin would have been grateful to be given something to do, anything, that would make him feel secure on the show.

I looked up, startled. The section of audience sitting near me had just gasped. A large group of adults gasping in suspense can take your mind off anything. Their attention was riveted on the stage. On the

Kitchen Arena set, the two teams were chopping and filleting. The contestant chefs were working feverishly to get their pots of gumbo ready to cook. They were being judged on the grace they showed under pressure. On the side of the stage, a raised platform held the celebrity judges. Bowzer was hamming it up, his eyes circles, his mouth a gasping O. Belinda Holtz had drawn first blood. She had stabbed herself while trying to shell too many shrimp too quickly.

In the audience section nearby, Belinda's new boyfriend jumped up in agitation and shouted, "Get the medics!" All the other contestants went back to their intense work, but Chef Howie was there in an instant. He consulted with the team, checking Belinda's finger as she rinsed it in cold water.

Randy East's concerned voice filled the room, booming out over the rock and roll crescendos of the band. "This could be a crushing blow for a team of plucky individuals who overcame their own personal differences to cook together here tonight. Did you know that since winning on *Food Freak* earlier this year, Bruce Holtz has opened his own handmade ice cream shop in Wilmette, Illinois? And his ex, Belinda, has taken her quarter million and traveled around the world, tasting the best cuisines at the very best restaurants. Let's see what Chef Howie and the judges say."

Belinda's ex-husband, also an ex-marine, did a battlefield dressing, wrapping Belinda's finger tightly in a Band-Aid he had pulled out of his wallet. Then he kissed away her tears. The crowd screamed their approval. These two gourmets had determination and grit. Belinda said she wanted to continue and Chef Howie gave her the go-ahead sign. The crowd around me cheered their heads off. And the "Applause" sign didn't even have to remind them.

So Quentin had most likely written up the mangled bumper recipes, just doing what he was told, happy to keep his job. And this setup could very well account for all the cash Tim had resisted placing in a bank. A payoff for letting the bad recipes go out over the air and keeping his mouth shut. But what had changed? What had gone wrong?

I guessed that Tim was never let in on the truth. He didn't understand the deeper evil lurking behind those recipes. Maybe he resented getting mail saying his show's recipes weren't reliable. So he rebelled one time. On his own, he ordered that show number 10021 be fixed before it was broadcast. He must have found out soon after what those recipes were really used for—they represented addresses. And the person who lived at that altered address was soon dead. Immediately after that, Tim Stock ran.

Onstage, the clock was counting down the last few minutes of the cook-off as the rock band launched into their final song. Sydney Baker had begun to scoop out dollops of sour cream while her sister Marley was pulling fresh sourdough rolls out of the oven. Sour cream in gumbo? I was amazed. The Holtzes had recovered from Belinda's injury and were adding some last-minute crab legs to the pot. Chef Howie was excited and urging the crowd to go nuts. The audience screamed.

I turned to Holly as Randy's voice called out over the cook's melee onstage, "Don't go away! We'll be right back with the final revenge-filled minutes of 'THE FINAL FOOD FIGHT' . . ."

"Holly, come on."

"Where are we going?" she called out after me, and then caught up.

"I've got to call Honnett. I'm not sure how well I can hear my phone in here."

When we came to the heavy stage door, I pushed it open and found that the sky had gone dark during the time we'd been inside. It was nearly seven P.M. and the night air was chilly. When we were alone outside, I pulled my cell phone out and hit the Redial button. Noiselessly, it connected me with Honnett's cell phone in an instant. The marvels of modern technology. Honnett was just a button-push away.

"It's me," I said, breathless. "I've figured it out, Honnett. Not all of it, but enough."

"Where the hell are you?" His voice sounded agitated as it hit my ear. "I've got four uniforms out there and they have been on your lot for the past half hour. You aren't at your office. They checked."

"I've been down at the stage," I explained. "But it's okay. Holly is with me along with about two hundred healthy strangers in the audience. What's up?"

"We got a break," he said, his voice relaxing a little. "Look, I'm on my way over. I'll be there in fifteen minutes. Ten if I can manage it."

"You're coming here?" I was so relieved. I turned to Holly, who was rubbing her arms to keep them warm and told her, "Honnett's coming." And then I spoke to the cell phone, "I thought you were working on your Wednesday-night theory."

"It's all over," he said. "We've been there. We rounded up two real badasses tonight. We've made the arrests."

"What!"

"That address you gave me. We got over there right away. The guy who owns the place nearly wet himself when we told him there were some guys looking to whack him. He kept saying, 'Assassins.' "

"So he was involved with some drug dealers."

"Big time."

"What happened?"

"He was so scared that he might be on their hit list, he offered to turn state's evidence and we took him into protective custody. So we also got the name of three very rough dudes on arrest warrants tonight."

"I can't believe this."

"And then we had that house on San Gabriel Drive staked out and you wouldn't believe who walked into that net. We grabbed two separate guys out for a walk. Each was armed like you wouldn't believe. Both with priors. One actually broke into the house before we busted him. So that's two more scumbags on their way to jail tonight."

"So it's over?"

"It looks like we got pretty lucky on this end," Honnett said. "And I'm not sure how you figured it out. But until we know how your show got involved in this, you just stay put. Stay with Holly till I get there."

"Yes, sir," I said. "She's with me now. Aye-aye."

"Enough," he said. "You done good."

I smiled as I pushed the tiny "End Call" button on my cell phone. I turned to tell Holly all the news.

Only Holly was no longer standing a few feet away in the alley behind soundstage 9.

"You must be chilly, my dear."

The only other person standing out there was Artie Herman.

MUST have jumped.

"You nervous, Maddie?" Artie asked. His voice sounded some-where between disgusted and charming.

"Where's Holly?"

"While you were on the cell phone, there, I told her it was time for our celebrity judges to come onstage. She wanted to see them. Can you blame her? I told her not to worry about you. She said you shouldn't be left alone, so I volunteered to help out. Do you mind?"

"Let's go inside," I suggested. "I'm cold."

"Not yet," Artie said, his voice still low. "Let's talk first. I was just in-formed by the studio guards that there is a swarm of policemen at my office right now. Do you know about this?"

"No."

"Really? Well, that's odd, then. You see, they gave your name when they got to the guard gate. They thought you might need protection, Maddie. Why is that?"

"It's a mistake," I said. "But why are you so nervous, Artie? You seem pretty upset. Have you done something that might not look too good to the police?"

"Me?" he said. "I've done nothing."

A bulky man in a studio-guard uniform came around the corner. I was no longer alone with Arthur Herman, and I was incredibly relieved. I started toward the man who had come at just the right time.

"Yes, sir, you got trouble?" he asked Artie.

"Grab this girl and bring her inside. She's stolen material from my show."

"I have not!" I yelled, but the guard was twice as big as I was, and like a fool I had walked right up to him.

He grabbed me and twisted my arm in back and up high. Arms shouldn't go there. Tears leaped into my eyes. The pain was extraordinary and I couldn't think of anything else. The guard opened the soundstage door and thrust me forward down the little corridor. I yelled at him, "Please, this is a mistake. Let me go. The police are here, damnit. Go ask them!" But no one could have heard my screams. The band onstage was going nuts on their final song. The audience was whooping it up. Randy East's voice was amplified over it all as he counted down the seconds of the cook-off. "Six . . . five . . . four . . . three . . . two . . . one . . . IT'S ALL OVER!"

By the time it was officially "all over" onstage, I had the feeling it might be all over for me as well. I had been dumped in a tiny prop room in a remote corner of the huge soundstage. I was screaming as loud as I could, but no one could hear me now.

"Should I go get the cops, Mr. Herman?" asked the studio guard after he shoved me into the room.

"Let's not bother with that," Artie said. "It's much better to keep these things in-house and out of the papers. Just stand in the hall, in case I need your assistance."

"Sure thing," he said, despite my screams that Artie was going to kill me. Who would believe that? And he left me alone in the prop room with Artie.

"So what do you know, I wonder?" Artie asked, worried and angry. He made that sound I'd heard before, pushing a few puffs of air out his nostrils as he thought over what to do. "What have you told the police?" he asked me.

"Artie," I said, trying not to sob, "Artie, what are you doing? You don't want to hurt me. Let me out of here."

He blocked the door with a chair and sat down in it. "You'll forgive me for not offering you a chair," he said. "I just need a minute to think what I'm going to do."

I stood there, wondering if I could overpower him. He might be seventy, but he looked solid enough. And then there was the studio guard who would come to help him.

"So, what did you discover here, Miss Madeline Bean, in only two weeks of working on my show, that made you sic the police on me?"

"Nothing, " I said.

" 'Nothing,' " he repeated, looking up into my eyes. "I could almost believe you, cookie. What could a girl like you discover in two weeks? I'm frankly surprised you learned how to write a decent game-show question in two weeks. You are smart, my dear, but you are not that smart." He looked me over. "Who told you about it?"

"Look, Artie. I don't know what you are talking about."

His light eyes danced and he grew even angrier. "Was it Stock?"

"Artie . . ."

"Was it Stock?" he asked, making the accusation and looking at me for confirmation I shook my head. "Don't lie. It had to be. Tim Stock put you up to this, didn't he? Tim told you everything, that bastard. That bastard. Even though he swore to me up and down he would go away. He would just disappear. He promised on his mother's grave that he wouldn't tell a soul. Not a soul. I knew I shouldn't have trusted him. But I'm an old fool. Sure I was fond of Tim. Sure I was. But now I have a new problem."

I watched him as he tried to work it out. I kept hoping he'd say something that explained how he was connected to the trouble, but he was just rambling.

"And I won't let my family suffer, you understand? I won't make that kind of bargain. They come first. You can understand that, can't you? I should have kept my mind on my own troubles. I should have thought of Neal first. Sure, sure. But then, I couldn't let them kill Tim, could I?"

"You're saying you saved Tim?"

"What are you asking? Sure I did. Do you think I wanted to see anyone get hurt?"

"How can you ask that question, Artie? Look at what you've done to me."

"I have no choice. You gave me no choice. There were police at the gate. They had to be admitted, I was told. They were going to search my office. Why did you bring them here? Answer that. Why did Tim betray me when I went out on a limb to save his life?"

"Save his life? You got Tim into trouble, Artie. He was inserting those bumper recipes into the scripts for you, wasn't he?"

"Why ask me that? If Tim told you this, you already know!"

"And you paid him all that money to shut him up."

"Yes, they paid me and I paid him. I didn't take one penny. Not one. How can you blame me for that? Tim's the one who needed money. I just made sure he got paid in cash. He was going to England, he said. All right, so he helped me get the recipes in the scripts. That was his job, wasn't it? He worked for me. The extra money was a bonus."

"Then why did he change that one recipe? Why did Tim order the looping session?"

"Why?" Artie looked like he wanted to pull his fluffy white hair out. "Why? What kind of a question is that? You and Tim have been in on this together. You know why! Tim is no saint in this scheme, cookie. He agreed to look the other way and not get too involved with the bumper recipes. When this all started, I tried to keep him out of it, but he had too many questions. He was always a meticulous head writer. The best. So I had to offer him the deal. Money for his silence. At that time, he was just bugged the recipes were so damn inaccurate. He didn't know what the recipes meant, you see. Neither did I. We were both in the dark. The men who were behind this told us nothing. I swear."

"So they passed you the address information each week and you constructed the recipes and handed them to Tim."

He nodded.

"Then Tim gave them to Quentin, who submitted the material as his own," I said. "But what did you think it all meant? Why were those men paying Tim so much to keep quiet?"

"Tim already told you this," Artie said, disgusted. "We thought it was about the drugs. The whole thing was a mistake, I realize that. But we had the best intentions."

"You mean about your son. About Neal?"

"Yes, I'm sure you know all this. Neal has had some problems. All boys do sometime or another. He got in trouble with these men."

"Your son was selling drugs?"

"I don't know that. I just know they said he owed them a lot of money. Of course I was upset. I'm a father. Sure, I said, I'll pay his debts. They were going to hurt him, Madeline. My son. They said they didn't want my money. I told them I'd pay extra, anything, send my boy back home. But they wouldn't listen to me. They said they needed a good example. They said that if they killed Neal, it would teach the others out there what happens to someone who tries to cheat them.

"I couldn't persuade them. I tried. I have plenty of money, believe me, but they laughed at me and my money. They said it was too late for Neal to pay back his debt. He'd had his chance. So I went to them and begged. I'm an old man and I begged. I cried. He's my son. They must have sons. What could we do? How could we work out a deal?"

A tear escaped, and then another. Artie was reliving his worst nightmare. "They were only interested in my show," he said. "You'll love this part. These men. These animals. They were all big *Food Freak* fans. Can you imagine that? Well, why not? Forty million other people are addicted to the show, why not these drug-dealing swine. And they thought it would be funny if they could use my show to do their dirty work. They offered me that. My only deal. Take it or leave it. They would kill my boy as an example, or I could put these little recipes in each week's show. What was the harm?"

"Didn't you know the recipes were really addresses in code?"

"Sure, sure, I figured it out with Tim. We both knew they must be addresses. But we didn't know what they meant. We never dreamed the addresses would be used by hired killers. We figured it was about drug shipments, that sort of business. It was hard enough to live with the idea that we were probably giving drug dealers out there in America the address where some shipment was arriving or something like that. We didn't like it, but what were we going to do? When Tim decided to make that unauthorized change in one of the recipes, that's when we discovered the truth. Tim was the one who brought in the *L.A. Times* the next morning. He was physically ill. He figured we were being used to give out the addresses for some kind of gang murders. And because he changed those numbers in the recipe at the last minute, some poor woman had been killed by accident. I couldn't believe it." Artie, who had always looked more youthful than his years, was now an old man. He looked at a point somewhere beyond me and swore. "Those bastards! Those filthy bastards tied me and my show to something much worse than some dirty drug deal. They had turned my number one television series into an accomplice to murder. What was I going to do then?"

"That's when Tim went into hiding."

"Of course he did. Of course. I told him to go. I saved his ass."

"The people you were doing this for, they got angry when the recipe was altered," I said, filling in the pieces.

"Sure they were angry. Up until that week, they had been laughing at us. They had used my beautiful show for their dirty work and they laughed at us because we didn't even know what we were helping them do. But after that lady was killed and her address was in the paper, we knew. They couldn't allow us to have anything on them, you see, so they were going to kill Tim and make me help them do it. That way they could trust me again, they said. They said put Tim's address in the next show." Another tear fell down Artie Herman's old cheek.

"And you couldn't do it. You told Tim to hide?"

"Sure I told him to hide! I told him to stay away from that house like it was the plague. That house would be a deathtrap. What else could I do? I couldn't ignore their orders or they'd kill my boy, Neal. I had to put that recipe on the air to show them I was not going to cross them. But I told Tim to stay away. If you don't believe me you can go ask Fate. She was in my office when I spoke to Tim on the phone. She didn't know squat about what we were saying, but she heard me loud and clear. I told Tim not to go near his house on Wednesday night. And even after that. Once that address had been broadcast, who knew how greedy some of these contract killers might be. They could stalk that house for weeks, months, until they had their kill and could collect their reward. I didn't want Tim's blood on my hands. I didn't want any of them."

"But what will you do now?" I asked him. "You keep getting in deeper and deeper. Tim may have been kept safe, but Quentin Shore died last week. Tonight, you put another address out there. Did you think of that?"

Artie wiped away another tear. "I have to save my boy. That's my job. These are gangsters you are worried about getting killed."

"Are they going to kill me, Artie, just to shut me up? Are they going to find Tim and kill him, too, now? You can't pretend you aren't responsible."

"Why did you have to get involved?" he asked, angry again.

"It's over now, Artie. The police know all about the addresses."

He stared at me, a lost old man.

"They went out to that home on San Gabriel Drive tonight. They arrested two men who were caught trying to get into the house. And tonight's intended victim? He is going to testify against the men who put out the hit over the air on your show."

"How do you know that?" he asked.

"My friend is working on the case for the LAPD," I said. "I was just talking to him on the phone when you got rid of Holly and dragged me in here, against my will."

"Just to talk," Artie said, starting a fresh tale.

"You can't twist the truth anymore, Artie."

"It will be your word against mine," he said, angry again.

"Not exactly." I pulled my cell phone out of my bag. This was the reason I had been so calm. This was what had given me strength. The phone was on. I held it up so Artie could see the elapsed time still ticking off the seconds of the live call. "The police have been listening in. They've heard every word you said."

The moment Artie had surprised me out in the alley, I had just ended a call with Honnett. It took only half a second to push the Redial button and drop the tiny phone into my purse before Artie had any ideas about taking it away. All that time, I knew Honnett was tracking our conversation, so I pushed Artie for more answers.

"Can I go then?" I asked, rubbing my sore arm.

Artie stared at the phone, his eyes desperate now. "The police? What have I said? I never hurt you or threatened you! I'm an old man, Madeline." Artie's forehead showed beads of sweat. "Sometimes when I forget to take a pill, it can leave me disoriented and I don't know what I'm . . ."

"It would look better if you turned yourself in, Artie," I said, holding up the phone. Every word we spoke was being heard.

"Give me a head start," Artie said, making a final deal. "I'll meet the police in a few minutes. I was a pawn. You know that. I was being blackmailed and coerced. These men, these scum, were threatening to kill my son. I had no choice. And, look, Madeline, I had no idea what those men were really up to. They never told me. So I was a victim, too. I will testify. I am a respected businessman. My testimony has to be worth ten times what that drug dealer's testimony is worth. Let me go and I'll be back in a minute."

"The police are probably all over this studio by now."

"I know a shortcut," Artie said. "I just need to gather my thoughts. That's fair, isn't it?"

I watched as Artie Herman moved the chair aside and slipped out of the prop room. I ran to the door, but when I opened it, he and the guard were gone.

I put my cell phone to my ear, so relieved it was over and Honnett had heard the whole thing.

"Honnett? I'm safe."

"Maddie!" The voice was not Honnett's. It wasn't even a male voice. And there was a hint of an Asian accent, too.

"Who is this?" I asked, shocked.

"This is Anna," said the voice. "What is going on there? We were worried."

I looked down at my phone. I had not redialed Honnett's number. Oh my God. I must have hit the speed dial button by accident. All the time I'd been pushing Artie to confess, I'd been connected to the receptionist at the May Moon Nail Salon.

30

HIS is the best thing I have ever tasted."

I turned and saw a good-looking guy, tall and thin, dip his spoon into the steaming bowl of gumbo. He was leaning against the wall next to the buffet table, chatting to Holly, who was serving up hearty bowlfuls to all of the cast and crew of *Food Freak*.

"I'd marry a woman who could cook like this," said the tall blond guy.

Holly grinned and pointed to me. "There she is."

The tall blond guy looked over at me and smiled. His eyes were friendly and I tried to place where I'd seen him before. Obviously he worked on the crew of *Food Freak*, but he didn't look like crew. He looked more rock and roll. That was it. He was one of the musicians in the show's band.

As wrap parties go, the one for *Food Freak* was looking to be a knockout success. After slaving away to prepare the "Final Food Fight" episode, we were all long overdue for a celebration. Our decision to serve Cajun cuisine turned out to be extremely popular after that night's cook-off. It seemed everyone's appetite had been whetted watching the contestant chefs preparing their versions of the spicy stew. Gumbo, as I wrote in my first and, alas, last job as a TV writer, is a Louisiana soup that blends the rich cuisines of the Indian, French, Spanish, and African cultures.

Holly left her post behind the buffet table and joined me as I scoped out the party in progress. "Hey," she said, as we walked together to get drinks. "You got yourself a very cute fan back there."

"He looks young," I said, smiling.

"He looks gorgeous," Holly replied. "If I didn't have extreme news right this very second, I'd go for him myself."

"News?" I stopped. We had come to the area near the stage where the bar had been set up. "Wait a sec," I told her and then I ordered a Diet Coke from the gal who was tending bar. "Want one?" I asked Holly.

But she had moved over to the punch station. Wesley had designed a display that featured a series of retro punch bowls, which had been artfully lighted. In the center of each bowl was a different culinary-themed ice sculpture. One sculpture showed the *Food Freak* logo; one was of Chef Howie's head. The crystal punch bowls contained different flavors of Kool-Aid.

"This is so neat," Holly said, filling her cup with a ladleful of bright blue liquid.

"Did you know that Kool-Aid twists come in Berry Blue again?" I asked her, excited to share the news. Wes and I had gone on the Web and had just found out. "Isn't that awesome?"

"Why, Maddie. I never realized you were such a connoisseur of packaged powdered beverages."

I laughed. The things I had gotten into.

"And did you know," she asked me back, "that Kool-Aid makes a new Magic Twist that starts out one color but then changes into another color?"

"Whoa!" I realized I was in the presence of someone who had an even deeper knowledge base. "I defer to your greater wisdom on this subject."

"Schnitzel!" Holly cursed. "Oh, rats! This sweater is brand new."

She had turned too quickly and a slosh of Berry Blue Kool-Aid had splashed out of her cup and onto her white silk sweater. "You think that will come out?"

I smiled up at her. "Not a chance."

The music had been going strong throughout the night, but now that dinner was being served, the four big-screen televisions had been tuned to the network as the final episode of *Food Freak* aired on the West Coast.

"What's your news?" I asked Holly, hoping to take her mind off her turquoise-spotted sweater.

"Oh, Mad. I've got to get Donald. We've got to tell you this together." She looked over the crowd and waved. Donald, dressed in black, crossed the floor to meet up with us at the Kool Aid bar.

"Sweetie," Holly said. "You've gotta taste the Berry Blue!" And she turned and ladled him a cup.

"Hi, Maddie," he said to me. "So, what do you think?"

"I haven't told her yet," Holly said.

"Holly and I are getting married," Donald said, with a big smile.

"We're driving to Vegas tonight," Holly added, giggling and handing over the cup to Donald. "Isn't that the best news you ever heard in your life? I'm so happy!"

"Honey!" I said, hugging Holly and then hugging Donald.

"Do you give us your blessing?" Donald asked, beaming. Just then Wesley walked up to our group.

"Hi, kids," he said. "Well, I can't believe the buzz we're getting over the Kool-Aid. It's just hitting everybody's spot. Mad, you are a true kitsch genius."

"Did you hear Holly and Donald's big news?" I asked, still stunned. "They are getting married."

"No!" Wes said, as shocked as I was.

"Tonight," Holly added.

"Get out!" Wes said, shocked even more.

"We're eloping," Donald said. "Isn't that fun?"

"But, Holly," I said, whining a little bit. "I want to see you get married."

"Both of you come with us," Donald offered. "It'll be great."

"Well," I said, looking at Wesley.

"Well, why not?" Wesley answered. "We'll be dead tired, but why not?"

On the big screen nearest us, I noticed that the first segment of *Freak* was just ending. Randy East's voice was describing the perfect recipe for guacamole. When I heard him read off the ingredients, I became quite still. I turned to see if Honnett had made it to the party yet.

There he was, standing toward the back of the large room, apart from the crowd.

"Later," I told Holly and Donald and Wes, and I walked over to talk to the cop in my life.

"Say, it looks like one hell of a party," Honnett said when I joined him.

"Wes did most of it. It's been fun, for once, to be a guest at one of our parties."

"So you know we took your boss in for questioning."

"Artie? I figured you would."

"He was unexpectedly candid in his statement. I believe I've got you to thank for that. He seemed under the impression I'd already heard it before."

"A gift," I said, unwilling to go into further details about my manicurist.

"We'll need to get a statement from you, but right now I'm not sure we can charge him with much more than accessory to murder-for-hire on one of the hits."

"Will you let him make a deal?" I asked, aware again of how much life imitates game shows.

"We'll see. Probably. Doesn't look like we can prove he had any idea what those recipe-addresses meant until after the woman was killed in Burbank. We're better off getting him to help us put away the drug dealers. They are the guys we want off the street."

I nodded, thinking of how everything in life seems to be a trade-off. "Once you make L.A. safe from drug traffickers, you can then move on to cleaning our streets of game-show producers. It's priorities."

Honnett gave me a wry smile. "Glad you understand how it works."

"Have you figured out any reason why Quentin Shore was over at Tim's house last Wednesday night?" I asked Honnett.

He just shook his head. "We may never know. Wrong place at the wrong time."

Over at the bar, there was a commotion as a short, heavyset young man was complaining about his drink to the bargirl. I was surprised to see such ugly behavior at a private party where, at any rate, most of the staff had just started drinking. "I'd better go see what that's about," I said to Honnett.

"No, wait," he said. "That's the guy I'm looking for. That's Neal Herman, the son. Looks like he's pretty wasted."

"That's Neal Herman?" I looked at him and realized there was a resemblance to Artie there. Neal was like a fleshed-out younger version. "You know, he's listed as one of the writers on the show."

"His dad sends him his paycheck. That's about the extent of his involvement," Honnett said. "That, and dragging his father down with him. I'm going to take him downtown and get his statement, too."

"You've got to go?" I turned and held Honnett's arm, looking up at him. "I wish you could come to Vegas with Holly and the rest of us. She's getting married tonight. Isn't that insane? I don't know whether I should try to talk her out of it, or just keep my big mouth shut. It's not like I'm one to give advice about relationships." I gave him a smile. "Although we're doing pretty well, don't you think?"

"Oh, Maddie." Honnett looked away. "You are not making this easy."

And then I woke up. Something had been strained between us, but I'd thought it was a little something. I sipped my Diet Coke and waited.

"Look, Madeline, I have to tell you something. It's not about you and me. It's about the other part of my life."

"You being a detective, you mean?"

"Well, no. About my wife."

"Your . . . wife?" I have prided myself in handling shocking news. I love nothing more than being truly accepting of life's slings and arrows. Stay detached, that's my motto. What goes down must come up. But all the platitudes and Buddhist sayings in the world had not prepared me for that one word.

"My ex-wife," Honnett corrected. "I told you I had a past. You knew I'd been married before."

"Ye-es."

"I've been married twice. I told you that."

"So what is it with your ex-wife, then?" I asked, my voice sounding tenser to my ears than I'd hoped.

"Well, not exactly 'ex' yet. Marie and I have been separated for two years. And now she wants to see if we can give it another try."

"What? What are you telling me?" I looked at him hard. "Are you saying you want to go back to your . . . your *wife*? I can't believe we're actually saying these words. I can't believe you lied to me. You said you were *divorced*. Twice." I have zero patience for women who date married men. And now, it turned out, I was one of them. "Damnit, Honnett! You said you were divorced twice. What was that? A convenient way to seduce me? You're a freaking cop, Honnett. You're not supposed to lie!"

"I said I'd been married twice, Maddie. I didn't say I was divorced. I told you I'd been living on my own the past two years. I didn't lie."

I stared at him, my eyes stinging. "You didn't lie? What did you think? I would date some guy who still had a wife?"

He looked away.

"Look," I said, calming my voice the hell down through an extreme exertion of will, "I can't talk about this right now. I've got to help—"

"Madeline!" Greta Greene walked into the party and spotted me off to the side.

I turned to Honnett and said, "Good-bye. Good luck."

"Maddie . . . ," he said, taking a step after me, but I wouldn't turn back. I couldn't bear to look at him, with his beautiful eyes and his sexy cheekbones. Instead, I made myself walk over to greet Greta.

"Maddie, I can't believe how brilliant this party is!" Greta was celebrating, and not with plain old Kool-Aid. "See, I told you we'd do it up right, and you certainly did."

"How are you?" I asked, making it all the way over to where she was standing without looking back. Greta, her petite figure enhanced by a stylish emerald-green pantsuit, lifted her glass of champagne in a toast.

"Here's to a dozen years at the top," she offered. I clicked my Diet Coke glass to her champagne flute. "Artie called me an hour ago," she said. "All is forgiven, he said. He wants me back. He's made me executive producer, and get this, he's retiring."

I realized Artie was true to form. After humiliating Greta and firing her in a rage, he now needed her more than ever.

"He's so sorry he unloaded on me, but you know, sometimes these creative guys can really lose it."

"Tell me about it," I said. "Did Artie mention anything about the police?" I asked.

"No. Why? Is this about the fire at Tim's house?" she asked, suddenly very interested.

"You'll hear all about it later. So," I said, adjusting to the fact that Greta was back, again, "did you see the final show? Did you like it?"

"It's horrible!" Greta said, aghast, pointing her champagne flute in the direction of the giant television monitor closest to us. "The music's not bad, but the look is all wrong." We watched a little of the program together. On camera, the contestants were just learning that the surprise dish they would be preparing was gumbo.

On camera, a very relaxed and charming Chef Howie was explaining, "Gumbo is a Louisiana soup that blends the rich cuisines of the Indian, French, Spanish, and African cultures. The word 'gumbo' is derived from an African term for okra, 'gombo,' and the very first recipe for this dish appeared in print in 1805. One of your most important ingredients in preparing gumbo is filé powder, which we use as a thickener. It is actually made from ground sassafras leaves and came to the recipe from the Choctaw Indians. There are no hard-and-fast rules for making gumbo beyond the basic roux, okra, filé powder, *and* your imagination. So get ready! There are probably as many distinctive recipes for gumbo as there are cooks in Louisiana. Or cooks right here, in *Food Freak*'s red-hot Kitchen Arena!"

"I wrote that," I blurted out, unable to shut up about what little parts of the show had been my personal contribution.

"That was delightful," Greta said kindly, and I instantly suspected she didn't really mean it. Ah, well. "I knew Artie would go down the toilet without me," she continued, returning to her original point. "But, next season we'll get back on track. My only foreseeable problem is Fate Finkelberg. God save me from Fate!"

I toasted her on that one.

"Oh," she added, in great spirits, "did you hear Chef Howie's news?"

I shook my head.

"He's been cast in the new Spielberg."

"You're kidding."

"I wouldn't kid an old friend like you," she said. "I believe they are doing a remake of *Marty* and they want Chef Howie to be Marty."

"No way," I said, laughing. "Will Chef Howie play the Ernest Borgnine role?" I couldn't stop laughing at the picture of the pretty-boy chef playing a lonely aging momma's boy. What a town.

On the big monitor, the last episode of *Food Freak* was still playing. The show had progressed to the part where the contestants had begun the final cook-off. I was mesmerized by how different the show looked from how I remembered it. As I had watched it during the taping, it seemed like a manic play. I was struck by the energy of the room, the reactions of the audience, the live spectacle. On the screen, now, I noticed that the show was more about fancy hand-held camera angles and quick cuts. I had to admit, the close-up views of butter melting in a black skillet juxtaposed with hands sprinkling flour a little at a time to make the basic roux and then a quick cut to the faces of each of the contestant-chefs was effective. With the rock-music background, the final cook-off looked like a great big sexy rock video where gumbo was the star. This must be part of the attraction of this series. The director, Pete Steele, deserved a lot of credit. I thought I'd look for him and tell him.

The crowded party scene was warming up. Most of the guests had, by that time, made their way through the buffet line. Many were seated at the clusters of tables positioned around the Kitchen Arena set, enjoying their dinner by candlelight. Wes had scattered dozens of chunky white block candles around the tables and their warm glow made the large set seem cozy and intimate.

At the serving table, two of our waiters were helping the last of the guests. I was reassured to see there seemed to be more than enough oysters Bienville left. More than enough is exactly the quantity we caterers aim for. The oysters had been baked on the half shell and then topped with a sherry-flavored béchamel sauce mixed with sautéed chopped shrimp, shallots, and garlic. Out in the mobile kitchen, one of my chefs was baking them in batches, to keep the dish that was named for the second colonial governor of Louisiana fresh. For those who stayed away from seafood, we were offering grilled andouille sausages and Cajun dirty rice. We also had platters of Southern-fried chicken. For dessert, three chefs were out front making our version of bananas Foster we called Mad Banana Crepes.

"Oh, Mad," Holly said, walking up to me. "Your cell phone has been beeping." She handed it to me. Holly had borrowed it a while back and I'd completely forgotten about it.

"Did you answer it?" I asked.

"Yeah. A guy called you. Maybe two or three times. Said his name was Karl. Said he met you at the Swine Bar."

"What?"

"That's what he said. Where is that Swine Bar? On Sunset?"

"I don't know anyone named . . ." Wait a minute. At Pierce College. The farm manager. I had given him my card.

"Not the Swine Bar," I said, laughing at Holly. "The swine *barn*. I met this guy in a barn, Hol. With pigs."

"Whatever," she said, shaking her head. "He left this number." She handed me a slip of paper.

I moved away from the diners to a quieter spot and dialed. The cell phone reception was spotty inside the soundstage, but I got enough of a signal to hear the call go through. I counted the rings. After the third, I heard a man's voice. "Hello."

"Hello. This is Madeline Bean. Is this Karl?"

"Sort of," the voice said.

That stopped me. I mean, either you are or you aren't. "Are you the guy I met at Pierce College?"

"Yes," he said. "You gave me your business card, remember?"

"Yes," I said, feeling back on firmer footing. "I'm in the middle of a pretty loud party right now," I explained, "and I—"

"I know," said Karl. "I'm here, too."

"Wait. You're at the *Food Freak* party? Right now?" I swung around and scanned the crowd. Had Susan invited her friend from the farm to our wrap party?

"No, but I'm here on the lot. Look, I need to talk to you," Karl said. "Could we meet up somewhere a little more private?"

"How about outside?" I suggested. "In the mobile kitchen. Know where that is? It's a big orange-and-white tent."

"I'll find it. I have a surprise for you."

31

A SURPRISE? I thought about what sort of surprise the good-looking farm manager could have for me as I edged my way through the crowd on the dance floor and then walked to the back of the soundstage building. Perhaps he was going to suggest some summer classes in animal husbandry. I pushed open the heavy stage door and exited. In the night air, I smelled the smoke of a few nearby cigarette fiends, outside catching up on their nicotine. They said hi. Then I turned the corner and headed for Wes's mobile kitchen.

The smell of grilled sausage and Cajun spices greeted me at the door to the tent. Several of our catering staff were cleaning up and taking breaks. Wes was there, having a glass of champagne, and when he saw me enter, he picked a half-empty bottle of Crystal out of a bucket of ice, gesturing. I nodded. I was ready to relax and I sighed as I watched Wes pour.

"What's new in there?" Wes asked as I took a sip of champagne.

I looked at my watch. "Show is still on for another half hour. And dinner is going very well. It's a great wrap party, Wes."

"What I like to hear," he said, smiling.

"I'm supposed to meet a guy," I said. "Someone I met out at Pierce College."

"That the one?" Wes asked, looking back over my shoulder.

At the entrance to the tent stood Karl, the guy from the farm. Next to him was Susan. Just what I had imagined.

"See you in a bit," I told Wes and then walked over to Susan and Karl. "Want something to drink?"

"No thanks, Maddie." Susan smiled at me shyly.

"Karl, I presume," I said, turning to the guy I remembered from the college, the one who'd evicted me from the pigpens. I noticed that he was still packing some nice muscles under his sweater.

"Well, actually, *not* Karl," Susan said. "Tim."

That would be the absolute last time I was ever tricked by an embroidered name on a uniform shirt. Honestly.

"This is *Tim*? Tim Stock?"

"Yes. Hi." Tim held out his hand to shake mine.

Well, well, well. I finally got to meet the man whose office had provided me with such a fine assortment of new experiences. Or, perhaps I should rephrase that. We'd already met, but I had never suspected who he really was. He'd been out at the swine barn wearing a shirt sporting the name "Karl," so I'd never imagined he didn't belong there, right along with the hay and the mud. I recalled the note Susan had left for Tim on the subscription card in the *Gourmet* magazine — "6 A.M. Thursday." Apparently, Tim was there at the appointed time after all.

"Nice to see you again, Tim. Finally. Well, I guess you heard what happened tonight."

"We heard," Susan said. "Is it all true? Is Artie going to jail?"

"I wouldn't put money on it," I said. "But the men who have been threatening Tim are as good as gone. There are a number of people who are telling the police all they know, including Artie. Those drug dealers will not be bothering anyone for a long, long time."

Susan buried her head in Tim's shoulder and he squeezed her in a big bear hug. They were just so darn cute, those two.

"So I guess you are free to go home," I said.

"Thanks, Madeline," Tim said, meeting my eyes. "Susan told me everything you have been doing for her. You've been an incredible friend. I don't know how you managed this, but we are truly grateful."

"We're moving to England," Susan said. "Isn't that crazy? I can't believe it, but we're going to take the boys and move."

"You can take the dogs?" I asked.

"I was worried, but then Tim figured out the perfect plan. They have a new program. We get the boys microchipped, blood-sampled, and vaccinated by our own vet, and once we get an all-clear at six months, Niko, Khailo, and Thorn can travel with us without the quarantine. Tim knows everything."

"I knew Susan wouldn't leave the boys," Tim said. "And I couldn't leave them either."

"Tim's going to buy us a country house with a patch of pasture."

"For Susan's flock," Tim said, looking at Susan like he couldn't believe his luck.

"About the money I found in the cookbooks," I said, "my partner, Wesley, has been keeping the fifty thousand dollars in his safe and—"

Tim held up his hand and interrupted. "No. Please. I could never keep that money. I wish I'd never had anything to do with it."

Susan met his eyes and Tim sighed.

"Would you do us one more favor?" Tim continued, his voice calmer. "Could you turn it all over to one of the police investigators?"

"I know just the one," I said. Cop cheats on me with his own freaking non-ex-wife and I hand him the fifty grand to seal his case. That's just the kind of good-natured woman I am.

"Thanks, Maddie," Susan said.

It would be safer this way, I knew. Once the drug gang heard the cops had confiscated the payoff money, they'd lay off and leave Tim alone. He and Susan would be free of it all.

"So we'll have a little less to start our dream on," Susan said, not sounding in any way put out. "I can work a little. I'll sell some of my fleece and hold dying workshops."

"And I'll keep writing questions, part time, while I work on my book," Tim said. "I know a guy who is starting an interactive quiz game on the Internet, so I can work from home."

Maybe it wasn't as ideal as their original dream, but, honestly, what ever is? It got them out of Hollywood and out of game shows. They'd be fine.

"Look," Tim said, "another thing. That night you were hit on the head . . ."

"You know about that?"

Tim nodded. "I was in the hidden bedroom, right next door. I heard a noise, which must have been you falling down. Then it got really quiet. I was worried, so I opened the bookcase and there you were. On the floor. I didn't know what to do. I mean, I was still in hiding, but . . ."

"So you were the one who picked me up? You carried me over to the sofa?"

Tim nodded. "I wish I had been able to do more. You seemed to be okay, just knocked out."

"Did you see who did it? Do you know who attacked me?"

"I'm not sure . . ." Tim shook his head.

"Tim thinks it was Artie," Susan said. "He saw Artie hanging around when he should have been up in his own office. Luckily, Artie didn't see Tim. But we thought you should know."

"Artie attacked me?"

"I don't know," Tim said. "Maybe he was worried about what else I'd uncovered about his dirty deals and thought he'd look around my office. He probably figured the office would be empty that late at night. But there you were. He probably thought you were such an over-achiever, you'd be working there all night."

"So that angry, bitter egomaniac just decided to bash me over the head and get on with his errand? What a frightening little man."

"I'm so sorry," Tim said.

"*Food Freak*," I muttered.

"Great job, eh?" Tim asked, and smiled at me.

"I want to do something special for you," Susan said, holding my hand. "We would like you to come out to England next spring. We should be settled by then. Tim's going to go up to London to do his research on day trips, and I'll be home tending my sheep."

"Will you teach me how to dye wool?" I asked, smiling at her.

"Of course. We'll have a great time. But I want to do something more. I want to name our first lamb after you. Our first British-born lamb." Susan's eyes were bright behind her tiny wire rims. "Madilamb Bean."

I was speechless.

"And if there is anything I can ever do to help you," Tim said, "like if you need something researched . . ." He laughed. "But now that you are a game-show writer, I guess you can do that for yourself. You have all the questions and answers you need."

"I guess the only answer I'm missing is what really happened to Quentin Shore. Do you have any idea what he was doing at your house the night of the fire?"

Tim looked down. "I can't believe he's dead. I can't explain how horrible I feel. Like it happened on my property, so I'm responsible. Like I should have warned everyone in the universe to stay away. But I had never invited Quentin over to my house in my life. I didn't even realize he knew where I lived. I cannot imagine what he was doing there that night."

"Tim feels a lot of guilt, Maddie," Susan said quietly.

"Of course I feel guilty. While Quentin was being murdered, the killer thought he was killing me."

Susan turned to me. "But Artie made Tim promise not to tell anything to anybody. Not even to me. That's why Tim dropped out of sight. And for the past week he's been living with my sheep."

"Excuse me," I said, shocked at the revelation that had just hit me. Now I remembered what Artie had said. Looking at everything from a new angle, it had all suddenly come into focus. "I've got to see someone right away." And before they could question my incredibly rude behavior, I ran out of the tent.

Inside the soundstage, "*Food Freak* Revenge: The Final Food Fight" was on all the video screens, playing down its final minutes on the air. The celebrity judges were being interviewed. Four giant shots of J.Lo's perfect complexion filled the monitors.

I found the woman I was looking for sitting alone. The candles on her table had burned hollows under their wicks. Pools of clear melted wax shined under the dancing flames.

"Fate," I said. "May I join you?"

"Why not?" Fate Finkelberg turned to watch the last moments of *Food Freak* on the monitors.

"Quite a show," I said.

"Not bad," Fate said, not turning to look at me. "Howie is getting up-staged by that awful Tobey Maguire, but that's what we get for letting a hack like Pete Steele direct. Next season he is gone."

"I guess you heard that Artie is talking with the police," I said.

That got a quick glance from Fate. "So?"

"So, he's telling them everything. He's cooperating fully. I think they'll let him off with just a hand slapping if he gives them what they want to lock up the really bad guys."

"I haven't followed it closely," Fate said, waving a hand.

"Of course, he told them he knew there was going to be a hit or-dered last week. He knew it because he was coerced into putting Tim Stock's address out on the air. In code. You knew about that, right?"

On the big screen, Chef Howie was in a close-up. He was telling us we'd get the judges' final verdicts after these commercials. With only a Subaru ad on the screens, Fate turned back to face me. "I didn't know anything," Fate said, her expression like stone.

"Sure you did," I said. "You knew that some very dangerous men were going to be stalking anyone who was found at 12226 Lemon Grove Drive, because you were in Artie's office when he was telling Tim to stay away. You overheard it all. Artie didn't realize how clever you are. He al-ways underestimated the women he worked with, didn't he?"

Fate continued to stare at me. She said nothing.

"Then," I went on, "you found out about Chef Howie and his ro-mantic fling."

Fate flinched at that word.

"So you had Howie followed. You hired a private investigator. You told me all about it, remember?"

"So what? That means nothing."

"No? I suppose you didn't finally get a report from that investigator. A report that proved your husband was just as unfaithful as you had suspected. And your PI wouldn't be able to provide the police with a copy of the photos he made?" Fate looked extremely uncomfortable but I pressed on. "So, then you're all right."

"What do you want from me?" Fate hissed. "What did I ever do to you?"

"Not that much, I guess. But then, you really didn't have the time. You were too busy sending poor Quentin Shore on an errand over to Tim's house. Perhaps you suggested he might be the one to take over as head writer on *Food Freak* next year? He just needed to do you one favor, I bet you told him. Like get some records that were being stored in Tim Stock's garage. Go after the show airs on Wednesday night. Don't worry. No one will be home. Just wait there for you." I looked at Fate. "Does any of this ring a bell?"

"Shut up. Shut up! None of this is true. You're insane."

On the big screen, *Food Freak* had resumed. It was time for the final announcement of the show's new champion chefs. We were about to learn who would win the fairy-tale chateau in France. This was the part I had missed last time.

"Tell me what you want." Fate's harsh voice rasped. "Money?"

"Shh," I said to her, holding up my hand. All around us the cast and crew were quieting down to watch the final moments of the show. "I want to see this."

Fate was growing more and more agitated. She reached out her hand to grab my wrist and in the process knocked over a candle. Hot wax spilled over the white damask tablecloth and a few drops splattered on Fate's arm. "Ahh!"

"Shh," I chided.

"So you know everything. Did you know I'm the one who turned Tim's office upside down? I had to figure out what Artie was talking about. He told Tim not to go near his house, but I had to know why. I used my key to get into the office while you were out at that meeting. I found the newspaper article he had clipped about that woman's murder. I looked through all the old scripts and I figured it out. Those stupid recipes. They were sending out hit men and the best part was, the killers didn't even know who they were intended to murder. How could I let such a perfect opportunity slip away?"

I wasn't looking at Fate, but I was listening. Her confession almost made me miss the crowning moment of the show, when the judges awarded the grand prize by a vote of two to one to the Baker sisters. The winner's theme music blasted out over the speakers and everyone at the party cheered. The three Baker siblings, standing near the Kool-Aid bar and enjoying their victory once again, came forward and took a little bow.

"And I'm going to get away with it," Fate told me. "I will deny everything. All you have is a lot of speculation and there is no way to prove it. So go ahead. Pat yourself on the back, Maddie. You're a smart girl. Now you will just have to live with knowing what you know and still having nothing you can do about it. When you think of it that way, not everything is worth the pain to figure it out, is it, smart girl?"

Fate jumped up from the table and walked straight out of the room.

I got up to follow her, not that there was anything I could do to stop her. She was right. On my way to the door, I was approached by Dawn Weiss, *Food Freak*'s receptionist. "Hi, there," she said, stepping in my path.

"I'm sorry, Dawn. There is someone I have to see."

"That's okay," Dawn said. "I'm going that way, too. I'll walk you."

I was moving quickly across the stage and Dawn had no trouble matching my strides. "I owe you a big thanks," Dawn said as we walked outside. "You got me the break I had been looking for."

I couldn't see Fate. She could have gone in any direction.

"So thanks," Dawn said, her voice happy.

"Thanks for what?" I turned to Dawn

"I was hired as a game-show writer," Dawn said, her cheerleader smile at its zenith of cheeriness.

"You what?"

"And it's really thanks to you. Remember this morning? You told me about that cat?"

There was no use in my trying to find Fate Finkelberg. What could I do now, anyway? I tried to refocus on Dawn. What was she going on about?

"The cat?" Oh, yes. The CAT. I had to smile at that. "So you found him?"

"Oh, yes. Darling lion, isn't he? And then I found out that *Let's Make a Deal* was back in production and looking for writers."

"Really?"

"Really. And I submitted material this afternoon, and I was hired by five. You know, Artie was not doing anything for me. I tried to call him all afternoon, so he could make me a better offer. That bastard. He never even called me back. I'm sorry I wasted a few good evenings on the jerk."

I daresay. "So when do you start your new job?"

"I've already started. We're taping tonight on soundstage two. You should come by after the party and check it out. Only be careful. They are keeping our 'cat' on soundstage three. Just a word to the wise."

"Thanks, Dawn. And good luck."

"No luck needed," she said. "I've got a plan. I'm only twenty-four and I'm already joining the Writers' Guild." With that, she gave me a killer smile and turned toward soundstage 2.

Plans are great, I thought, but you need luck in life, too. Wait until Dawn was as old and wise as I had become. I smiled.

The door opened from our soundstage. Some of the show's crew were already departing. It was after ten o'clock, the broadcast was now over, and these guys had put in a long day. One of the handheld camera operators was walking with his wife. He left her for a moment to go back in and get his DVD player.

She smiled at me. "Did you watch the show?" she asked. She was a pretty woman with red hair and a few extra pounds.

"I'm one of the writers," I said, and then smiled to myself. First and last time I'd get to say those words.

"Congratulations. I thought it was a great show. I was here for the taping, too. The sisters," she said, chattering on, "those great sisters. I thought it would go to the Holtzes because when Belinda cut her finger and kept on going, she really won my heart over. But it was the sisters who got the castle," she said. "I think it was because of the guys on the celebrity jury. You know?"

"You think the guy from Sha Na Na appreciated their charms?" I asked, intrigued by the psychology that goes along with these reality-based shows.

"No doubt," said the redhead. "You don't really have to know how to cook if you look like they do."

I shook my head. Is this what my short visit to planet Game Show had all boiled down to? As if the game wasn't insubstantial enough, the *real* reason people were hooked on the show turns out to be even shallower than that?

And yet, to me, the attraction of a game goes much deeper. I am taken with the idea that in one short show all the questions are answered. The ones who are right are rewarded; the ones who are wrong lose. It was simple. I wanted simple answers. Couldn't life be like that?

What I hated was ambiguity. That's why I had been so upset with the trouble at *Food Freak* from the start: a man was missing. There is nothing so frightening. I had learned that very young. If they never find a person, how can you tell it's okay to grieve? If you stay detached, you don't feel it that much when a man goes missing. Like with Honnett. And with Arlo, my past boyfriend. And with Xavier, my former fiancé. And with Simon. With each passing man in my life, I had managed to stay just that much more detached.

I felt the urge to cry but it never came to the surface. When men go missing, what can you do? You have to carry on, right?

I stood there, alone in the silent street, outside soundstage 9. I knew I should go back in. I wasn't dressed for the cool of a fifty-five-degree March evening in Los Angeles. But I stayed there a bit longer, just thinking. I heard the stage door open again and I waited until the next departing crew members passed me on their way to the parking lot.

"You look cold."

I turned my head.

It was the tall blond guy, the musician. "Hi, I'm John Quinn," he said.

"Madeline Bean."

Just then Chef Howie came out of our soundstage, looking worried.

"Madeline," he said, coming up to us. "Do you know where soundstage three is?"

"Soundstage three?"

"It's around there," John said, pointing.

"I just got a call on my cell phone. Fate wants to leave. She has been out here in the cold walking around, she said. Now she wants me to get the car and pick her up. She said it was too cold outside, so she was going to wait for me inside soundstage three. What is with that woman? Is she crazy? I don't want her to be all alone at night in some deserted, empty soundstage."

The quiet night became a little less quiet just then. A disturbing sound came from the direction of soundstage 3. The sort of sound that is only heard at night in Kenya. Or in one of those wild animal parks. Or in a zoo. It was the roar of a hungry lion.

"What was that?" Chef Howie asked, uneasy as a tribesman on the Serengeti.

Tonight, I recalled suddenly, soundstage 3 was not altogether empty. Justice takes many forms.

But John wasn't listening to any roars or even to Howie. He was looking at me. "So what are you doing later?" he asked, his voice warm and low.

And then, most unexpectedly, I felt a weight lifting off me. I almost felt the sky was getting lighter, but I suppose that was just a lighting effect. I turned to John Quinn.

"Do you like Vegas?"